the boys across the street

the boys across
rick the street
sandford

ff faber and faber, inc.

an affiliate of farrar, straus and giroux

new york

For
Avraham and Yaakov
and
Moshe and Yitzchak

Faber and Faber, Inc.
An affiliate of Farrar, Straus and Giroux
19 Union Square West, New York 10003

Library of Congress Cataloging-in-Publication Data
Sandford, Rick, 1950–1995.
    The boys across the street / Rick Sandford. — 1st ed.
    p.   cm.
    ISBN 0-571-19960-7 (alk. paper)
    I. Title.
PS3569.A5163B69   2000
813'.54—dc21   99–38697

acknowledgments

I would like to thank the following four men. There are so many others whom Rick loved and who loved Rick not acknowledged here. I thank these men because I believe that they were instrumental in bringing Rick's writing to book.

Rick met Robert Drake in 1988 in a writing group led by Robert. Rick was angry, suspicious, and vulnerable. He was also an exquisite writer—that's what Robert saw. Without Robert Drake there might be no book. He never abandoned Rick as a writer despite publishers' fears about Rick's work. All of us—you, Rick, and I—have Robert to thank for this book and for Rick's stories coming to print; without him, they would live only in my boxes of Ricky's things. Thank you, Robert.

Peter Cashorali met Rick in Robert's group as well. They loved to play Jesus and Simon Peter. When Rick died, Peter prepared his body for the journey. I know Ricky would have laughed heartily while basking in the comfort. Thank you, Peter.

Peter Choi provided Rick with the means to sustain himself financially without too much effort. He continued to be there as a practical and loving friend through Rick's dying. Thank you, Peter.

Don Bachardy loved Rick, which was a source of great pride and joy for him. Don gave Rick the grace of deep acceptance. His gaze reflected Rick as beautiful, strong, courageous, and wanted. Thank you, Don.

I thank these men for Rick. I cannot know if he would have fulfilled his dream of writing without them. I do know they contributed to the pages that open before you.

For myself, I would like to thank Rick Sandford for staying alive as long as he did, for being my friend, my nemesis, my husband for a day, and a constant love in my life for twenty-seven years.

—Stacey Foiles, Executor, the Estate of Rick Sandford

introduction

I first set eyes on Rick Sandford from the stage of the Gershwin The-ater in 1979. I was singing in the chorus of *Sweeney Todd*, and Rick was seated near the front between his friends Christopher Isherwood and Don Bachardy. Rick and Don were passing a bottle of poppers back and forth, sniffing and grinning up at the huge industrial set.

After the performance the four of us went for drinks at Wienerwald on Seventh Avenue. This had all been arranged by my ex-lover, who knew of my reverence for Isherwood. In the faux beer garden, Rick (then twenty-eight) functioned as talk-show host, filling the gaps, as I was too tongue-tied to do more than bare my teeth in imitation of a smile. I remember Isher-wood saying, "When it comes to plays, it doesn't matter if you have a really good plot or any of that business; the audience will stick with you for the whole way if you have one really good character they can watch."

The Boys Across the Street has, among many other astonish-ments, one really good character to watch. The character, Rick Sandford, lives alone in one room; when not having sex, working out, or earning what little cash he has as a stand-in on TV shows he is unable to watch—he has no TV—he is collecting unemploy-ment and reading. The supreme autodidact, he devours philoso-phy, poetry, plays, novels, criticism. And he *watches*. Since he doesn't have the income or inclination to buy a car which might enable him to go places and shop for things he doesn't need, he fills his free time with the pursuit of physical pleasure and the nearly equal pleasure of gaining knowledge. His only other social activity is to go to practically every movie ever made. No one I have ever known has had a more encyclopedic knowledge of movies.

But we're talking about a character, the protagonist of a fiction. I hope no one will ask or try to determine what part of this book is "true." It is all true, whether any of it happened or not.

Rick lives across the street from an Orthodox yeshiva, and his interactions with the students make up nearly all the action, told in a lucid and unadorned prose more Cather than Updike. The boys are drawn to Rick because he speaks to them openly, without design or condescension. Coming from an all-male environment where they are daily required to thank God they were not born female, the boys are fascinated by Rick's candor and iconoclasm, particularly about sex.

In a very real sense the other major character is the street which divides these believers from the non-believer, the Jews from the Gentile, the virgins from the man who claims to have slept with two thousand men, and most significantly the (presumed) heteros from the homo. What unites the two sides of this chasm? In addition to their estrangement from mainstream American culture, Rick and the boys also share a need to belong to something, someone, and a deep curiosity—a seemingly innate desire for truth and knowledge. Admittedly, this gets beaten out of most of us, and Rick watches as it happens to his boys.

The motivation behind much of Rick's own behavior, increasingly provocative and bizarre, is at first opaque to him. But unlike so many, he is willing to be in the uncomfortable place of *not knowing*, to keep asking why he does what he does, until he hits upon the truth: his own intrapsychic, previously unconscious reason for disguising himself as what he is not—a Chassid.

But it is not his attire which most deeply offends the boys: it is Rick's homosexuality. "We don't believe in that," they insist.

Noam Chomsky has observed that if you speak the truth to

people who have been lied to all their lives, you will sound as if you are from Neptune—crazy, criminal, or both. Rick frequently strikes the boys (and sometimes the reader) as just that—except that his voice has none of the hallmarks of insanity: he speaks rationally, he stops throughout to question his own perceptions, feelings, and beliefs. What is he, then, a mystic? If so, his only god is cock, and the taste of sperm his holy communion.

When I first knew the real Rick, his lovemaking was vehement and overemphatic; he could take two cocks up inside him, but it was more like an Olympic event than an expression of love; he could deep-throat, but it was brutal, insistent. Blood came out of the head of my cock after he sucked me off. What drove him to this seemingly desperate desire to consume the other man? And so many? What in the world had happened to this child?

Rick, the character, wishes he hadn't been born and is not afraid to die. This astonishes the boys. They have been taught to "be fruitful and multiply." Rick thinks it is the worst possible sin to bring a child into this world and that self-pity is the most disgusting of human traits.

The real Rick could not understand what was wrong with the actions of the character of Louis in *Angels in America*; he thought no sick person had the right to expect to be taken care of, even by a lover. When everyone rallied around Rick during his final illness in 1995, he was completely gobsmacked. It was as if he had never before taken in the simple reality that he was loved. And among many other things, the book is an attempt to make the imaginative and necessary leap from Rick's terrible experiences to his capacity for love.

It grows increasingly clear that the American Dream is death—and I don't mean that the American Dream is killing us, which it may well be—I mean that what we seem to be dreaming about and striving toward is death. Movies, TV, and journalism are filled with ever more startling and gruesome images of human destruction. We want to know how fast the car was going when the celebrity was eviscerated. Whole evenings can now be spent watching real people die in avalanches, tornadoes, tsunamis, fires, and sports accidents. We are kept sufficiently entertained by the massacres of other people's children and the various ethnic cleansings, and though we believe that the government and media lie to us, we also believe that we can do nothing about it. We are a nation of know-it-alls who have no power, so we wait for death, getting high on various substances while we stare at televised drivel.

The enemies of culture, then, in my view include ignorance, distraction, knowingness ("Been there, done that" cynicism), and speed. Plato says that you can't think when you're in a hurry, and it's true. You also can't think when you're working yourself to the bone at a meaningless job or when you're perpetually distracted—watching endless sitcoms or whatever human disaster currently occupies the airwaves. As Pierre Bourdieu has persuasively argued, "Television poses a serious danger for all the various areas of cultural production—for art, for literature, for science, for philosophy, and for law."

Here, then, is an anomaly: a work of art narrated by someone who doesn't own a TV, whose quiet days are his own, who admits to knowing very little, possesses almost no creature comforts, doesn't habitually indulge in consciousness-deadening drugs like alcohol or pot, doesn't have children or even much of a future. Someone striving toward consciousness without the familiar carapace of "knowingness." Someone who reads and questions and arrives at his own beliefs instead of simply receiving them. A life-affirming novel by a real man who has died.

Maybe there is hope for us yet.

—Craig Lucas
September, 1999

the boys across the street

1 / isaac and moshe

The two boys were sitting on the steps of a walkway across the street. All dressed up in black suits, with little black beanies on the back of their heads, they didn't seem to have anywhere to go or anything to do. They had been wandering up and down the street for a while, but now they were still, and their attention was settling on the person directly across them: me.

I was reading.

I'd brought my canvas-backed director's chair out of the house and was sitting in it facing the sun. It was the last Saturday before the end of the year and the weather was beautiful: all I had on was a pair of gold-colored trunks. My feet were propped up on one of two low brick walls that bordered the walkway leading to the courtyard apartments where I lived, and on it I had arranged my dictionary, my binoculars, and a cup of coffee.

But I was finding it difficult to concentrate. I had moved into my apartment thirteen years ago, the Jewish school across the street had opened shortly thereafter, and in all that time I had never really engaged any of the students in conversation. I guessed the two boys across the street from me to be about fourteen. They were Semitic-looking and the taller of the two was rather attractive.

I knew how to begin the conversation. I had imagined it in my mind a hundred times, and now, as I looked down at my book, and back over at them, I wondered if this was the moment. What the hell.

I looked at them directly.

We were definitely looking at one another.

Okay:

"Do you believe in God?"

They both immediately stood up. Not only were they being addressed by an adult, they were being asked the most basic question about the only thing that really mattered.

"Yes—of course. Don't you?"

"Of course not," I answered, matching their self-assurance. "I think life is meaningless," and I had to catch myself before I added, "and stupid." If life was meaningless, it couldn't also be stupid.

"Then how did all this come to be?" one of them asked.

That sounded like a trick question. I answered cautiously, "I don't know."

"You don't know," the shorter of the two boys said, very satisfied, "but I know."

"How do you know?"

"It says in the Torah."

"That's just a story."

"It's God's revelation."

"Men wrote that book—not God."

Stalemate.

In the silence, a car passed between us. When it had gone by, there was a sudden interjection from up the street.

"The Jews killed the son of God."

I turned around in my chair and saw a fat man in a torn T-shirt leaning against a car, his arms folded over his belly, a smile on his face.

"That's ridiculous," I said, and turned back to my book. I was baiting the boys, but not like that. His was a conversation I didn't want to take part in, and I was willing to sacrifice my talk with the kids to avoid it.

I don't know what happened to the fat man, but as I sat there trying to read I became aware of the two boys approaching me. They weren't just walking toward me across the street, however; they had split up and were coming at me from two different directions. One of them was angling down the street and then back up to me, while the other was making his way from behind: they were reconnoitering a target.

When they had at last regrouped, they were standing just beside me. My chair, however, was on an embankment several feet above the sidewalk, so, from my perspective, they were slightly below me and looking up. I acknowledged them with a nod of my head: Yes?

The smaller of the two boys began the offensive: "If there is no God, then how did all this happen?" He made a gesture indicating the street, and meaning the world: the apartment houses, the palm trees, the parked cars, and the sky.

I gave a different answer this time: "Arbitrary accident."

Both boys scoffed at this.

"Do you think this is a perfect world?" I asked them. "Do you think this is the only way things *can* be or ought to be? I think that shows a lack of imagination."

"Then how did you get here?"

"I don't know."

"You don't know." The smaller boy, in particular, was contemptuous.

"But I have the courage to admit that I don't know. You have to be very courageous to believe in nothing," I told him.

The little boy came right back at me: "You have to be very courageous to believe in something."

I was willing to concede that point. "That's true. Sometimes." But I wanted to get back to the question of this inevitable, perfect, and created world. "What about the Holocaust? Do you think God wanted that to happen?"

This was obviously a tricky point for them. They weren't agreed on how to answer me. The taller of the two boys, the better-looking, the more thoughtful, let his friend answer. "God wanted those people with him."

"And so he made them suffer?"

"Maybe they did something bad."

I looked at him in disbelief.

He hurried to offer an explanation. "Let's say a man is good, but he isn't circumcised, then he will have to come back in his next life to get circumcised."

I wasn't exactly sure how this related to the Holocaust and God's existence, but I'd never heard of this before. "The Jews believe in reincarnation?"

Both boys answered me at the same time. The taller boy said "No" and the smaller one said "Yes."

I gave them a shrug: What gives?

They went into a conference. The taller boy answered. "Yes, the Jews believe in reincarnation, but it's a special thing. Not everyone gets reincarnated."

"The Anointed One gets reincarnated," the smaller boy said.

"He is always with us, yes," the taller boy affirmed.

"He's alive." The little boy seemed to be emphatic about this.

"What's the 'Anointed One'?" I asked.

"That's what we call the Messiah," the taller boy explained.

"You think the Messiah is alive?"

"He is always with us. He returns with every generation. We're just waiting for him to reveal himself."

I didn't quite know what to do with this information. I had a momentary vision of a second—*first*—Messiah coming here on Alta Vista Boulevard. "Aren't you going to be mad at him when he does come for not revealing himself during World War II?"

"No," and here the taller boy seemed to be making a special effort to clarify an important point. "You see, the Jews weren't ready then. Before the Messiah comes, we have to be prepared and ready as a nation."

This was really shocking to me: the regulation of collective self-hatred. Well, for now, for the moment, I would offer myself as another possibility, a window on the outside world and—maybe even—a salvation.

"Do you believe in Moses?" I asked.

"He saved our people," the smaller boy said.

"That's the story. That's what it says. But except for the Bible there is no other historical evidence for his existence."

"His name is Moses," the taller boy said, indicating his friend.

I looked at the boy with his rounded, almost chubby face. "Your name is Moses?"

"Moshe," he said.

I turned to the taller boy. "What's yours?"

"Isaac."

"My name's Rick."

We looked at one another: we all had names.

"I just wanted to make the point," I said, "that all recorded history is within the last five thousand years or so, and in the scheme of things that's nothing. I just read a couple of weeks ago that they discovered a genetic link that indicates that every single person on this planet is descended from a woman who lived in western Africa one hundred and fifty thousand years ago. Can you imagine how long ago that is? The Torah was written, at the most, three thousand years ago. I mean, there's no difference between the Torah and the old Greek gods. I just finished reading the *Iliad*, and they thought the gods all lived on this mountain in Greece—"

"That's just a story," Moshe asserted.

"I think what you believe is just a story," I said.

We looked at one another and once again we seemed to be at a stalemate.

"Have you read Leviticus?" I asked.

"We've memorized the Torah in Hebrew."

"You're kidding!" I was horrified. "Really? The first five books of the Bible?"

"It's *not* the Bible," Moshe said, exasperated.

I excused myself and ran into my apartment. I grabbed my 1611 King James Version of the Bible and came back outside. I opened it to Leviticus and looked up one of my marked passages. "So, if I ask you what Leviticus— chapter 20, verse 13— is, you can tell me?"

"It's not like that," Isaac said. "It isn't written that way."

"It's on scrolls," Moshe explained.

"It doesn't say this?" I asked, and proceeded to read the Leviticus passage to them: " 'If a man also lie with mankind, as he lieth with a woman, both of them have committed an abomination: they shall surely be put to death; their blood *shall be* upon them.' "

The boys reflected on these words.

"Do you think that's true?" I asked. "That men should be put to death for having sex with each other?"

Moshe felt there was a distinction to be made here. "Before they're married?"

Isaac tried to cover up for his friend's misunderstanding. "That isn't the real Torah," he said. "You have to read it in the original."

"Well, the reason I read the 1611 King James Version is that, apart from any value the book might have in terms of its content, it's a very important book for the history of English literature and the English language. I think what it says is stupid, though."

Moshe looked at the book as if it were contaminated. "If my

father found that book in the house he would throw it out so fast . . ."

"That isn't what we've memorized, anyway," said Isaac.

"It's bigger than that," Moshe asserted, still looking at the Bible suspiciously.

I separated the first five books and held them between my fingers. "You're just talking about the Torah, right?"

"It's much bigger than that," Moshe declared.

"You're talking about the Talmud," I suggested, "with all the commentary and explanations."

"It's not exactly the Talmud," Moshe was a little bulldog now.

"It's called the Mishnah," Isaac said.

"What's that?"

"It's like the Torah, but it's not."

"Hmm." I didn't know what they were talking about. "Well, if you have an English translation I'd like to see it."

For a moment we remained suspended there with our unresolved thoughts, and then I asked them, "Why do you wear those things on your head?"

"It shows our respect to God," Moshe said and then, in case I didn't know, "They're called yarmulkes."

"Do you wear them all the time?" I asked.

They both nodded, and Isaac further explained, "It represents our humility before God."

I thought about that for a bit, contemplating the yarmulkes on the back of their heads. It looked to me like the revenge of bitter old men with bald spots, coercing young men into an eternal condolence for the ravages of time.

And then I began to wonder about their haircuts: they each had a lock of hair on either side of their faces, from the temples down over the ears.

"Do you wear your hair that way on purpose?" I asked.

They both simultaneously moved a hand to the side of their heads and said, "Peyos."

"What's . . . peyos?"

"It's one of the commandments," Isaac explained. "We're not supposed to cut our hair."

"Why?"

"We have to remember God," Moshe said.

How weird it all was—all this effort for the sake of Nothing.

"So what do you think is the point of life?" Isaac suddenly asked me.

"The 'point of life'? Well, I don't think there is any. Except to be happy and have fun."

"And what's that?" Isaac asked.

"Well, for me, fun is reading books and having sex."

This was true, and I said it with full awareness of its power to engage. And it really was amazing: with what other teenage boys in the United States could you use the question of God and the reading of books as a means of seduction?

"Are you married?" Isaac asked.

I winced. "Ooh. No." And then I elaborated. "I only have sex with men."

Moshe was curious. "You have sex with men? How do you do that?"

"What do you mean, how do I do that?" I asked him rhetorically. "How do you think? I suck cock and get fucked."

Moshe was insistent. "How?"

"How? How do I get fucked? Up my ass."

Now Moshe was incredulous. "It's not possible."

"Of course it's possible. You can even go over on Melrose and rent a video and see me getting fucked by two guys at the same time."

"I don't believe you."

"I used to make porno films," I told them. "I made thirteen. Wait. I'll show you," and once more I jumped up and ran into my apartment. This time I went to my file cabinet and got out the issue of *Skinflicks* with the interview of me inside. I ran back out to the boys, and opened the magazine to a page showing two cocks pushed together with me trying to engulf them both in my mouth. "That's from the *Gold Rush Boys*. I got fucked by both those cocks in that movie."

"That's you?" Isaac asked doubtfully.

"Well, that was what? Seven years ago."

"It would hurt," said Moshe.

"Well, it can be a little difficult at first, but men have a prostate gland inside them, and when it's massaged—like with a penis up inside them—it feels great."

"What's a . . . prostate . . . gland?" Isaac asked.

"It's this little organ inside your body that helps produce semen."

The boys turned the pages of the magazine.

"When I made movies my stage name was Ben Barker. That was my only interview."

The boys had turned to a color picture showing my tongue reaching out toward a huge uncircumcised cock.

"I wish my cock was like that," I told them.

"Why?"

"Because it's so big, and if I wasn't circumcised my cock would probably be more sensitive and I'd have stronger erections."

"But being circumcised is better," Moshe said. "It's cleaner."

"I don't think it's worth it. Being mutilated."

Moshe looked at the picture. "He's circumcised."

"No he's not," Isaac said.

"Isaac's right," I said. "You can't even see the head of his cock because of his foreskin—and that's *with* an erection." I pointed to a picture on the opposite page. "*He's* circumcised. Can you see the difference?"

Moshe contemplated the different pictures.

"It's hard to tell in that picture," I said, indicating the circumcised penis, "but I think that's the biggest cock I've ever sucked. He was great."

The boys handed the magazine back to me. They hadn't even dared to touch the Bible.

We were all quiet for a moment. I wondered if they would dream about these pictures tonight, if they would dream about me. I mused aloud, "I love semen."

Moshe was adamant: "Why?"

"Because it tastes so good. Because—I don't know. I guess because it's the original life force."

We were all quiet again.

I had an afterthought: "It's so spectacular when it shoots out."

The boys were looking at the ground, apparently deep in thought.

"This morning," Moshe said, "there was this sticky—"

"That's a wet dream," I explained.

"I didn't have a dream."

"You don't *remember* having a dream. That's great. You're lucky."

Moshe was obstinate: "*Why* am I lucky?"

"Because your sex life is just beginning. It's been more than two decades since I've had a wet dream. You have a lifetime of ejaculations stretching away before you . . ."

The two boys and I looked at one another over an abyss of more than twenty years, the boys concerned with their nocturnal emissions and I with the specter of fading potency.

Isaac looked at his watch. "We have to go."

I smiled at them. "Have a nice day."

And as they walked away I imagined myself in their dreams, in those oh-so-wet dreams, that "sticky" splashing *me*: their— blissfully—anointed one.

2 / boy friends

It was about ten o'clock at night and I had just bicycled to the
store to get something to eat. On my way back home, as I rode
past the school, I noticed a number of the boys sitting on the
porch of one of the two school buildings that faced my street.
They were smoking. One of them said hello, and I circled
around in the street, pulling my bike up alongside the fence surrounding the school.

"How are you guys doing?" I asked.

They said they were fine.

"I wrote a story about you guys, about a conversation I had
with two boys named Isaac and Moshe."

"You wrote a story about us?"

"I think it's good, too."

"What's it about?"

"It's just a conversation I had, but it's about everything: God
and sex and the meaning of life. Do you want to see it? I'll go
get it," and, very excited at the prospect of their actually reading
my story, I cycled over to my apartment.

Some of the high school boys board at the school and late at night, when the adults are gone, they start their socializing: playing basketball, taking walks, or just sitting outside and smoking. I was fascinated with this world of theirs, a world of uniforms and studying and masculine camaraderie. I grabbed a copy of my story and ran back across the street.

They had all come down from the porch and gathered together near the fence. Some of them climbed over, while others came around through the gate. I handed the story to one of the boys, who started to look through it.

A tall boy with glasses, looking over his shoulder, turned to me. "Who're Isaac and Moshe?"

"I don't know. They were just these two boys I spoke to one day."

"Were they dark?"

I shrugged my shoulders. "I guess."

"I think I know who you mean. They're from Israel; they don't go to school here."

One of the smaller boys looked up at me. "Did you put in the Jews' point of view?"

"Well, I'm not a Jew, but I wrote down what the boys said to the best of my ability."

"So what's the point of the story?" asked the boy who held it in his hand, a serious young man obviously disinclined to read the whole thing.

"I guess it's best summed up in the last paragraph." I turned the pages, directing his attention to the final lines: "And as they walked away I imagined myself in their dreams, in those oh-so-wet dreams, that 'sticky' splashing *me*: their—blissfully—anointed one."

He read it over a couple of times. "What does it mean? I don't understand."

"Well," I explained, "you have to have read the whole story, but when Isaac and Moshe walked away I was imagining them dreaming about me. If you'd read the story, you'd know that 'sticky' was a word that Moshe used, and I was imagining myself as their Messiah, being anointed when they jacked off on me."

The boy just looked at me. Had I blasphemed? Or was that only to be expected from a person such as myself? He handed the story on to some of his friends, who started looking through it.

"I'm getting my first story published this year," I told them. "It's about the Jews, too. It's about Auschwitz. It's my ultimate fantasy. I'm a commandant in a concentration camp, and I get to have sex with all the Jewish boys I want. I wait at the train unloadings, and when they get off, I just choose the ones I like best."

The boy continued to stare at me in silence. I don't think he knew if I was kidding or not.

"So what do you do for a living?" one of the other boys asked. "You're a writer?"

"I'm a writer, but I make a living, I pay the rent, by being an extra in movies and TV shows."

"What movies have you been in?" another tall boy asked me, this one with a rather goofy grin on his face.

"The last couple of years I've been a stand-in on some TV shows, but I was in *E.T., 1941, Streets of Fire, 2010, Pee-Wee's Big Adventure, Lethal Weapon*: I even got to be a Nazi in *To Be or Not to Be* by Mel Brooks."

"What's a stand-in?"

"Well, on a TV show, after the actors rehearse the scenes, they have to block it with the cameras—there's usually three cameras on the shows I work on, and that takes a lot of time, so they have people like me, stand-ins, watch the rehearsals, and then when the camera crews come in, we do what the actors do until they have it all set up."

The boys were looking at me with blank expressions. I sighed: How do I explain this?

"My job exists as a courtesy to the actors, so they won't get bored while the cameras set up their shots."

The boy with the goofy grin was staring at me as if I were an alien. "Who were you in *E.T.*?"

"Remember when the government men came to the house, and there were all those men in white outfits? I was one of the guys in the front yard with a Geiger counter."

Now that I had impressed them with my Hollywood credentials, I wanted to get the conversation back to them. "So what do *you* do? Do you guys ever jack off together?"

"No."

That was too easy. "Is anyone homosexual over there?"

"No."

"Does anybody over there ever stop believing in God?"

"No."

"Are you guys all virgins?"

"Yes."

"Really?" I was stunned: teenage boys admitting their virginity—wasn't that a contradiction in terms? "None of you has ever had sex?"

"No."

"Really?"

"Mendel did."

"Who's Mendel?"

"Me."

The boy who acknowledged this distinction was very cute, with tight curly brown hair and an impish grin.

"So do all the boys look up to you?" I asked.

"No, we're ashamed of him," someone said.

"Are you glad you're not a virgin?" I asked him.

He said, "No," but I figured he was lying. He had a big smile on his face at thus confounding me and my expectations.

The boys stood there, proudly confronting me as one big implacable force.

"Are you aware that your sexual peak is at eighteen? And then it's all downhill after that? It would be too bad if you wasted your youth on renunciation. You should have fun while you're young."

"We're not going to have sex until we get married," one of the hard-liners proclaimed.

A younger-looking boy elaborated. "Sex is like a beautiful rare jewel. If you had a beautiful rare jewel, would you show it to just anybody?"

"Why not? If it was so beautiful, why shouldn't as many people see it as possible?"

"But wouldn't you be afraid someone might steal it?"

"I don't think it's good to care too much about things. You know what the anarchists used to say? 'Property is theft.' "

"If I had a rare jewel . . ." The boy was persistent in contemplation of his precious stone, almost conjuring it before me: it was a ruby. "If I had a rare jewel, I would protect it."

"Well, I think you're wrong," I said. "Haven't you ever heard the old adage that you can't love someone unless you love everyone?"

"I've never heard that before."

"Well, think about it. I think Christopher Isherwood said that, but it might have been Nietzsche."

Another boy joined in the conversation. "Having sex is just like being an animal."

"What's wrong with that? We are animals—"

"But we have to rise above that!"

Finally, I deigned to use their terminology: "I don't think God made our minds and bodies so that one would have any particular ascendancy over the other. I think he made them so that they should both be utilized equally."

Met with silence, this last remark seemed to have some impact on them.

———

The next evening a friend of mine named Josh stopped by to talk and get stoned. He was thirty-two and trying to become a more than occasional filmmaker. We were sitting outside and I was telling him about my experience with the boys when one of them came across the street toward us.

"Hey, Rick!"

It was the serious young man I'd first given my story to the night before. He'd brought along three of his friends, and they stood behind him, dark and solemn.

I was gratified to see "from my lips to God's ears," and went out to meet him.

"Tell them what you told me," he said. "They don't believe me."

"About what?"

"The concentration camp."

"Oh." I didn't quite see how I was going to manage it. "Well, I mean I was being sort of facetious, but I'm attracted to Jewish boys, and my story that's getting published is about these two boys who are friends in Germany. One's Jewish and one's not, and when the boy who isn't makes a pass at the one who is, the Jewish boy rejects him. The other boy becomes a Nazi, and at Auschwitz he has sex with Jewish boys who remind him of his boyhood friend."

They looked at me in silence for a moment and then a car drove by. We moved over to the curb on their side of the street. As we re-formed our little group on the sidewalk, Josh came over to join me.

"What does 'facetious' mean?" one of the boys asked me.

"Well, 'facetious' sort of means you're kidding, like you're not totally serious. I mean, I wouldn't *really* want to be a Nazi."

"The homosexual Nazis were pretty much wiped out by 1934, anyway," Josh explained.

"This is Josh," introducing my friend to the group.

"Are you Jewish?" one of the boys asked him.

"Yes."

"Are you gay?" another inquired.

"No."

I had an explanation: "Josh and I are like brothers. He does things I can't do, and—"

"He does things I *won't* do," Josh finished for me.

More boys from the school joined us on the sidewalk, and in a few moments there were two little groups, one around me and the other around Josh.

"Why do you like Jewish boys?" one of them asked me.

"Mostly, it's guilt by association. I used to be in love with this boy—he was adopted and raised Catholic, but I think he was really Jewish—and after our relationship ended I was attracted to other guys who looked like him, and they all turned out to be Jews. Sometimes they might be Italian, but mostly they were Jewish. And of course, the main thing—even though it's not always true—I like Jews because they have big noses, and that's an exciting phallic symbol."

"What's 'phallic'?"

"Having to do with penises, cocks. You know what they say: guys with big noses have big dicks. I mean, obviously that's not necessarily true, but it's a nice idea."

The boys reflected on all this for a moment, and then the Serious Young Man asked, "Which of us standing here do you think is attractive?"

"I think you are," I said.

"Why?"

"You have a nice nose, you wear your glasses well, and you have a clear, bright expression."

He wasn't about to give in to me. "Who else?"

I looked around and saw an Arabic-looking boy talking with Josh. He had thick black hair and an aristocratic bearing. "I like him," I said.

This delighted the boys I was talking to, and one of them

called over to their friend, "Hey, Mordecai, you got a boyfriend!"

Mordecai joined us for a moment, to size up this person who thought he was attractive. He had dark, beautiful eyes.

"I think you're sexy," I told him.

His friends hooted and hit him on the back, and he moved away from me.

I was aware that Josh was talking to the boys about metaphysics: it was the element about my "Isaac and Moshe" story that he liked best (he wanted me to cut out the "clinical" parts). Every now and then I would hear snippets of his conversation: ". . . You really think, you *literally* think, the world is 5,750 years old? . . . What about the dinosaurs? What about carbon dating?"

But while our two conversations continued, his audience dwindled as mine increased.

"When you have an erection," I explained to them, "you're very vulnerable. When a man and a woman have sex, they can *only* have sex if the man has a hard-on. The woman doesn't have to *do* anything; that's why *she's* in the more powerful position. The one that *does* something is always in a weaker position. *That's* why I'd rather get fucked than fuck someone: because *I . . . like . . . power.*"

The boys just looked at me, and in the sudden silence we could hear Josh, trying to make points with the only boy still talking to him.

"I think there is an eternal consciousness that we are all a part of—"

"But isn't that God? What's the difference?"

I looked at the boys around me and tried to impart my philosophy of life to them as simply and completely as I knew how.

"You only live once, you're only young once: you should have fun. You should have as much fun as you possibly can."

"What's 'fun'?"
"*Anything* you want it to be."

Later Josh told me they had asked him if he knew I was gay.
   "Yes."
   "Did he tell you?"
   "Yes, but I already knew that."
   "You did? Then. . . ."
Josh said their deliberations died away.
Then: *How could you be friends with him?*

3 / the other side of the street

It took me more than two years to read the Bible, and as I neared the end I would stay at home on the days I wasn't working and set myself up outside with my director's chair, binoculars, and cup of coffee, as well as my dictionary and *Asimov's Guide to the Bible*, and I would read. The sun would traverse the sky, I would turn pleasing shades of brown, and as I read I would keep tabs on the neighborhood: the ravens building a nest in the eucalyptus tree above me, the mockingbirds with their territorial imperative, and, of course, the descendants of the people I was reading about, the Jewish boys across the street.

On weekdays in the afternoons, they would leave the school in varying groups and classes, and go up Alta Vista on their way to the park, where they would play ball. After an hour or so they would return, straggling back down the street to the school. On Fridays, in deference to the coming Sabbath (which begins at sundown), they would go and come back earlier.

I regarded the boys across the street almost as an alien

species, ignoring them as they ignored me, but occasionally I'd ponder their visual assertions: the skullcaps, their dark suits year in and year out, and the strings hanging down the sides of their pants.

When the school first opened, before they soundproofed it, there had been a mini-riot on our street over the noise they made. The police were called, and a rabbi and some of the students were arrested. The next day there were notices distributed up and down the block by the Jewish Defense League: "WARNING to all anti-Semites in this area (straight or gay). We of the JDL will NOT tolerate any attacks on Jews. We are on patrol to defend this community. If one Jew is bothered, YOU will pay in blood. NEVER AGAIN." A week or so later everyone on the street received a letter from the school saying they wanted to cooperate with their new neighbors and listing phone numbers to call if there were any problems.

For the most part, there weren't. One Friday night, though, a car caught fire, and the next day when the owner found out that the Jewish boys had watched the incineration without calling the police or the fire department (they're not allowed to use telephones on the Sabbath), he got really mad and ran around in the street cursing and yelling.

As for myself, I'd spoken to them only once. One day when I was trying to read they had some horrible Israeli music blaring and I went across the street to tell them to turn it down. They'd been very obliging and, other than that, we'd had no real communication until I spoke to Isaac and Moshe in December.

By March the TV season was over, the show I was working on had finished shooting, and hiatus had begun. Workless days stretched before me, and since I'd finished reading the Bible other projects took its place: catching up on two years of unread newspapers, cataloguing Christopher Isherwood's library onto my computer for his estate, and then thinking about my next big undertaking: the writing of a blasphemous, homoerotic gospel in the style of the 1611 King James Version of the Bible.

As time went by, the boys became steadily more aware of me. When they came clanging out of the gate on their way to the park, I would put down the book or paper I was reading and watch them.

Sometimes they would look over at me.

Sometimes we would even acknowledge that we were looking at one another.

Since the boys all dressed the same, it was almost impossible for me to know which ones I had spoken to before, but there was only one of me, and since my name was written on the back of my director's chair they very definitely knew who I was.

"Hey, Rick, how's it going?"

I would nod, sometimes I would answer, and I could feel the attraction growing: they wanted to know about me as much as I wanted to know about them.

When I started work on the Isherwood library I had to stay indoors, but my desk was just to the side of a large window that faced the street, so I could keep an eye on things. One afternoon while I was at my computer I noticed a couple of the boys running up the street.

I decided that was a good excuse to stop working, so I grabbed my director's chair and a book and set myself up in front of the apartment.

A few minutes later three more of the boys came out of the school, talking together as they walked up the street. When they

saw me, the one in the middle—very cute and gregarious—
called out to me, "Hey, Rick!"

It was Mendel, the only Jewish boy over there who wasn't a
virgin.

"Hello."

"You're looking good, Rick!" he yelled over to me.

I laughed. I wasn't sure what the joke was, but at least I had
the presence of mind to call back, "You look good, too."

They were a ways up the street by now, but I could see
Mendel getting teased by his friends. Trying to make amends, he
rejoined, "I'm just kidding!"

I was definite in my response: "I'm not."

That stopped them. Mendel's two sidekicks really started
laughing and giving him a bad time.

For a moment I had him flummoxed, but then he did manage
to get in the last word: "Rick—you're a funny guy."

After the boys had gone to the park I decided to stay outside
reading until they came back. Since my apartment is on the west
side of the street, if I want to get sun in the late afternoon, I have
to reposition myself drastically to avoid the shadows of my
building. If it's hot enough, late in the day I move my chair
across the street and set it up on a little paved walkway in front
of a seldom-used gate to the school.

This I did, taking my chair and book with me.

During the daytime, the area between the school buildings
and the fence is used as a playground for nursery school children, and several jungle gyms have been built there for the kids
to play on. The kids are usually supervised by one or two
women, invariably pregnant and wearing horrible wigs (I later
learned that it's a custom for the women to cut and cover their

hair after marriage so as not to be attractive to other men). Around five in the afternoon, when the children are picked up by their parents, the street is logjammed and, while bearded men dressed in black parade about imperiously and bewigged mothers navigate in huge beat-up station wagons filled with kids, one of the women oversees their comings and goings with a megaphone. All in all, it is quite a spectacle.

After I'd set myself up across the street and was comfortably reading, I heard one of the five-year-olds, looking at me through the fence, say in a kind of wonderment at my near-nakedness, "There's no sand or water!"

Before long, other small children were gathering together behind the fence to look at me. Tiny little boys and girls began trying to get my attention, but I wouldn't look at them and continued reading my book, *Words with Power: Being a Second Study of "The Bible and Literature"* by Northrup Frye.

After a while they started to call me names and ascribe outrageous behavior to me, the worst of which was "You eat the toilet!"

When this didn't work, they gathered together and started spitting at me. I was far enough away and they were young enough that their little liquid projectiles couldn't reach me, but occasionally, when the breeze was right, I would catch some of their spray. Finally I turned around. "Stop that."

They screamed and ducked behind the wall and ran away, but after several moments they were back in their places, once again spitting at me.

One of the women who supervised the children, seeing so many of them grouped together in a corner of the yard, finally came over and asked them what they were doing.

"That man talked to us," one of them said.

"What did he say?"

I wondered what incredible story they might make up. After all, if I could "eat the toilet," I could do anything.

"He said, 'Stop that.' "

"Well, he's right," she admonished the children. "Don't bother the man."

I was amazed. They might look at me and conjecture the worst of all possible behavior, but when push came to shove, they respected their elders enough to tell them the truth. The little girl who had answered the adult had quoted my words exactly: "Stop that."

Some time later, as I continued reading, the boys began returning from the park. Seeing me on their side of the street, some of them, I could tell, were a little disconcerted.

"Rick, put on your shirt!"

I looked at them as they passed behind me. "How can I get sun if I put on a shirt?"

"It's not modest. Put on a shirt!"

I had an idea: "If you take off your yarmulkes, I'll put on my shirt."

They scoffed at my proposal and sullenly walked on past me.

After most of the boys had come back from the park and it was starting to get a little chilly, two of the homelier boys made a tardy return to the school. They had apparently gone to the store to buy something, because one of them was carrying a bag. As they neared me one of them called out, "Rick, put your shirt on!"

I turned in my chair to see them better. They were both very unattractive.

The uglier of the two boys spoke. "You offend the women without your shirt."

I smiled at his preposterous assertion, but the other boy backed up his friend's allegation. "You really do."

They'd stopped walking and were standing several yards

away from me. We looked at one another and I tried to imagine those women, perpetually pregnant, wigs covering their heads, veritable baby-making machines, being offended by my naked chest.

I offered them my proposition: "I'll put my shirt on if you take off your yarmulkes."

The uglier boy, the one who had told me I was offending the women, reached up and took off his yarmulke and held it at his side.

I was surprised, and expressed it in my look to him.

Then I turned back to my book.

I couldn't even focus on the page: How contemptuous was I? *Was* my proposition just a lie?

I looked back at the two boys, still standing there, the uglier one with his yarmulke still clasped in his hand. There was a look of profound disgust on his face, and when I made no other move to cover my nakedness he replaced the yarmulke on his head.

That look was a little too much for me. To see someone so unattractive, someone who would have to work hard all his life for any kind of acceptance; to see someone so disadvantaged make such a pathetically gallant gesture; and to see such disfiguring emotion pass over an already misproportioned face—all this was daunting enough, but it was the nature of that emotion that caught me off guard. Not only was he disgusted at me for my lying Gentile ways, he was even more disgusted with himself for actually having deigned to meet my challenge to his beliefs.

As it happened, I couldn't have put my shirt on even if I'd wanted to. I didn't have one with me; I hadn't brought one outside.

It was getting too cold to get sun anyway, so, as they passed behind me on the sidewalk, I got up, gathered my chair and my book, and crossed back to my side of the street.

4 / sightings

It was after two o'clock in the morning. A man in a car was following me. I thought he might be attractive, but I couldn't be sure. He would slow down, take a good long look at me, and then move on, park, wait for me to get close and then drive ahead, go around the block, overtake me again, pull in a driveway, watch me approach, and then pull out and drive back past, wait for me to turn around and then, just when I was within speaking distance, gently step on the gas and drive out of range. I had finally decided that it wasn't worth it, to play that game: walking around the block again, loitering x more minutes on some street corner or another, and eventually finding myself stumbling to bed around dawn. So, walking east on Waring, I headed home.

The guy was still following me, but I didn't care anymore. I just kept on walking. He drove past me very slowly and then pulled over just ahead at the corner.

Okay: if he stays there I'll try just one more time.

When I got to the corner we were parallel with each other. I

turned to get a look at him. He looked back. I stepped toward
him. And then he started the car and turned the corner.

Fuck it: I've got some poppers at home, I'll go jack off and
I'll be fine.

I came to my street, Alta Vista, and turned right, heading
north toward my apartment, four lots up the block. I was
almost home when I noticed a lighted window across the street
in the dormitory of the Jewish school.

Facing toward me (looking into his own reflection) was a
good-looking boy with dark hair. He didn't have a shirt on and
he had an incredible body: massive pectoral muscles, large
potent nipples, and a Davidesque stomach.

I stopped, dumbstruck, and stared. He was lifting weights,
pulling a barbell up to his chest in a measured rhythm, and
straining the muscles and veins in his arms. Two younger boys
were in the room with him and, much more typically, they were
in their casual Jewish regalia, the white shirts, black pants, and
yarmulkes. They had pale funny faces and under their dumpy
clothes there was a sense of misshapen bodies. Like me, they
were watching the half-naked young man.

I'd seen him in the window for the first time the night before
when I'd come home late from a dinner with friends. Then, as
now, I'd been stunned. It was like coming across a giant movie
screen that somehow, in the middle of the night, on my street,
was showing one of my favorite movies. I'd gone into my apartment, grabbed my binoculars, and come back out and found a
place on the lawn directly across the street from his window.
For the next hour or so I watched him as he went through his
workout. He didn't do just one exercise and exhaust it, but went
from one thing to another, sometimes going to the floor and disappearing out of sight, but always returning to the exercises that
allowed him to confront the glass and watch his reflection
against the dark of the night. Through the binoculars, he was
practically staring me in the eye. The boys in the room looked

up to him with adoration, relishing the presence of this big beautiful man among them, and he glowed in their admiration as a hero: obliging, considerate, and wise.

Watching him again now, I guessed he was about nineteen. He was wearing wire-rimmed glasses and, like his little friends, he had a yarmulke on the back of his head: he was an apparition of beautiful, physical intelligence.

The man in the car drove past, and I felt his eyes on me. There, on the sidewalk, I was a pillar of salt looking back at . . .

The light in the window went out.

"Faggot!"

Dark and quiet.

Me?

Receding taillights.

Did a Jewish boy call me faggot?

Earlier in the day I'd asked one of the boys who'd been in the room with the beautiful weight lifter the night before if he was going to be a bodybuilder, too. He had stopped and looked at me carefully. "Did you watch?" he asked. When I told him I did, he turned and went away.

And now they were calling me faggot. I wanted to yell "Jew!" back at them, but it didn't come. The man in the car was turning around up the street. I dashed over to my apartment to get my binoculars and sit outside: maybe if the guy in the car saw I had other more important things to do he'd stop and talk.

Or something.

By the time I got outside again they'd turned the light back on across the street. I sat on the raised portion of the walkway in front of my apartment, lifted my binoculars, and focused. I could see one of the boys with his hands pressed up against the window looking out. Were they *really* so aware of me? *Could* I be such a threatening presence? I felt so invisible.

The man in the car pulled up just in front of me and

stopped. Once again he was watching me watching them. He didn't drive on.

Had I made my point? This was obviously where I lived. If he wanted to, we could just go inside and have sex there. All he had to do was park. Was he interested? He must have been; he was just sitting there. He couldn't just want people to follow him around, could he? Okay: one last time. I stood up and walked down the steps, out between two parked cars, and into the street. I was almost to the passenger window, and about to lean down to say hello, when—

He gave the car some gas and oh so slowly drove on down the street. What bullshit.

Asshole.

I was the asshole.

I turned back toward my apartment and sat down on the raised part of the walkway. The light was now out in the window across the street where the boys were, but I could hear the side door over there opening, and voices. The thought just passed through my mind: Could they be coming over here to confront me?

Some deliberation was going on beside the door, by the side of the building. And then there was some sort of resolution as three boys started out from the shadows and into the pale orange of the streetlight. They headed right for the gate, which clanged shut as they left the school's enclosure, and then, crossing the street, they made their way directly toward me.

A tall boy, the bodybuilder, was in front, his two acolytes trailing respectfully behind him. He was wearing a long blue robe. In contrast to the usual Orthodox disdain for color, it was very striking, its skirtlike aspect emphasizing, as perhaps mere nakedness could not, the sheer physicality seething beneath.

"Is your name Rick?"

He had stopped on the sidewalk about five yards away from

me. His little friends were grouped together in the street behind him.

"Yes."

"Do you like watching guys work out with binoculars?"

I had a bit of difficulty measuring the weight of the accusation. Would a religious boy actually hit me? My answer was tentative:

"Uh. Yes?"

The boys in the street had to shift their positions as the watcher's car drove slowly past again; I wondered what *he* was thinking.

"Well, I don't appreciate it. I'm not working out to have some . . . guy . . . watch me."

You're lying. You love having those boys hang on your every word, you love having them watch you, wishing your body were theirs—

"Well, actually, I was wondering . . ." I was having a little trouble getting my position together. "I mean, I watch guys work out at the gym all the time . . ." I don't *have* to watch you. "And I've been talking to you guys and you talk about the importance of the mind and the spirit over the body, and I was wondering: just what *are* you working out for?"

"For girls!"

This was the last word and he practically spit it at me. He turned away and started walking back across the street, striding past his two little friends, who continued to look at me. In the middle of the street he suddenly turned back to get in the last word yet again: "I'm working out for girls—*not* guys. For girls!"

He led his two charges back through the gate and they marched up beside the building and into the shadows, but they didn't go inside. They were probably assessing the battle, or rather *he* was. Did the two boys still look up to him? Was he a hero?

Did he win?

He won.

I guess getting the last word in *is* the measure of victory. My fantasy rejoinder came too late.

"You're working out 'for girls'? That's very naïve. Obviously you don't know very much about women. If you can say 'I love you' with a straight face, that'll get you further than the best body in the world. 'Girls' don't care about great bodies. Guys do."

The side door of the school finally opened and the boys went back inside. The light came back on in the workout room and the boys put up some brown paper they used to cover the window when Mr. Bodybuilder wasn't working out. I sat there on the walkway by myself for a long time: I couldn't go in, I couldn't let my defeat show. Let *them* make the retreat.

"If you don't want to be looked at, then why have the window wide open? To get a little air? You *know* people can see in, you *know* you have a great body, and you *know* you want anyone to see it who can. You're lying if you say you don't."

This confrontation was just a little show for his friends. And what a pathetic little show, really: making a stand in support of some stupid idea of masculinity, and one, come to think of it, with its roots in the dreary old strictures of the Bible.

I put the binoculars to my eyes and looked up at the moon. It was full, and I felt reassured somehow seeing Tycho, that crater near the bottom of the sphere with its emanating rays.

Checking in with eternity.

The lights went out across the way. Had I actually broken off his workout? And what *was* he doing working out after two o'clock in the morning, anyway? And . . .

Was it an infringement of privacy to use binoculars to look at your neighbors?

I'd bought the binoculars (Army, 7 × 50) for a very specific purpose: to see Bruce Springsteen in concert. And when the concerts were over I'd introduced them into other aspects of my life. Mostly I used them when sitting out in front of my apartment reading, lifting them up to watch people down the street or, more often than not, to observe mockingbirds.

This wasn't the first time I'd been called to account on my use of them, however: when I was standing in on *The Hogan Family*, I'd been watching one of the stars during one of the rehearsals and, aware of my observation up in the stands, he had suddenly turned to me and given me the finger. When I didn't put the glasses down, he'd given me the finger with the other hand as well. I never brought them to the set again.

The street was empty, the watcher in the car hadn't come back, and I felt slightly sick. Like I was *wrong*. But I didn't know *how* exactly.

I *am* vicarious, therefore—

I am invisible.

But I'm not.

I'm *here*.

I guess that's how I'm wrong.

There was a movement just across from me, and when I turned toward it I was startled to see a fairly large creature come sniffling around the corner of my apartment. It wasn't one of the cats and it wasn't a dog—it had a long nose to the ground: it was a possum! An opossum, here in the middle of Los Angeles. I put the binoculars to my eyes, but I couldn't make them focus. It was too close. I put the glasses down, but the moment had passed.

The creature had turned about and disappeared behind the building.

5 / the accident

I was sitting at my computer when suddenly there was an incredibly loud noise just outside, coming from the street. It obviously involved a large mass in some sort of collision, and yet it didn't sound like the only thing it could be—a car crash. There were no screeching brakes or full-throttled horns.

I waited a moment to hear how the noise was going to resolve itself, to see if the aural picture might come through my window, but there were no lightning flashes or explosions, the loud scraping finally stopped, and the night became as it was before. I got up and went outside.

In the street, right in front of my apartment, a large car was turned over on its side, the top facing me. Two boys were crawling out from under it, through the driver's side window, which was raised somewhat off the pavement. They were obviously a couple of boys from across the street, with their black pants, white shirts, and those strings hanging down the sides of their pants. The smaller of the two boys kept repeating over and over, "Oh, I'm sorry, I'm so sorry."

My next-door neighbor, Kimberly, an engineer who wanted

to be a social worker, was just coming home and had seen what happened: the car had been parked in front of the school; the driver pulled out very fast and veered across the street, side-swiping two cars parked there; then the car swerved back toward the other side of the street and smashed directly into another parked car, the impact turning it over on its side.

While we were talking, our neighbors started gathering on the street and Jewish boys began coming out from the school to see what had happened. The boys who had been in the car had disappeared.

Chris, one of the guys who lived in our building, joined Kimberly and me on the sidewalk. He was an aspiring writer in his late twenties with thinning, wispy blond hair. As we wandered out on the street, he recognized one of the demolished cars as belonging to Diana, a pretty girl who lived next door to him.

"She's going to freak out," I said.

Chris and I looked at one another. Suddenly the idea of how upset she was going to be, the sheer random bad luck involved, and the fact that it was, after all, only an assault against a material object, passed between us as a kind of exultation. In a moment we were racing each other from the street, up the steps, and down the walkway of our courtyard apartments in order to be the first to tell her and see the look on her face.

Chris had the lead, but just before we got to the door he stopped running and I "won." I knocked on the door and turned to Chris. "Why'd you stop?"

He was just about to answer when Diana opened the door.

"I think one of the Jewish boys just hit your car," I told her. She was on the telephone, she said she already knew about the accident, and our chance to see dismay cloud her features was not to be. As we returned to the street, slightly dispirited, Chris suddenly turned to me. "Why did we just do that?"

I shrugged. "Fun?"

Coming upon the scene of the accident again, we found an

almost carnival-like atmosphere: people were everywhere, and far outnumbering the few civilians were the Orthodox Jewish boys.

They were swarming all over the place, pouring out of the school like some kind of bothered insect colony, all of them so alike in appearance: the yarmulkes, the black pants, and the white shirts not tucked in. Tonight, however, some of them were in a state of undress, and I could see that over their undershirts they were wearing some loose, sideless, free-flowing garments. It was then I noticed that those strings I'd seen hanging down the sides of their pants were actually a part of these things. I'd always assumed that the strings were just attached to the belt loops of their pants.

"Hey, Rick," one of the boys called to me, "put your shirt on!"

I'd been writing without a shirt on, and it amused me that the sight of my naked torso remained such a worrisome thing to these boys.

Another one of my neighbors, Tom, joined us on the street. Tom was a blond New York transplant, a member of Queer Nation. While we were going over the details of the accident, he suddenly realized that his brand-new sports car was one of the two that had been sideswiped. Tom took this with a measure of grace and, after appraising the damage, went back to his apartment to get his camera.

"Rick, put your shirt on!"

As the boys milled about, recounting the accident, examining the particular indentions of the crushed metal, and even taking pictures alongside the upturned car, they would pass me with a mixture of curiosity and disapproval.

Tom came back outside with his camera and took pictures of his car. While I was talking to Kimberly and Chris, passersby stopped to see what had happened and to listen to further retellings of the story. All the while the boys continued to wander about.

"Rick, put your shirt on!"

I turned around to see who had said this and saw a boy looking at me with an impish grin on his face. It was Mendel, the non-virgin, and I smiled at him. As I turned back to my neighbors I suddenly realized that I could make a statement: my putting a shirt on didn't necessarily *have* to be an acquiescence to their value system. I ran into the house and put on a pink T-shirt that had a message on the front in big block letters: CHRISTIANS ARE ASSWIPES.

I came back outside and got a few laughs from my neighbors and we even started taking pictures with Tom's camera. Chris, very influenced by Thomas Pynchon, wouldn't have his taken, and when I went after him so that we could be immortalized together, he ran away.

Puffing my chest out, the better for the letters on the T-shirt to be seen, I went out among the boys. Although several of them hailed the covering of my torso as a victory for modesty, they were a little disconcerted at the message on the shirt itself.

"What does it mean?" one of them asked.

"It's my tribute to you boys," I teased him. "No, actually a friend of mine made this up for me when we went to the opening of *The Last Temptation of Christ* and the Christians were protesting."

Some of the boys gathered around me to see what was going on, to see what the shirt said. Another boy asked me what it meant, and as I turned to him I noticed Mendel standing a few feet away from me. I pointed to him.

"Mendel told me to put a shirt on, and I said I would but he would have to pick it out. So we went in my apartment and looked through my shirts and he said he wanted me to wear this one."

Mendel laughed and waved his hands "no" to me. "Don't you be telling anyone I was in your apartment—"

I teased him. "But you told me you wanted me to wear this one—you said it was the prettiest!"

Mendel laughed but backed away and went off to where the police were just arriving. Their car pulled up, and as one of them got out and started walking toward the upturned car he made a joke: "So where is he? Where is Evel Knievel?"

While the police started making out their report I began to wander about the accident site. The boys had separated into various groups, and I approached first one and then another of them as nonchalantly as I could, but invariably, when the periphery of their circle was transgressed, they would casually disperse and realign themselves somewhere else.

At the center of one group of boys, on the other side of the overturned car, I noticed a young man holding court authoritatively. He had one of those sideless shirtlike things on. He was tall and gangly, with short dark hair and glasses; his nose had a bump and his chin an unruly mass of half-grown whiskers.

"So do you know who was driving the car?" I asked.

"Yeah," he said, with a what's-it-to-you attitude.

"Who?"

Another boy answered me. "It was Zvi Ritchie."

I looked back at What's-It-to-You. "Who is Zvi Ritchie?" I asked.

"He's ju-just this kid," he stammered.

"He's sixteen," the boys filled in. "He just got his driver's permit today."

I looked at What's-It-to-You for confirmation, and since the information I'd been asking for had already been (too freely?) revealed, he summed up Zvi Ritchie for me: "He's a genius geek."

I loved that definition. "Are *you* a genius geek?" I asked.

Some of the boys laughed and one of them said he was just a geek. What's-It-to-You walked away, not to be bothered.

"Who is he?" I asked.

"His name's Avi," I was told. "We call him Catfish, though. That's his nickname."

I thought I might keep an eye on this Avi and was about to follow after him when the tow truck arrived. I stopped and watched as a man got out and began to attach something from his truck to the car. As I stood there in contemplation of this man's work I became aware of someone standing just behind me. I turned around and saw a younger-looking boy standing by himself. He seemed familiar. He had one of those shirtlike things on over his undershirt, with the strings.

"What is that?" I asked.

"What?"

"That thing you're wearing, with the strings?"

"Tzitzis," he said, without elaboration, and as he looked away I remembered who he was: he thought sex was a "beautiful rare jewel."

"What does it mean?" I asked, and I reached over and took hold of the strings hanging from one corner of his shirtlike thing.

"It represents the six hundred and thirteen laws of Moses," he said.

That sounded like Leviticus to me.

I stood before him, rolling the strings of his—tzitzis—between my fingers, raising the shirt aspect of it from his body, and feeling the oh so easy possibility of just pulling him to me, the eroticism of that strange underwear of his linking us together.

He seemed to be getting nervous and I wondered if it was blasphemous if a stranger held your tzitzis. He gently stepped away from me, trying not to appear rude, but I wouldn't quite let go the strings, and the shirt part of it was lifted tentlike between us.

There was a sudden loud scraping noise and I looked around: the overturned car was being dragged slowly down the street, pulled at an angle by the tow truck. I could feel the strings of the tzitzis slipping from my fingers. And then the car was tipping, with a painful crunch of metal, tipping back over onto its wheels. As I let the strings go, the car finally banged down into its upright position and there was scattered applause.

When I turned back to my little friend he was gone. I caught just a glimpse of him as he disappeared among some other boys.

I walked down into the street where the car had been, and watched as it was hauled away around the corner, scraping against the pavement. Most of the boys were going back to the school and I was sorry that the excitement was all over.

I wanted some kind of consummation.

I wanted an eradication of race, creed, and religion.

I wanted to share a "beautiful rare jewel."

6 / the yarmulke

Several days after the accident, I noticed that the room across from me, the room where I'd seen the bodybuilder, was now apparently being occupied by Avi, the "Catfish." He took down the brown paper that had covered the window, and whenever he was in his room I would watch him. I used my binoculars only after dark. It was fascinating to see him wandering around in there, sometimes with just his pants and tzitzis and yarmulke on. Sometimes his friends joined him and they would sit around, often involved in heated discussions, and I longed to know what they were talking about, what their priorities were, what they cared about—their lives seemed utterly mysterious to me.

But I *had* begun a communication of sorts with them, and so I decided I would try to approach them more on their own terms. The first thing I had to do, of course, was get a Jewish version of the Old Testament, so that when I talked with them I could use a text they would respect. I went to a Christian bookstore in Westwood and found a copy in Hebrew, but I couldn't find a Jewish version in English. I finally went to one of the bookstores on Fairfax, the center of the Jewish community in Los Angeles, and started asking around.

It turned out that the Old Testament was called Tanakh: The Holy Scriptures, and it was divided into three parts: Torah: The Five Books of Moses; Nevi'im: The Prophets; and Kethuvim: The Writings. The most official version of the Tanakh in English was published in 1985 by the Jewish Publication Society and included translations by a novelist I'd heard of, Chaim Potok.

To compare it with the King James Version, I immediately turned to the Twenty-third Psalm. Both versions begin the same way, "The Lord is my shepherd," but whereas the King James then has "I shall not want," the Jewish version reads: "I lack nothing." Compared with the 1611 version, this new Jewish translation, though perhaps more accurate, seemed pretty crude.

"I am that I am."

So God calls himself in Exodus 3:14. I was reading Northrup Frye again and he suggested that, instead of a noun, "God" might better be understood as a verb. This seemed like a revolutionary concept to me and I wondered what the boys would think of it.

Several of them passed me on their way to the park, and we acknowledged one another. I had now become a recognized part of their world. I had been spoken to and, since it had been established that I was homosexual, some of the boys, when they saw me looking at them, would either strut with a proud and adorable arrogance or do a contemptuous limp-wrist act, while still others ignored me. It was a fascinating thing to watch, and as I developed my ability to catalogue these various reactions I noticed that the better-looking boys were usually the flirts, and the taunters were invariably the ugly.

More boys came out from the school and started up the sidewalk toward the park, and as I watched them engrossed in deep conversations—watched the way they grouped themselves and the way they related to one another—I wondered what they were talking about. I longed to be one of them but with my hard-won self-assurance, that self-assurance I didn't have when I was their age.

The best I could do was watch and contemplate and impose myself upon them, just letting them know that across the street there was someone who coveted their animal bodies, and longed to bear witness to an unholy spilling of seed . . .

When yet another group of the boys went by, I decided I would just go ahead and ask them about "I am that I am," or "Ehyeh-Asher-Ehyeh," as it is in the Tanakh, and I got up and ran across the street to them.

"Excuse me, do you know about these words?" I asked, stopping them in the middle of the street and holding the book open for them to look at.

They gathered around me and looked where I was pointing.

One of the boys began a translation of the words: "I am that—"

"It's *Shem*," said another.

"It's God's name—you're not supposed to say it out loud."

I turned to the boy who'd pronounced this abjuration. It was the Serious Young Man, the boy who hadn't believed my fantasy about being a Nazi.

"Do you consider this—these words—a noun? Or a verb?"

"It's God," the Serious Young Man said. "It's a noun, a verb, an adjective—it's everything."

I looked around at the boys to see if they were agreed about this, and was just about to say something when Mendel came up to us with a friend of his, a fat redheaded kid.

"Hey, it's Rick the faggot," the fat kid said.

I tried ignoring him and turned back to the Serious Young Man. "Well, in the sentence you just said, when you said 'God,' it was a noun."

The Serious Young Man shrugged his shoulders, his silence

indicating he now felt it necessary to respond to me on the fat redhead's terms.

"In English, 'God' is a noun," I said, "and I was just thinking, wouldn't it be amazing if it had been translated wrong and 'God' was really a verb?"

"It's God's name," the Serious Young Man said, obviously uncomfortable and willing the conversation over.

One of the other boys must have felt the unfairness of this exchange, for he suddenly spoke to me with genuine interest. "It's everything—it could even be a preposition."

"What's it like being a faggot?" the fat redhead asked.

I turned on him. "You know," I said, "if you worshipped the penis instead of God you wouldn't be such a bitter little boy."

And I turned on my heel and left them, the little group standing in the middle of the street, absolutely quiet. I could just imagine *that* going around the school: what a revelatory, utterly blasphemous, mind-boggling concept that must be for them. Great!

As I walked back to my apartment, they didn't call anything after me, not even "Faggot!"

There was a knock on the door, and when I answered it, my neighbor Tom was standing there. He had found a nicer apartment up near the Sunset Strip and was moving his things there piecemeal. I think his car getting sideswiped had been a sign for him that it was time to move on. He said he had a present for me.

This did not particularly thrill me, since I felt that it would be almost impossible for anyone to give me a present that might actually mean something to me, and I dreaded having to feign pleasure.

He extended his hand and offered me a small piece of sheer material.

It was a yarmulke.

"*Really?*" and I took the little skullcap in my hands. I was suddenly thrilled with expectation: What would the boys say?

"Do you like it?"

"Tom, I love this! This is *exactly* what I've wanted—and I didn't even know it! Where'd you get it?"

"I went to a funeral for this friend of mine who was Jewish and they gave them to everyone."

The yarmulke was made of a cheap flimsy material, the barest excuse for the purpose it was meant to serve. I put it on and looked at myself in the mirror next to my door. I turned to Tom. "Well? Do I look like a nice Jewish boy?" and I twisted my neck to see it better. "I don't believe it! I really like this, Tom. This is great! Are you sure you don't want it?"

"Positive."

"Well—thanks. I really do love it. Thank you."

After Tom left, I wondered what I should do. I felt I must go out immediately, somewhere, anywhere, maybe up to the store. But if I bicycled to the store, how would the yarmulke stay on? I looked around and went to my desk. I had some paper clips, and using one of them, I fastened it to my hair.

I got my bike and, checking myself out in the mirror one last time, prepared to confront the world as a Jew.

What *would* they say?

On the way to the store I passed a couple of the boys, but they didn't seem to notice me and I made no particular effort to call attention to myself. They must make the discovery themselves. And, of course, they could only really see it as I bicycled away from them, when it would be too obvious if I looked back.

At the all-purpose drugstore I got some cookies, and as I approached the checkout counter I noticed there were a couple of lines, and in one of them the last person was an Orthodox Jewish boy. I went and stood behind him.

Sensing someone beside him, he looked around and our eyes met for a moment: there was recognition—he knew who I was and/or he could see the yarmulke on my head—and then he turned back to make his purchases.

After he had paid for his things and was preparing to leave, he acknowledged me. "So, what's with the yarmulke? Are you becoming Jewish?"

"A friend of mine gave it to me: he got it at a funeral, and he thought I might like it. I've never had a yarmulke before."

I had to step to the counter to buy my cookies. As the clerk rang up my purchase, the boy turned and left the store. He hadn't seemed amused, nor had he indicated any enthusiasm at our continued conversation, but I was still very excited.

By putting on the yarmulke, I had immediately become one of them: as far as the outside world was concerned, I was a member of their community. No matter what they might think of me individually, whether they liked me or not, we—they and I—were representatives of a single idea, whatever that might be, and as I got back on my bicycle, I was thrilled.

This association absolutely demanded communication!

I cycled down Poinsettia, past the park where the boys played ball and past the Orthodox Jewish boy I'd met in the store. As I rode past him I felt his eyes on me and I felt proud.

I could also feel the wind playing around the edges of the skullcap, wanting to blow it away.

The next day I made a point of sitting outside with my yarmulke on. When the boys came out of the school and started up the street on their way to the park, there were the usual greetings, the whispered jokes and laughter, the flirtations. I couldn't tell if they saw my yarmulke or not. Had the boy I'd spoken to the day before said anything to anybody?

A few minutes later two boys who were straggling behind started up the street, and suddenly one of them called out to me, "Hey, Rick, why the *kepa*? Are you becoming Jewish?"

As I turned around in my seat to see them better they crossed the street toward me. They stopped in the driveway several yards away. The boy who'd spoken to me was tall but ensconced in a baby fat well on its way to becoming chronic obesity.

"What's a *kepa*?"

"Yarmulke. It's another word for the same thing."

"It's Yiddish?"

"Hebrew," he said impatiently. "So why are you wearing it?"

"Well," I began my explanation, "I'm writing a gospel, the story of Jesus, in the style of the 1611 King James Version of the Bible, and since the Bible was written by Jews I want to feel like a Jew while I write it."

The boy with the baby fat looked at me in silence for a moment, and then shook his head. "You're a strange guy, Rick."

An hour or so later when the boys came back from the park, I was sure the boy I'd spoken to would have told all his friends that I was wearing a yarmulke, and anyway when they came down the street, approaching me from behind, they would be sure to see it as they got near me.

Usually when the boys cross the street, either coming from or going to the school, it is at the driveway for the apartments next door, or at some other point farther up the street. Very seldom do any of the boys actually walk down the sidewalk in front of my apartment.

But this day when they returned from their playing, a group

of them came right on down the sidewalk and stopped beside me. I looked up from my book. "Hi."

The Serious Young Man was among them and he stepped forward to confront me. "What are you doing wearing a yarmulke?"

"A friend gave it to me."

He indicated his little following. "Do you know why we wear them?"

"To show your respect to God?"

"That's right."

One of the other boys suddenly interjected a question: "Do you believe in God?"

"No. But that's not why I'm wearing it," I told them. "You have *your* reason for wearing a yarmulke, but that's not necessarily *my* reason."

"What's your reason?"

"I'm wearing it because you're wearing it. It's my tribute to you boys."

The Serious Young Man was outraged. "You have no right to wear it! You're an animal! You don't even know what being Jewish means."

I sat up in my seat. Now I really *was* interested. "Oh? And what does being Jewish mean?"

The Serious Young Man looked at me for a moment, his various retorts competing for verbalization in his mind.

He must have decided that the best answer was no answer because he started to walk away, but before he had completely turned his back on me he said, "It's too complicated to explain."

Realizing the bind he'd got himself into and as disgusted with himself as he was with me, he crossed the street to the school with his friends trailing him. Even with the last word he hadn't achieved a clear victory.

My answer to him came later: "It's all right to have a long answer, but you should have a short answer, too."

7 / tzitzis

I started wearing my yarmulke all the time. I wore it when I went to the gym (although not during my workout), I wore it when I went to the movies, and I wore it when I went to the store.

For the most part, there was no reaction from anybody. My friends indulged me: some thought it was cute, others thought I was crazy, and one, a Catholic, said I had no right to be surprised if I got beaten up. Josh thought I might get some sort of anti-Semitic reaction, but if I did I was never aware of it.

One day, while I was at the check-cashing place I usually went to on Santa Monica Boulevard, there was a black woman standing behind me in line. She must have been in her fifties. As I came away from the window with my money she approached me. "Are you Jewish?" she asked.

"No," I said. "I'm just wearing this because—well—"

"They're good luck," she said, interrupting me and saving me an awkward explanation. She reached up and touched my yarmulke, repeating, as she did so, "They're good luck."

But what I was doing didn't have as much to do with the

outside world as it did with the boys, and my primary aim was to have it on at all times whenever I was out and about in the neighborhood. The news that I was wearing a yarmulke had spread throughout the school, and I never wanted the boys to see me without it. When they came out to play or go to the store they would all look to see if I had it on and then talk about it among themselves, and I guessed it must have thrown a monkey wrench into their sense of propriety. What did it mean? Was I becoming Jewish? Was my wearing a yarmulke a compliment or an insult? Was I emulating them or making fun of them?

They kept asking me why I was wearing it, and my answers varied, but I usually said that I wore it because of them, "because I like you." One of the boys, when I told him that, flung his arms out in a gesture of despair and, spinning himself around in a circle, exclaimed, "Oh, man!"

My yarmulke had become a part of my person and it fit so neatly atop my head that I didn't really need the paper clip unless I was on my bike or the wind was really blowing. But one morning, while I was taking a walk with a friend of mine, my yarmulke did blow away. The wind wasn't much more than a breeze that day and I hadn't taken the time to clip it to my hair. I wasn't aware my little kepa was gone until sometime later when I reached up to make sure of it and it wasn't there.

The next day I returned to Fairfax and the store where I'd bought my Tanakh. In the back there was a rack filled with yarmulkes. I pondered them, feeling a little nervous about actually trying one on. As I held them, one after another, and examined them, some adorned with elaborate embroidery, I realized just how flimsy and insubstantial the yarmulke I'd been wearing was.

I found a simple black velvet yarmulke that seemed big enough for my head, and I went to the counter and asked how much it cost. Five dollars. That wasn't too bad. I went back and looked at the other yarmulkes some more, to make sure I had the one I wanted, and then I saw some little packets labeled "For Your Yarmulke." I picked one of them up and looked at it more closely. Inside were four strips of Velcro that would adhere to the underside of the skullcap. A notice on the packet said it wasn't good for men who had lost all their hair. One package cost $1.75.

When I went to the counter with my purchases a young woman helped me. I braced myself for the question: "Are you Jewish?" but she didn't ask it. Instead, she just rang up the prices, accepted my money, and put the things in a bag.

When I got home I opened the packet, took the paper from the back of the strips of Velcro, and, spacing them apart evenly, stuck the pieces on the inside of my yarmulke. Then I put it on and, as the instructions stated, pressed down where the pieces of Velcro were. I shook my head and, sure enough, the yarmulke didn't come off!

I looked at myself in the mirror. The black velvet was much prettier than my first yarmulke had been, and it offset my brown hair in a cute sort of way: beneath a rather sober symbol of spirituality, my unruly mass of hair stuck out in all directions.

I looked great.

That Saturday night I was in my apartment reading when I heard loud singing coming from the school. I already had my yarmulke on, and as I went outside I grabbed my binoculars. I walked down the sidewalk a ways until I could see where the music was coming from.

In the parking lot on the other side of the buildings that faced my street was a crowd of men. They all had beards and were dressed in black, with old-fashioned dress hats instead of yarmulkes. They had their arms around one another and were dancing in a circle and singing loudly. As they danced around together they seemed ecstatically happy.

I looked through my binoculars and tried to see if I could recognize any of them, but I didn't. I wasn't even sure who they were but suddenly I felt very excluded. I wanted to join them. I wanted to dance and be happy.

And then the noise and the movement came to an end. They were laughing with a kind of exultation and they all started hugging one another. In another couple of minutes they were getting in buses and cars and then they were gone.

I didn't know it then, but the spring break for the yeshiva had just begun.

All at once, the neighborhood was unusually quiet. There were no more boys going up and down the street to the store, or to the park to play ball; there were no more late night conversations going on in the dorm rooms, and as the entirely uneventful days passed, I realized I was lonely.

It was strange. I hardly ever feel lonely: I always have the gym to go to, or books to read, and the only time company with myself seems particularly burdensome is New Year's Eve, which also happens to be my birthday. It struck me as slightly unnerving that I felt a loss at the boys' absence.

But as the days passed I got an idea that excited me: when the boys came back from their vacation, I would look just like them. I had a black coat and some black pants, and I already had my yarmulke. As soon as my unemployment check came, if they didn't cost too much, I would get some tzitzis. I couldn't do the peyos, the long hair on the sides, or a beard unless I let my hair grow—but I *wasn't* working, so I didn't *have* to get a haircut, I didn't *have* to shave: I *would* grow peyos!

I've never shaved on my cheeks, and my beard and mustache are so light they could never really amount to much, but I could still do it. I could look like that boy they called Catfish.

When my unemployment check finally came I went back to the store on Fairfax and in the rear, behind the rack with the yarmulkes, were shelves of tzitzis. They were made of several different kinds of material, some of them were striped, and they had different prices. I chose a white, fine-textured cotton one for ten dollars. Again, when I went to buy it, I expected the girl to ask me if I was Jewish, but she didn't, and as I left the store I felt I had achieved some kind of coup.

I now had the capability of passing as an Orthodox Jew.

8 / avi

Orestes called me and asked me if I wanted to come over and have sex later that night. I said I did. Orestes was Latin and my whole Orthodox outfit probably wouldn't mean much to him, but it was the first excuse I had to get all dressed up. I put on my black pants and shoes, a T-shirt, the tzitzis, a white shirt over that, the black coat, and my yarmulke.

When the boys are in school or just hanging out, when they aren't all dressed up for services, they usually wear their shirt-tails out, giving them a rather unkempt appearance. Now, as I looked at myself in the mirror, I began to understand why. If I tucked my shirt in, and wearing a coat seemed to demand at least that much, there was suddenly a problem with the tzitzis: they were very uncomfortable.

The whole point of the tzitzis is that they should be seen, but since they were part of an undershirt I was wearing beneath my dress shirt, I had a problem. A knot or two inevitably ended up between the waistband of my pants and me, digging an impression of itself into my side. It was not a good feeling.

But at the moment I didn't care about that so much. I just cared about how I looked and I thought I looked great: if anyone saw me they would think I went to the yeshiva.

I wasn't going to see Orestes until nearly midnight, so I decided to go to the gym wearing my yarmulke and tzitzis. I got a few looks when I arrived and left, but for the most part no one seemed to care. The ones who would definitely notice me were the old Jewish men who came in the morning, but now, in the early evening among the bodybuilders and the socialites, I was just an insignificant aberration.

When I got back home I was at loose ends. Orestes and I weren't getting together for several hours yet, and I didn't really have anything to do. What I wanted was to have some kind of interaction with the boys. School had begun again the day before, but I still hadn't found an opportunity for showing off my full regalia.

I went outside and walked the length of one of the walls that bordered the walkway. Across the street the school was quiet; a light was on in one of the windows. Looking down toward Waring, the nearest cross street, I saw two of the boys walking west. They were probably going two streets over and then down to Melrose, to the little convenience store there.

I decided to follow them. I ran back in the house just to make sure how I looked. My yarmulke was in place, I had my shirttail in, the tzitzis were hanging at my sides, and, all in all, I looked passably Orthodox.

I walked to the store instead of taking my bike, and as I strolled along the street, my hands in my pockets and my eyes cast down, I began to feel romantically "religious." When I got to the store one of the regular bums there asked me for a quarter. I had a pocketful of change, and a quarter was practically in my fingers. I handed it to him, and felt I had thereby exonerated any hint of mocking that my clothes might imply.

At the door I noticed one of the Orthodox boys by the newspaper stand; the other one, tall and gangly, was in line at the cash register. As I walked in, the boy reading the paper by the door didn't look up but the other one, at the cash register, immediately took me in, and as our eyes met I recognized him: it was Avi, the boy they called Catfish.

Avi wasn't the only one taking me in. Right behind him in line was an acquaintance of mine, Sam, a musician friend of my neighbor Chris. Sam had been one of the first people to read my story about Isaac and Moshe, and his comments had impelled me to make the ending more explicitly sexual. He was Jewish, and as he looked at me now in my full Orthodox outfit he had an absolutely incredulous grin on his face: he couldn't believe he was seeing what he was seeing.

It was a weird moment. As I walked in the store I was approaching both Sam and Avi, my attention on the Catfish, but my obligation of communication was with Sam.

"You haven't converted!" Sam exclaimed. "I don't believe it—you haven't become Jewish, have you?"

I pointed to Avi, just ahead of him in line. "He converted me," I said. Avi was looking at me, and as I defined him as a catalyst in my life, I felt in him a sudden falling away of understanding. He knew I was kidding, he knew it wasn't true, but he still wasn't sure what the joke was.

There was an awkward several moments: purchases were being made, there were other people in line, and in a way I had begun two conversations at once. I retreated down the aisle away from the cash register and got some peanut-butter cups. After Sam bought his beer I explained to him that I *hadn't* become Jewish but I *was* emulating their fashion sensibility. Sam laughed, and after we said goodbye, Avi and his friend approached me. I didn't know the friend, a rather nondescript boy, but he was the one who spoke to me first.

"Why are you wearing tzitzis?"

"I'm wearing them because you do," I said, indicating them collectively.

"But you're n-not Jewish," Avi stated.

"So? Not everyone who's Jewish wears them."

"But the Orthodox do," Avi's friend said. "The Chassidim do."

"What's that—what's—" and I tried to say the word I'd just heard.

"Chassidim; that's what we are. Chassidism is the kind of Judaism we practice."

I thought about this for a moment. "When I bought my tzitzis, the woman in the store didn't ask me if I was Jewish."

"Do you know what the tzitzis mean?" Avi asked.

"They stand for the six hundred and forty-three laws of Moses," I said.

"Six hundred and thirteen," the friend corrected me.

"Six hundred and *thirteen*," I repeated carefully, to set it in my memory.

"Where'd you get them?" Avi asked, at the same time as the nondescript boy asked my name.

"Atara's on Fairfax," I answered Avi, and then gave my name to his friend.

People were passing us in the aisle and it was getting crowded. I excused myself and made my way to the counter to pay for my peanut-butter cups. Avi and his friend went outside, and as I paid for my candy, I could see them through the window talking together and waiting for me. When I joined them the nondescript boy regarded me for a moment. "Your name is Rick?" he asked and then, "Are you gay?"

I answered in the affirmative.

"We d-don't believe in that," Avi said, setting up a boundary for definitions.

"I know: Leviticus. Men who are homosexual should be killed. That's one of the six hundred and *thirteen* laws of Moses, isn't it?"

Avi nodded, and with this framework established, we looked at one another, not really knowing where to go with it next.

"You have sex with men?" the Nondescript Boy asked, repeating his question about my homosexuality, but this time a little more explicitly.

"Yes."

"Isn't that disgusting?" he pursued, and I felt a really interesting conversation between Avi and myself slipping away, a philosophical inquiry into the ramifications of Judaism, while I had to—once again—define homosexuality for a boy who had never met me before.

"Why do you think it's disgusting?" I asked. "Do you find your own body disgusting?"

"No."

"So why would you find another man's body disgusting?"

Since we were all going "home," they to their rooms at the yeshiva and me to my apartment across from them, we started walking back up the street together, three guys with yarmulkes and tzitzis engaged in conversation.

"Have you ever had sex with a woman?" the Nondescript Boy asked.

"No. I think their bodies are repulsive. I don't like soft things. I like hard things, men's bodies with strong muscles and big hard cocks."

They thought about this for a moment and we walked on a bit in silence. I had a suspicion they liked big hard cocks, too. After a moment the Nondescript Boy asked me when was the last time I had sex.

"Well, I had sex about an hour ago at the gym," I said.

"At the gym?"

"In the sauna. Me and a couple of guys jacked off together."

"How long did it t-take you to spit?" Avi asked.

I shook my head: to what?

"You know, to squirt, pop your nut, shoot your load, what? Thirty seconds?"

I was surprised and impressed with Avi's stockpile of slang. "Well, actually I didn't come," I explained. "I'm going to have sex later with a friend of mine, and I didn't want to get off yet. But the other guys jacked off."

"You just jacked off in front of other guys?" Avi asked rhetorically. "That's n-not having sex."

I shrugged: then I didn't have sex.

I watched Avi as he loped along and I tried to imagine his life: dressing in funny clothes, studying ancient scriptures all day long, incessantly praying to a god that doesn't exist, a prisoner of his virginity, and yet feeling that jacking off with a bunch of guys was not having sex.

We reached the corner at Waring and were about to head east, back toward Alta Vista, when the Nondescript Boy suddenly spoke up. "So, Rick, do you like me? Do you think I'm good-looking?"

"No," I told him, and I pointed at Avi. "I like him."

With this determination of his attractiveness, Avi jumped out into the street, pounding his fist into the air victoriously.

The Nondescript Boy made the best of his rejection. "It's a good thing you said no, or else I would have told you to get the hell out of here."

I started to explain my philosophy to him. "I like big noses—"

But Avi, who'd apparently heard all this before, interrupted me. "I have a big nose but a small cock."

"Oh?" I asked. "How do you know? Do you guys have contests to see whose dick is the biggest? Do you know who has the biggest cock over there?"

They dismissed this supposition, but I detected a certain

ambivalence. *Did* they know who had the biggest cock? Or was it simply that once the question was posed, it wouldn't go away unanswered?

"Oh, by the way, speaking of big cocks, whatever happened to that bodybuilder that used to work out in your room?" I asked.

"He was n-nuts," Avi said.

"They kicked him out of the school," the Nondescript Boy explained. "He wasn't a real Chassid."

"Well, he sure was beautiful," I mused. "You know, I think all you boys should work out more—"

The Nondescript Boy suddenly interrupted me. "Aren't you afraid of getting AIDS?"

God, I hated this terrible and inevitable association of homosexuality and disease. "Look," I said, "I've known about AIDS since the early eighties, and for a while I really was afraid of getting it, especially around 1984 and 1985, but you just can't hold on to that kind of fear forever, you just can't do it. So, no, I'm not afraid of getting AIDS."

"You don't care if you die?" the Nondescript Boy asked.

"I don't *want* to die," I told him. "I mean, think of it this way: I wasn't alive in 1945 and it didn't bother me, so why would it bother me if I'm not alive in 1995?"

"So, do you have AIDS?" Avi asked.

"No," I said, simply and definitely, but the quiet with which this was received compelled me to amend that answer: "I don't *think* so. I'm part of a group called the UCLA Gay Men's Study, and they've tested me every six months since 1984. They send me my cell counts after each visit, and so far I haven't gotten sick. Actually, I don't even know if I've been exposed to the virus. They'll tell me if I ask, but I don't want to know."

"Why don't you want to know?"

"I don't see the point. If I find out I've been exposed to the

virus, that means I'll feel guilty and inhibited whenever I have
sex, but, on the other hand, if I *haven't* been exposed to it, that
means I'll probably be afraid to have sex. Either feeling—guilt
or fear—seems horrible."

"You're not afraid to die?" the Nondescript Boy asked
again. He still didn't see how I got around that one.

"Two people I had sex with died this week. Forty people I
know have died of AIDS so far. What am I supposed to do?" I
suddenly felt that I had to cut through these boring rationaliza-
tions. I decided to let Avi and his friend be my catalyst for seeing
what all this might be about: "I knew this boy named Paul K.
We had sex once, and he was absolutely beautiful and full of
life, and he was a really good person. And he got sick and died,
and you know what I felt when he died? What good is all this?
Life. Why should I care about being alive if Paul isn't here? If
Paul isn't here, then how important could life really be after all?
I'm forty years old, I've had sex with—I guess—two thousand
men. I've had a great life, so why should I care if I die? Just so I
can hold on to getting old? I don't think it's worth it."

"So, if someone wanted to kill you, you wouldn't care?" the
Nondescript Boy asked.

"Well, I don't *want* to die," I began again, but it didn't feel
right. "*Intellectually*, I can say I don't care if I live or die, but I
know that a part of me, my *body*, wants to live. In 1971 I was
living in Sacramento and I was hitchhiking one night and these
boys picked me up in a car and I very stupidly got in the back-
seat between two of them. They asked me for some money and
I said I didn't have any—"

"But did you?"

"Yes."

"How much?"

"I don't remember. But let me tell you. The guy in the passenger seat pulled out a gun and put it to my head, and the boy

in front of me, and the two boys on each side of me, pulled out knives, and they asked me for my wallet, and when they found out I was lying they got mad."

There were various ways to tell this story: I could go into all the details or just skim the surface. Avi and his friend were listening to me very attentively.

"They made me get undressed and then they threw my glasses out the car window, and then they drove me to a dirt road south of Sacramento and beat me up. But the point I wanted to make was that when they put that gun to my head I could say in my mind that I didn't care if I died or not—I mean, the car could have hit a bump in the road and the gun could have gone off: *anything* could have happened—and I remember very clearly the feelings I had. I was thinking that it didn't *really* make any difference whether I was killed or not, and yet at the same time I was very aware that everything I was doing, every action and everything I said, was based on the imperative to save my own life no matter what."

"So you *did* want to live," the Nondescript Boy said, satisfied that the world was as he felt it must be.

"My *body* wanted to live," I said, and I wondered if I should tell them what I did to save myself. What the hell. "I was a Christian then, and you know what I said to them? I told them that I felt God would take care of me no matter what happened. I think that freaked them out a bit and I think that's why they didn't hurt me any more than they did."

We reached the corner of Waring and Alta Vista: the school was just across from us and my apartment was just up the street. It was time to go our separate ways.

"Do you use c-condoms?" Avi asked, and as I looked at him he suddenly seemed to me such a kid. He had a few pimples on his face and his light beard really was a scraggly mess. The self-assurance that had charmed me the night of the accident was now, in this more intimate conversation, much more tentative.

He seemed to be having some sort of problem talking, some speech impediment, almost a stutter, and I wondered if I made him nervous. I suddenly wanted to wrap my arms around him and hold him and gently kiss all his insecurity away.

"No, I don't use condoms," I answered him and then explained, "I don't fuck people and the men I have sex with don't usually go down on me, so there's no real reason for me to use them. And I don't want the people I'm with to use them."

Avi started off across the street, but the Nondescript Boy stayed beside me, just looking at me.

"You see, I have a specific sexual proclivity," I told him, and then I raised my voice to make sure Avi heard me. "I love the taste of semen: I'm a cocksucker."

Avi called to his friend, and the Nondescript Boy jogged across the street to join him.

"Do you boys sleep together?" I called over to them as I made my way up my side of the street. I watched them as they arrived at their gate and started working on getting it open.

"Now, don't be getting any ideas, Rick," the Nondescript Boy answered back.

They were having some problem with the lock and finally Avi jumped over the fence and opened it from the inside. He let his friend in and then the gate clanged shut after them as they started up around the side of the building.

I called after them once more, "Have fun!"

They didn't answer me.

When Orestes and I finally got together he was slightly amused by my transformation into an Orthodox Jew, but it didn't kick any of *his* fantasies into high gear.

He slipped a video into the VCR and it was one of my old movies: *Games*, with Al Parker and Leo Ford and Brian Nichols.

And me.

Ten years ago.

Worshipping cock.

I was beautiful.

We took drugs and then Orestes fucked me: he fucked my mouth and he fucked my ass . . .

And when at last I finally came, I watched my dick *spit* its stuff all over my chest . . .

It took six hours.

9 / crystal

I've only taken crystal about half a dozen times, but I think I've discovered the trick of how to avoid messing up your metabolism's whole inner time clock. If you take it at night (and "it" is a high-intensity speed experience) and you start to crash in the morning, the key to not letting your waking and sleeping schedule get completely out of whack is to force yourself to stay awake until evening comes around again.

After I left Orestes I went to the gym and worked out. It was just after six in the morning and I was still fairly high. There was a real exhilaration in stretching my muscles and actually enjoying the employment of my body's energy, without the usual feelings of boredom and the concomitant daydreaming about anything but what I was doing.

By the time I got to the sauna I was feeling great. It wasn't even seven o'clock in the morning and I'd already had some great sex and a great workout. I was by myself in the sauna when one of the old Jewish men came in. He took note of me and ambled over.

"Real estate today," he said and shook his head. "I'm lucky, I made most of my investments thirty years ago."

When I first joined the gym it had been called the Beverly Hills Health Club and its clientele had been almost exclusively old Jewish men (which was fine with me: without working out, I still had practically the best body there), but when the new management took over, most of the old men left. The few holdovers, with their lifetime memberships, usually came to the club early in the morning, and over the years I had struck up an acquaintance with a number of them, but I didn't recognize the old man speaking to me now.

"Thirty years ago," I ventured. "That would be about 1960."

"That's right. I moved here in 1959."

"Where are you from?" I asked.

"Belgium. I still go back. I have a place there."

"So, where were you during World War II?"

The old man suddenly extended his left arm toward me, showing me a tattoo there. "I was released from Buchenwald."

Though I'd written a story about the concentration camps, since I hadn't been alive then I found the history of that time pretty much one with all other history previous to my existence. It always amazed me to come across people who actually had memories of what were, for me, just words in books.

"How old were you when you went in?" I asked.

"Twenty-five, in 1942. I was twenty-eight when I got out in 1945."

"How were you captured?"

"I was in a café and the SS came in and I had some papers— you had to have papers and they stamped if you were a Jew or not—and mine were stamped 'Non-Jew.' "

"So how did they know if you were Jewish or not?"

"Because of the people I was with."

"What happened then?"

"I was in a camp in Germany for most of the war—I was lucky, it wasn't so bad. They sent me to Auschwitz in 1942, but the worst camp was the one in Belgium. I saw a man I knew there, a man I knew in school. We saw each other and he said, 'I know you, we sat on a bench together.' "

"You mean, one of the other prisoners?"

The old man shook his head. "No, one of the ones that ran it."

I was amazed. The story I'd written had been about two friends who later meet in a concentration camp, on opposite sides, but I'd heard of that actually happening only once. "Did he help you?" I asked.

"No."

"Were you friends?"

He shook his ahead. "No. Me and another boy were the only Jews in the class and he picked on us."

"So it didn't surprise you?"

"No."

My biggest argument against the existence of God, at least as far as the boys across the street were concerned, was the Holocaust, and I asked the man, "Were you ever religious? Before or after?"

"No. You couldn't be religious—you had to be tough. But, you know, I wasn't religious before that—I had to work. I worked seven days a week."

"I live across the street from an Orthodox Jewish school," and then I tried to be more specific and say it right: "A—Chassidic school . . ."

"They're the ones. It was the Orthodox that caused it to happen. They're the ones responsible, always trying to be different. It never would have happened if it hadn't been for them."

I was stunned. I'd never heard that accusation before. I didn't know what to say.

The old man started pacing back and forth, looking down at the ground as he did so. Suddenly he came over to me, as if he'd just remembered the answer to a difficult question. "My son?

He won't pick up a penny. Says it's not worth it. I say to him, you just keep dropping the pennies—I'll pick them up."

And then he left.

I stayed in the sauna for quite a while longer, deliciously sweating in the heat, and then I took a whirlpool. As I was getting dressed to leave I modeled my outfit for some of the men downstairs in the locker room, but, for the most part, none of them seemed to care or even notice that I was wearing a yarmulke and tzitzis. By the time I got home it was nearly ten o'clock, and the beautiful day stretched away emptily before me.

I made myself some coffee, took my director's chair and set it up outside, and, dressed only in shorts with my yarmulke and tzitzis, picked up my book. I was reading *The Antichrist* by Nietzsche, but it was hard to concentrate, and more often than not I found myself staring off into the distance, the book resting in my lap, and my mind deep in contemplation of the life around me.

What were those mockingbirds doing? What were their lives like? Where did they live? How important was a nest to them? Did they sleep standing up? What did their twittering mean? What did my chirping imitations sound like to them?

What did they think about *me*?

Time passed.

The Jews are the most remarkable nation of world history because, faced with the question of being or not being, they preferred, with a perfectly uncanny conviction, being *at any price*: the price they had to pay was the radical falsification of all nature, all naturalness, all reality, the entire inner world as well as the outer.

I tried to concentrate, but a single sentence of Nietzsche's would send my mind spacing out, and when at last I returned my gaze to the words on the page, the ultimate meaning of his thought would seem to be hiding in ever smaller increments, in

a phrase—"being *at any price*"—or even in individual words—
"nation," "pay," "all."

A boy rode by on his bicycle.

He glanced over at me as he passed and then turned back
with a classic double take, calling out to me as he did so, "Hey,
Rick!"

I stood up on one of the little walls bordering the walkway
and shouted after him, "What do you think of my tzitzis?"

He shouted back to me from up the street, *"Hot!"*

Once I'd stood up, I realized how lethargic I'd become, just
sitting there, and decided I'd go for a walk: maybe get a candy
bar or something up at the drugstore. I left all my stuff outside—
after all, who would take it?—and headed on up the street.

I was feeling great in a sharp-edged dreamy sort of way, and
the simple physical act of walking became a wonderfully affirmative experience. Just after I turned the corner and was walking
west on Willoughby, I noticed someone approaching me. The
sun was in my eyes and even with my dark glasses on I couldn't
tell who it was; all I could distinguish was the black pants and
the white shirt, indicating that it was probably one of them.

When I was abreast of the man I finally recognized him: it
was the tall boy with the goofy grin. Just as we passed each other
I realized he was doing a kind of double take over my tzitzis.

"Hello," I greeted him.

He said something I didn't catch, we continued on our separate ways, and then five or so paces later I turned back to look
at him, just in time to see him turning back to look at me.

It was a lovely concurrence.

He said something, again I didn't catch it, and then he was
gone.

When I got to the drugstore I scoped out the candy displays,
but the thought of eating any of it made me feel slightly nause-
ated—the crystal—and I was aware of myself as the chemical
composition I really am.

I began to mosey back home. I walked down Poinsettia, past the park where the boys played ball, and saw one of them walking slowly ahead of me. I realized I would catch up with him, with my brisker walk, and I wondered what kind of reaction he would have when I passed him. He was rather heavy and had a green shirt on. As I got closer I realized it was Baby Fat, the boy who'd told me what a kepa is.

He looked around to see who was behind him and then, before I could tell if he recognized me or not, he turned away and continued walking, but he seemed to be deliberately slowing down so that I would overtake him, and as this inevitability approached, I began to feel slightly apprehensive. As I came up to him I said hello. "How's it going?"

"Fine."

We were walking beside each other now.

"Where'd you get the tzitzis?" he asked.

"Atara's on Fairfax," I answered.

He suddenly stopped and confronted me. "Why are you wearing the tzitzis? And the yarmulke?"

"Because you do," I told him.

He studied me for a moment, assessing this comment, which *sounded* like a compliment, a crazy one perhaps, but not ultimately threatening, and he said, "You're a strange guy, Rick," casually dismissing me, the way he had when we'd spoken before. He wanted me to be a harmless curiosity, but as we continued on our way together, just the two of us, he apparently realized he couldn't leave it at that. "You know, these things *mean* something. They represent our continual awareness of God, and it isn't right for you to wear them."

"They mean that to *you*," I told him. "They don't mean that to *me*: that's not why I'm wearing them."

He suddenly became sarcastic. "Do you like wearing strings down the sides of your pants?"

I shrugged: I wasn't sure.

He was contemptuous: "Monkey see, monkey do," and then, as he continued talking, a kind of hurt crept into his voice. "These are holy things, and we don't want you wearing them."

"Why not?"

"We don't want people thinking you're one of us, we don't want someone to see you and think that you're—you're"—and he raised his arm before him and let his wrist go limp—"androgynous."

"What's that?" I asked.

"It means a man who acts like a woman."

I resented that. "I don't act like a woman."

"It's not right, you're not taking it seriously," he said, and I began to sense a kind of helplessness in him, an offense and a desperation. "By wearing these things you're mocking God, you're mocking religion . . ."

"I don't believe in 'God,' " I told him. "I don't believe in 'religion.' "

I felt like Baby Fat might burst into tears and I began to feel something of his pain: since he'd been raised to be a professional Jew, and brainwashed by his whole culture, his family and friends and teachers, obviously there must come times when he just had to crumple in the face of the lies he was defending.

At that moment one of the phys ed teachers (interestingly enough, *not* a Jew) came from behind us. He didn't say anything to me, but as he overtook us he put his arm around Baby Fat and walked him on ahead of me, down Alta Vista.

A moment later they were laughing: the teacher had somehow made a joke out of me or the situation, and as they walked on down the street together I was glad of that. Although I wouldn't mind being a catalyst for any and every kind of questioning, I didn't really want to hurt anyone.

But maybe that was a contradiction in terms.

10 / the blessing

On the following Saturday, the Sabbath, I was once again set up outside. All I had on was my gold trunks and my yarmulke. As I sat there reading (Plutarch's life of Crassus), one of the boys yelled at me from across the street, "Hey, Rick, where's your tzitzis?"

"It's too hot," I called back.

Another boy asked me where my yarmulke was.

My hair was getting so long that you couldn't see it unless you were behind me. I bent my head forward so that they could tell I had it on. It was just the slightest puncture in their potential self-satisfaction at my not being able to hack it as a Jew.

While I sat there and continued reading I noticed an attractive boy come out from the building and begin talking to some of the other guys, who were leaning out of their dormitory windows. He had some white sweatpants on, a light blue tank top, and over that his tzitzis. I picked up my binoculars and watched him in discussion with his friends, and realized it was the Serious Young Man. One of the guys he was talking to, a slim boy with short curly hair, told him what I was doing, and the Serious Young Man looked back across the street at me. He gave me the finger, and at that I got up and dashed across the street.

"Are you doing something wrong by wearing your tzitzis without a shirt over them?" I asked.

"No," the Serious Young Man answered, but somewhat bewildered by my question.

"It's okay," said one of the boys looking out of the windows. "He's not going anywhere and he's about to take a nap."

Two other boys arrived about that time with suits on and the old-fashioned black hats. I'd noticed that they usually wore the hats when they were dressed up. I asked them if they had their yarmulkes on under the hats. They said no.

"Hey, Rick, you're bothering me," the curly-haired boy said. "If you don't get out of here I'm going to call the police."

I pointed to the sign that had just recently been put up on the wall next to their windows.

PRIVATE PROPERTY

NO TRESPASSING
P. C. SEC. 602 (L)
NO LOITERING
P. C. SEC. 647 (G)
NO DRINKING
P. C. SEC. 647 F & G

VIOLATORS WILL BE
ARRESTED & PROSECUTED

"That was put up because of me, wasn't it?"

The curly-haired boy just smiled at me, and I backed up across the street. The other boys still wanted to talk and were calling out to me, but I ignored them and continued on home.

I went in my apartment, put on my tzitzis, and came back outside.

As I returned to my chair, the tzitzis waving about me in the breeze, a kind of shouting started up from the boys. I wasn't sure what they were actually yelling, or if they were really saying anything at all, but occasionally I could hear the word "tzitzis" ringing out in loud exclamatory tones.

The sound rose in volume and I began to feel as if I had just vanquished all irreconcilable differences.

It was a victory cheer.

Later, as I sat reading amid the lengthening shadows of the day, my tzitzis now on under a regular white shirt, I heard the sound of running bodies behind me. A moment later I was aware of two little boys standing on either side of me. I recognized them from the Orthodox family that lived in the apartment building next door. I guessed they must be about eight or nine years old. I said hello. They said hi. I asked them what was up, and they said they were just playing.

"Is it wrong to wear your tzitzis without a shirt over them?" I asked them.

The slightly taller of the two boys said no. Then they both explained that when they wore an undershirt, their tzitzis went over it, but when it was hot their tzitzis served as the undershirt.

"Do you say something in the morning when you put your tzitzis on?"

"The blessing."

"How do you say it? Is it very long?"

The boy standing behind my right shoulder said it wasn't long, and recited it.

"How does it go?" I asked, indicating I wanted to say it after him.

"*Baruch.*"
"*Baruch.*"
"*Atah.*"
"*Atah.*"
And then I realized I'd better write this down. I grabbed a section of the paper I was reading and started writing: "*Baruch,*" and I spelled it the way it sounded to me.

My instructor supplied me with the next word: "*Atah.*"

I wrote it down, saying it out loud to guide my spelling.

"*Adonai.*"

I didn't repeat that word, but as I wrote it down I translated it for him: "God?"

His reaction almost immediately crossed itself out, a surprise that I knew what a Hebrew word meant and a self-accusation answering that, of course, anybody would know God's name.

"*Elo-haynu.*"

I repeated the word to him. That sounded to me like another name for God, and I asked if that was so. He said it was, momentarily considering the two separate words and then deciding the difference wasn't worth going into, at least not now.

"*Melech.*"
"*Melech.*"
"*Haolam.*"
Long "i."
"*Ashair.*"
Astaire.
"*Kidishanu.*"

This was the funniest-sounding word to me: *Kiddy-shan-oo.* As I spelled it out I explained to my teacher that I didn't know how to spell the words, I was just going by the way they sounded. He was watching me, and the words I was writing, and he nodded to me that he knew that. He hadn't corrected me.

The next word was difficult also: "*Bimitzvazum.*"

I made a big guess at the sound of that word and the way it might be spelled.

"*Vitzivanu.*"

"*Vitzivanu.*"

"*Al.*"

"*Al.*"

"*Tee-lass.*"

"*Tee-lass.*"

"*Tzitzis,*" and, with a sense of conclusion, he indicated to me the strings hanging at his waist.

I looked at what I had written, and read aloud: "*Baruch atah adonai elo-haynu mellah hilam ashair kidishanu bimitzvazum—*"

And here the boys interrupted me. I hadn't got it right. I asked them to repeat it, and wrote what I thought I heard: "*Vimitz—*"

But my teacher interrupted me. "No, it's a 'b,' " he said.

"It sounded like a 'v' to me," I explained and changed the "v" back to a "b": "*Bimitzvoisum.*"

Voi instead of *va* and *sum* instead of *zum.*

I went through the blessing again, this time with the corrections, and all the way to the end. I then asked them what it meant and above each word wrote in small letters in separate parentheses the meaning: (Bless) (you) (God) (God) (king) (world) (that) (holy) (for) (on) (the blessing) (tzitzis).

The boys seemed to be satisfied with this performance, explaining particularly how you take all four strings together in your hand when you say the prayer, and then kiss them as they sprout above your hand when you're finished.

While we were talking, two little girls and a smaller boy they had been playing with came up to us. The girls didn't say anything, and that sense of propriety was pleasing to me: as men, the boys and I spoke of the absolute in abstract terms, which had nothing to do with them; *their* obligation was to just be quiet and listen.

"Do you have to say a blessing when you put on your yar-mulke?" I asked.

"No," he said, "but there are other blessings and prayers . . ."

His younger brother suddenly spoke up. "So many . . ." and then seemed to falter at the sound of his own words.

My teacher affirmed this, nodding his head and repeating the words: "So many . . ."

And like his brother before him, with the utterance of these words he fell away into a profound silence, the space around us suddenly filled with those infinite possibilities.

"But this is enough to start for a beginner," he said, using my ignorance to regain his bearings.

I was a "beginner."

How delicious that was, to sit there surrounded by children, an unborn thing in the cocoon of their presence. They stood around me, quietly, without any apparent inclination to do anything else, as if they were waiting for me to open my wings and reveal myself as the butterfly they knew I must inevitably be.

But then someone called them, our little group broke up, and the spell was broken.

11 / gentleman's agreement

The sound of breakers kind of lulled us into a state of laziness, when, suddenly, very loud there was a shot.

David yelled, "Oh, fuck," real loud. It was loud at first, then dwindled out as he fell limp in my arms.

An American voice yelled something. I heard another voice yell. "They're Americans, for Christ's sake. What German would yell 'Oh, fuck'?"

People were running around us. They helped me carry him to the fire and I prayed to God he wasn't dead. In answer I heard some soft mutter from David.

"It's the kike," someone yelled, as his features could be discerned by flashlights.

We laid him by the fire. His eyes were open and he seemed trying to say something, although his lips didn't move.

"Hey. Anderson shot the kike."

"Did I shoot the kike?" Anderson said and came into the fire's light.

David looked at Anderson for a second, then closed
his eyes and he was dead.
—Rick Sandford, "The Place of Sunlight"
(October 1967)

When I was a teenager I wrote several stories about anti-
Semitism, invariably from the outraged sensibility that such
prejudice could exist. I'd seen the movie *Gentleman's Agreement* and it had seemed completely mysterious to me: How
could you tell someone was Jewish by his last name? How could
someone be "partly Jewish"? And why would people not want
Gregory Peck to stay at their hotel just because he asked if it
was "restricted"?

The hook of both the book and the movie of *Gentleman's
Agreement* was the idea of a newspaperman pretending to be a
Jew for a story he was writing on anti-Semitism. Now, as I was
dressing up as a Jew day after day, with my yarmulke and sometimes my tzitzis—although never saying I was Jewish if asked—
I began to wonder about this early influence of mine. After
searching the book out in a number of used-book stores I finally
found a 1947 edition (eighth printing) with a dust jacket.

I'd read the book by Laura Z. Hobson when I was a kid
because it was on my very first self-imposed reading list: all the
works that were made into Academy-Award–winning movies (a
list which, eclectically enough, included Shakespeare's *Hamlet*,
Tom Jones by Henry Fielding, *Seven Pillars of Wisdom* by T. E.
Lawrence, and *Elmer Gantry* by Sinclair Lewis). Now, more
than twenty years later, I read *Gentleman's Agreement* in a couple of days, finishing the bulk of it in one long sitting on the first
Sunday in May.

For the most part it was a joke, skirting all the real issues of
anti-Semitism, and coming forward with standard propaganda:
Judaism is a religion, *not* a race, and Jews are just like every-

body else. *Why* anyone would be anti-Semitic is never gone into, and the people in the book who *are* anti-Semitic are so without any kind of rationalization. It all seems to be about some unspoken code of etiquette, and the only real reason even obliquely hinted at is the hoary cliché that the Jews killed Christ: "Nobody ever says, 'The Americans killed Lincoln.' " Near the beginning, when the writer is trying to explain what Judaism is to his son, as his mother looks on, the most important question in the book is raised:

> "Oh, they talk about the Jewish race, but never about the Catholic race or the Protestant race. Or about the Jewish people, but never about the Protestant people or—"
> "Why don't they?"
> Phil searched his mother's face. It was now impassive and definitely not helpful. He glanced at his watch, and a wave of relief rewarded him.
> "Hey, it's eight-forty."

The question "Why don't they?" is never answered.

The main character is defined as an "agnostic" whose parents *and* grandparents were Episcopalian. He's regarded as a Christian by others, and although "he'd always been deeply moved by certain parts of the Bible," you don't really get the impression that he's ever read the whole thing.

The most profound thing in the book is the recognition of the attraction of Judaism—its martyr sensibility—although that is admitted only as a cover-up for its racialism:

> They both laughed, and then Phil grew thoughtful. "There must be millions of people nowadays," he said, "who are either atheist, agnostic, or religious only in the vaguest terms. I've often wondered why the Jewish ones among

them, maybe even after a couple of generations of being pretty free of religion, still go on calling themselves Jews."

Now Lieberman became serious.

"I know why they do . . ."

"Why?"

"Because this world still makes it an advantage not to be one."

The description of the physicist Lieberman becoming "serious" is a revelation of self-righteousness, although it is not presented as such by Hobson. She cloaks with nobility that most despicable of human characteristics—self-pity—just at the point where she must defend Judaism as religion.

The real mystery of the book is the question of the author's own identity: Is she Jewish or not? In the book, "religion" is never conceived of as racial or political, in and of itself: it is *just* a personal, individual experience, more or less determined by upbringing. That read to me as a defensive Jewish position.

Jesus is never hinted at as being a Jew—in fact, the words "Jesus" and "Christ" are used exclusively as swear words. But then, maybe that's not a particularly Jewish prejudice: a Catholic acquaintance of mine once told me Jesus couldn't be a Jew because he was the Son of God.

But what really made me think Laura Z. Hobson was Jewish was the background she provided for her main character's father. This man, only briefly alluded to, didn't believe in interest and each year sent the money his money made to something he *did* believe in: an organization defending Russian political prisoners, a group fighting the Ku Klux Klan, and, finally, the Civil Liberties Union. With this description I sensed autobiography and the leftward leanings of an American Jew.

And so I sat outside, reading, with my yarmulke on.

Later, when it got hot, I put on my tzitzis.

It was pretty quiet for the most part, but in the middle of the afternoon I noticed some of the boys on the roof across the street, in particular a rather muscular boy with curly hair, whose yarmulke was so near in color to his own brown hair that he could almost "pass." I picked up my binoculars and watched. In a few moments he and another boy were over near the front of the building, taking off their shirts. This was unprecedented. They didn't seem concerned at all. The boy with the brown yarmulke had a nice body, but his friend was grotesque: the soft, white, muscleless skin haplessly containing his ill-regarded guts. Looking at him, I felt that his misshapen physique wasn't so much the fault of his body as of his mind and its creed: a perfect indictment of that myopic self-conscious thing peeping out through the lenses of his glasses, that thing that elevated "man," even as it denigrated "animal."

Sometime later another boy, also fat and self-conscious, came to the edge of the roof and called down to get some suntan lotion handed up to him. As he was taking the bottle from a boy on the balcony below him, he noticed me watching him with my binoculars. He turned and called back to his sunbathing friends and the muscular boy got up and joined him at the edge of the roof.

Their naked, immodest bodies were being observed by a known homosexualist.

The fat boy was truly stymied. I don't think it had ever occurred to him that his body could be considered a desirable thing (nor was it: it was a curious thing), but the muscled boy, almost "passing" as he did and attractive as he was, rather liked my attention. I think he felt it was his due. Holding himself erect, he stood at the edge of the roof looking back at me and my binoculars without flinching: he wanted me to see what he was.

Later, when they were dressing, he turned his back to me, pulled down his pants, and mooned me.

I yelled across the street to him, "Thank you!"

———

Late in the afternoon, as I was nearing the end of *Gentleman's Agreement*, I came across a passage that confronted me with my sixteen-year-old self, confiscating ideas in his desire to be a storyteller:

". . . There was a boy in our outfit, Abe Schlussman, good soldier, good engineer. One night we got bombed, and he caught it. I was ten yards off; this is straight. Somebody growled, 'Give me a hand with the goddam sheeny—' Before I got to him he was dead. Those were the last words he ever heard."

12 / yaakov

My unemployment checks came out to $133 a week. With that I could just barely pay the rent. If I wanted to eat, or go to the movies, or do anything else at all, I would have to get some work, so bright and early Monday morning, after a good workout and sauna at the gym, I got on the bus and went over to Burbank to have a new picture taken at Central Casting.

I wore my yarmulke and tzitzis, and had my picture taken in them. Of course, the picture is from the waist up, so you can't see the tzitzis, and I am facing the camera, so you can't see the yarmulke, but as I made my way among the casting people one of them (Jewish) asked me, "What did you do that you have to be a Jew?"

When I got home I took off my clothes, all except my shorts and yarmulke, and sat outside and started going through my unread newspapers. I made some headway, and late in the afternoon I brought my blanket out and took a little nap. It was a very hot day with the Santa Anas blowing, and it was wonderful to feel that wind without a breath of coolness in it.

I was lying on the blanket when a little boy who'd just

moved into the apartment building next door came and sat beside me. We'd passed each other a couple of times and said hello. His name was Yaakov and he was ten years old, swarthy and rather pugnacious. He offered me some gum, which I turned down, since I'd just put one of my teeth back in that morning with Krazy Glue, but I did accept his offer of a large red cherry-flavored candy.

"You should be careful lying down," he told me, explaining that the neighborhood was extremely dangerous and that just the other day a friend of his had been kidnapped and he had seen it.

"A Jewish boy?" I asked.

He said yes, but it was a Jewish boy who went to the public school. I asked who kidnapped him, and he said it was a *schvartzer*.

"Do you know what that means?" he asked me.

"A black person," I said.

He asked me if I understood Hebrew. I said I just knew the blessing for the tzitzis, and I said it for him. He corrected me on some of the pronunciation, and I practiced it again a couple of times.

Suddenly Yaakov nudged me and indicated someone walking toward us on the sidewalk. It was a large and surly black man dressed in white. We watched him as he passed on by.

"See that man," Yaakov said, and I watched the retreating figure. Suddenly the black man turned around and looked at us, and I shifted my gaze back toward Yaakov, who wanted to tell me about him.

"He heard you talking about him," I told Yaakov, who hadn't seen the black man turn around.

"He did!?"

"He heard you say, 'See that man.'"

Yaakov looked back and forth between me and the retreating figure of the black man, excitement at the potential danger brimming in his eyes. And then he told me a story, how that man had broken something at his father's workplace and pulled a knife on him, and how his father had jumped over *ten* benches. "I swear to God! You don't have to believe me if you don't want to . . ."

I told him I believed him (although I wasn't exactly sure how massive "ten benches" were), but I didn't understand why the black man did that.

"*Schvartzer*: he's crazy," he said.

Something in the look I gave him must have prompted his further consideration.

"Some white people can be crazy, too," he said. "Once I saw this white man with long hair and a big knife chasing some black people around a parking lot, and we called the police."

As I talked to Yaakov I wondered at his sense of time and his sense of reality. Were these the real considerations of young Orthodox Jewish boys—kidnappings and black people and knives?

In the scheme of things, I thought, my pseudo-Judaism and my queerness must be fairly lightweight stuff.

While we were talking, two of the high school boys came over. One of them was the Serious Young Man I'd spoken to about his tzitzis, and the other was a big ugly boy with a pimply face who started calling me "faggot!" and doing a little mincing act as he approached us.

I tried to get them into a discussion. The Serious Young Man wanted to talk, but the ugly boy just wanted to insult me. Pretty soon more boys came over, two of them on bicycles. The big ugly boy was still being abusive and told Yaakov if he saw him talking to me anymore he was going to tell his mother. Yaakov was indignant at being told what to do and began circling around us menacingly. At one point, while I was being called a faggot and being told how sick and disgusting I was, Yaakov came and took a stand in front of me. He planted his hands on his hips and, defying them all, asserted with authority, "He's my friend."

"No he's not—he's a faggot—he's sick—ask him."

Yaakov turned to me and asked, in a straightforward manner, "Are you a faggot?"

I said I was.

He was astonished, and stepped back across the brick partition of the walkway. He couldn't believe it. And in that moment I realized I'd missed a great opportunity: "You tell me what a faggot is, and I'll tell you if that's what I am."

They also told him I wasn't Jewish, and I could tell that Yaakov was offended at the allegation. A little boy sitting on one of the low walls bordering the walkway suddenly spoke up and stated the case with authority: "He's pretending to be Jewish."

Squeezing his hands between his knees, he smiled shyly at me with his understanding of my motivation. I think what made him so shy and pleased was the (incredible!) concept that an adult—me—was pretending to be something that he *was*; that I was, in a way, pretending to be *him*.

Yaakov looked at me and asked, "Are you Jewish?"

"No."

He was shocked, and I think he felt we were playing a joke on him. On the one hand I almost wanted to apologize, but on the other I wanted him to stand up and be responsible for his own feelings about things, and not just the labels applied to them.

A few minutes later I saw the Big Ugly Boy whispering something into Yaakov's ear. I was talking to some of the other boys and wasn't really paying attention, but then I noticed him as he passed in front of me and with great intent slapped his hand to his ass, all the while looking me right in the eye. The Big Ugly Boy and his friends laughed, and Yaakov grinned at his new-found favor.

The next day when the kids got home from school I said hello to Yaakov, but he was hurrying on across the street, and that gave him an excuse for not having to acknowledge me. Still later, he passed me again, and I asked him how it was going. He turned and shrugged an okay to me. There was just the slightest smile on his lips.

Poor kid. Do you treat someone as he treats you, or as someone else tells you to? Is someone who seems nice bad—just because he's a faggot and pretending to be a Jew?

13 / mendel

When I was talking to Yaakov, and the older boys came over from across the street, I had a sense of lines being drawn, that they were pitting themselves against me: normalcy over perversion, Jew opposed to Gentile, good versus evil.

Among the boys that joined the assemblage in front of my apartment was Mendel, of the impish grin. His tight curly brown hair had grown out some since I'd last seen him and wasn't as attractive: it made him look a little more conventionally Jewish, but he was as gregarious as ever and had the bright rambunctious attitude of a kid having the legitimate right to tease a small animal (me).

I told him I'd written about him and he was pleased, possessed as he was of the adorable arrogance that comes with being self-consciously charming. Some of the other boys wanted to see what I'd written and I told them it was on the computer, but that I could print it out for them.

I went in the apartment, turned on the computer, brought up my "Orthodox" file, and printed out the first nine pages. I scanned them as they began to come out and was surprised to find only one reference to Mendel and then not by name: it was the day he told me I looked good and then said he was only kidding.

When I returned with the first couple of pages I saw a man with a beard walking across the street toward the boys. Unlike them, he was wearing a coat. He told them to go back to the school.

"The faggot's been writing about us," the Big Ugly Boy said, and the bearded man—teacher? rabbi?—gave him an admonishing look.

The boys said they wanted to wait just a minute or two to see what I'd written about them. The bearded man leaned against a car in front of the nursery school next door and the boys gathered about him. Although he was arbitrating among them, I couldn't really gauge how important he was to the boys. They seemed to regard him more as an older brother than a father, and even though the argument/discussion seemed to be reaonably good-natured I could tell he was losing points.

"You don't get any respect," I called over to him.

"That's right," he said, and with that there seemed to be a consensus that they could stay to read what I'd written.

As the pages came out of the computer I brought them out in batches of twos and threes. They all crowded around to see them, taking the unnumbered sheets from one another, and passing them back and forth. After reading the first couple of pages Mendel suddenly looked up and asked me, "Do you think you're good-looking?"

"I'm old," I said.

When I finished the printing I gave the boys the last of the pages and then, sitting on my blanket, I watched them. They huddled around the car where they'd gathered away from me, leaning against it and sprawling over the hood and trunk. Occasionally one of them would look over at me, sometimes there would be a laugh, and I wondered: What *did* I write in those first nine pages? Could I really just hand them over without checking them? Was I really that sure I hadn't incriminated myself somehow?

After the bearded man had finished reading all the pages, he gathered them together, explaining to the boys that I needed them back. I told him I didn't actually, that they were all on the computer, and he asked me if he could keep them. Sure. I noted that the pages weren't numbered and he pointed out that the entries were dated.

Rolling the pages up, he escorted the boys back across the street to the school, with everyone in pretty high spirits, it seemed to me. I asked the boys what they thought, and a couple of them told me I was a good writer.

After they were gone I got my things together and retired to my apartment. Immediately I printed out another copy of the nine pages I had given them.

I reread what I'd written—pretending I was *them* as I did so—and when I came to my encounter with Mendel I cringed:

> . . . A few minutes later three of the boys came out of the school, talking together and going up the street. They were on the sidewalk opposite me, and when they saw me the cute one, gregarious, dark-haired, bright-eyed, called out to me, "Hey, Rick!"
>
> I called out hello to them.
>
> "You're looking good, Rick!" he yelled over to me.
>
> The boys get a kick out of complimenting me—in some strange way it's how they make fun of homosexuality: telling a guy he looks good and knowing, or thinking they know, he gets a kick out of it. I'm not quite sure. In any case, I had the presence of mind to call back, "You look good, too."

They were a ways up the street by now. But he and his friends paused just long enough for him to call back, "I'm just kidding!"

I was definite in my response: "I'm not."

This stopped them. The two boys with the speaker laughed and started kidding their friend. I think there is something humiliating for them in being thought attractive, although, of course, it must be very satisfying to be thought good-looking, and maybe even more exciting to be thought good-looking by another man. There is also the fact of their rigorous Orthodox upbringing in which a very strict dichotomy exists between "human beings" and "animals." I think this eschewing of the physical has something to do with this dichotomy and the fact that most of the boys, and Jews in general, are generally so ugly. Certainly, their whole presentation seems to be an emphasis on what is unattractive, as if to somehow deny themselves as "animals."

For a second I had him flummoxed, but a moment later he got in the last word: "Rick—you're a funny guy."

14 / baseball and velcro

After reading through my "Orthodox" file I realized how paltry a thing I really had. Although I'd defined my encounters with the boys in my mind, I hadn't actually written as much as I thought I had and what there was, more often than not, was just excerpts from letters. They made me see that if I was going to write seriously about the boys, not only would I have to start paying much closer attention to them—prying the individuals out and away from the nearly indistinguishable mass they confronted me with—but most important, as nearly everything they did and said was fascinating to me, I would just have to knuckle down and start writing more.

I was sitting out in front of my apartment and musing on these matters when the boys came out of the school and started up the street toward the park to play ball. As I sat there, watching them file past me, it suddenly occurred to me that I might go up to the park and watch them play ball myself. I didn't actually have any interest in sports, but the idea of watching these boys with their yarmulkes and tzitzis running around a field and chasing a ball suddenly seemed rife with possibility.

I put my chair and things back in the apartment, loaded my binoculars and a notebook in my backpack, and then cycled up to the park. When I arrived they had taken over one of the baseball diamonds and were picking teams for a game.

I climbed to the top of the bleachers facing the sun and unpacked my binoculars. I discovered that although I'd brought the notebook, in my hurry I'd forgotten to bring a pen. Oh, well.

I didn't want to seem to be intruding too obviously in their world, so I sat as far away from them as I could, just up from first base, but the fact that I was the only person in either set of bleachers and no one else was paying any attention to them at all couldn't be overlooked. Almost immediately they started calling out to me and one another, "Look, Rick's here! It's Rick! Hey, Rick!"

I only vaguely acknowledged their calling my name, acting as if I did this every day, and *they* just happened to be here. Besides, they had a teacher supervising them and I didn't want to get in trouble with him. I'd missed seeing how the teams got picked, and by the time I was all settled in they were just splitting up, half of them moving out to the field, the others behind home plate.

As the boys took their places I noticed Mendel and his friend the Fat Redhead, the one whom I'd made the remark to about worshipping the penis instead of God. Mendel called up to me, pointing to his friend, "Is this the fat redheaded kid you wrote about?"

I smiled in acknowledgment, and the Fat Redhead gave me the finger.

I don't know anything about baseball, but I thought maybe I could at least keep score since I was starting at the beginning, but barely a play into the game I was completely at a loss as to the big picture. I was too enthralled by the minutiae: how the boys interacted, how they responded to me, how they felt about pulling off a good play, how they dealt with defeat, and, most particularly, how they dealt with the problem of their yarmulkes.

Whenever the boys ran—after a hit or trying to catch a ball—either they would lose their yarmulkes or else their hands would inadvertently go to their heads in an effort to keep them on. Apparently, most of the boys kept their yarmulkes in place with bobby pins, and it was funny sometimes to see these little skullcaps bouncing up and down on the back of their heads. One of the boys—Meir, they were calling him—lost his completely as he went after a ball. After he tossed the ball back into the game, I watched him as he walked over to where his yarmulke was lying on the grass. He leaned over, picked it up, and casually replaced it on the back of his head.

There was something in his movement, some offhanded grace as he followed through on the retrieval of his yarmulke, that was very moving to me, and in that moment I realized he didn't have any Velcro for his kepa or else it wouldn't have come off so easily. Then I wondered if *any* of the boys had some . . .

I could give them those Velcro strips as a present!

What could be more perfect, more practical, or more appreciated? Once this proposition entered my head it became even more difficult to pay attention to the game. I picked up my binoculars and started watching the individual players. For the most part, I concentrated on the style of each successive batter, and, one after the other, as they stood there waiting to swing at the ball, their friends would tease them: "Rick's looking at you!" I tried not to play favorites, but the boys were aware of some of them.

They think I like Meir. The first time I really noticed him was the previous afternoon when the boys came over and I gave them my nine pages of notes. He didn't talk much, but I was aware of him because of his exotically dark skin and large

straight-lined nose that, in its distortion of his features, emphasized his shyness. Several hours later he and another boy were
going to the store, and I ran after them. I wanted to know what
they thought of what I'd written. As I approached them, the boy
with Meir took off like a shot and ran away up the street—in a
kind of fear, I guess. Meir said I should go after him, but I
declined his kind offer. I asked him what he thought of what I'd
written. He said I was a good writer. That was appeasement—
for all that he might have meant it.

Meir or his friend must have said something about our
encounter because now, when he was at bat, the other boys
started calling up to me, "Look at those legs, Rick! Aren't his
arms great!" Meir was embarrassed, but I continued to watch
him through my binoculars and was happy when he made a hit.

As the game proceeded I noticed that whenever the Fat Redhead passed by he would dart glances up at me. When he and
his team were not at bat, he and Mendel played the outfield,
carrying on a conversation with each other and not paying any
attention to the game. I wondered what on earth they were talking about.

A couple of times balls were hit to centerfield, and when the
Fat Redhead didn't run to get them his teammates yelled at him,
but he didn't really seem to care. Once, when his team was at
bat and he was waiting his turn, he came around to my bleachers and lay on the bottom plank, and then, several innings after
that, he approached me from the field. "Come on, Rick, you
don't hate me," he said, looking up at me through the fence, his
words more a plea than a question.

I shrugged my shoulders: Okay, if you say so.

He turned to his teammates. "See? We're friends. Rick
doesn't hate me."

I was impressed: the power of the written word.

Because of where I was sitting I was very aware of the two
first basemen. One of them was Mordecai, a young man I

remembered meeting before. He was an Arabic-looking boy with an aristocratic bearing and he hated my being there, watching them, watching *him*, and when he was at bat he was particularly vehement in giving me the finger.

Near the end of the game, while his team was in the field, someone got a hit. One of his teammates fielded the ball and threw it to Mordecai as the batter raced toward him. To catch the ball, Mordecai moved off the base by nearly a yard. A moment after he caught it, the batter touched base.

The teacher called the play: "Safe!"

Mordecai freaked out and started yelling, "He's out! He's out! I caught the ball! He's out!" It was an amazing display of an intensely volatile anger, as if somehow force and reiteration could change the truth.

He was consciously lying.

The game ended because time was up and the boys had to get back to school, but also because the teacher was exasperated with a heated disagreement that had sprung up about one of the plays. As soon as he said it was over I was down the bleachers, on my bike, and home.

A few minutes later, when the boys arrived back at the school, I was sitting out in front of my apartment with my newspapers in front of me, reading away, as if I'd never left. As the boys walked by there were a couple of calls to me and some queries as to what I thought of the game, but then a large antagonistic group came by led by Mordecai, and he was vociferous in his abuse.

I turned on him. "*Mordecai*, I saw you *deliberately* lie about getting that guy out at first."

This specific retaliation surprised them and there was some muttering ("Faggot!"), but, with this allusion to what they all knew to be true, the pack quieted down and straggled back across the street, Mordecai among them and in a rage.

Poor baby.

He may be trying to be a strong man and a good Jew, but he's just a sex object to me.

The next morning, after going to the unemployment office, I stopped by Atara's on Fairfax to buy some of those strips of Velcro for the boys. When I'd bought mine several weeks earlier they had been in a plain package and cost $1.75. This time they were packaged differently and cost only a dollar. It seemed to be the same product as before, only now it was cheaper and had a brand name ("Stíckíppah"). The label advertised it this way: "HOLDS ON TO YOUR YARMULKE / No more clips or pins/One size fits all / Works with all hairstyles/SIMPLE TO USE/COMFORTABLE TO WEAR." Unlike the kind I'd originally purchased, there wasn't a notice for men who'd lost their hair.

I bought five packets.

I gave the first to the boy with the brown yarmulke that matches his hair, the one who looks as if he could pass as a non-Jew, the one who mooned me. I was sitting in the bleachers waiting for the baseball game to start when I noticed him over on the basketball court, dribbling the ball and shooting baskets. His yarmulke kept coming off, to the point where it became an actual part of his routine: dribble, throw, retrieve ball, replace yarmulke; dribble, throw, retrieve ball, replace yarmulke . . .

I approached him and he backed away. "Get away from me."

"I have something for you. It's something I got at Atara's to help you keep your yarmulke on."

"I don't want it," he said.

"You really should have it," I said. "You spend so much time trying to keep your yarmulke on."

And I tossed the little package of Velcro down on the center of the court. I then turned and walked back to the bleachers to watch some of the other boys who were warming up on the baseball diamond.

I don't know if one of them picked it up, or if they threw it away, but it wasn't on the court where I'd thrown it when I left the park sometime later.

I gave two of the packets to Avi and his friend the Nondescript Boy. They accepted the little packages and thanked me.

"*Why* are you wearing a yarmulke?" Avi's friend asked, as if hoping to finally get it straight this time.

"I'm writing a story that is supposedly by a Jew and I want to feel like a Jew while I'm writing it."

"But you're not Jewish."

I shrugged my shoulders. "You know what I did for the first twelve years of my life?"

"What?"

"I worshipped a Jew."

"Who?"

I looked at the Nondescript Boy incredulously. "What do you mean, *who*? Jesus, of course."

"Jesus wasn't a Jew," the Nondescript Boy asserted.

Avi was embarrassed for him, and corrected him under his breath. "Yes he was."

"Well, he wasn't a Jew when he died."

Avi was even more embarrassed this time. "Yes he was."

"Well, he wasn't a good Jew."

"As far as I'm concerned," I told them, "there's hardly any

proof that he even existed at all. But, true or not, that *story* is the most important story in Western culture and I want to make a stab at it."

The boys seemed unimpressed.

"Have you read the New Testament?" I asked. "The Christian Bible?"

"No."

"You should," I told them. "I don't believe in any of it, to me it's *all* just a story, but it is very interesting. And, as literature, the Christian Bible is a sequel to the Tanakh. I think you would want to read it for that reason alone."

"It's not the word of God."

I shrugged my shoulders: What are you going to do?

A little later the Serious Young Man I'd spoken to a couple of times walked by with a friend of his. As they passed me, he said, "You're sick."

"Why?"

There was just the slightest pause before he answered, "You're a fag."

I watched them walk away up the street, past the next house, where a bunch of little kids were playing outside. The kids were aware of this brief conversation and I think its antagonistic tone made them nervous.

When the two boys walked past again, on their way back to the yeshiva, the Serious Young Man said something I didn't catch, and I came back with my planned response.

"You're sexy."

They stopped in front of me and the friend answered me, "Boys can't be sexy."

I laughed, and they walked on, but a moment later the Serious Young Man came back by himself. "Why are you wearing the yarmulke?"

We'd been through this before. "I don't know," I said. "I'm not really sure."

"You know that our religion and that—what you do—they don't go together."

"I know."

"So then why are you wearing it?"

I shrugged my shoulders.

"Why were you watching us play baseball the other day?"

"Because it's fun to watch you."

"Do you think we're good?"

"I don't know anything about baseball, but I don't think so."

"So, why?"

"Because I like to watch you play together. I like to see who's friends with who, and how you pick teams, and how you talk and relate to one another."

"It would be fun to watch girls do that," he said.

"I don't think so."

"Don't you like girls?"

"No."

"Why?"

"I don't like people who don't have sex organs."

"Women have sex organs," he answered me, but he didn't sound too sure.

I looked at him incredulously and then flatly contradicted him: "No they don't."

"They have breasts."

I snorted in contempt. "I don't like anything soft. I like hard things, hard and strong, and proud."

"Do you have sex with women?"

"No!" and I made a face.

"So how do you have children?"

"Children? I think having children is the most evil thing a person can do. I think it's sadistic, and horrible. There're already too many people on this planet. We don't need any more."

"But the Torah says to be fruitful and multiply."

I looked at him for a long moment, and then answered him slowly and distinctly. "I know it does."

"Then what do you do?" he asked.

"What do you mean?"

"How do you have sexual intercourse?"

"Well, I don't usually. Basically, I'm a cocksucker. I love a penis ejaculating in my mouth. I love the taste of semen. I think an erect cock is the most beautiful thing in the world. I think it is the closest thing I know of to God."

The Serious Young Man listened to my praise of the male sex organ and didn't seem completely contemptuous. I think he felt, instinctively, the contradiction of societal mores: that if he found the male sex organ repugnant, he would be finding *himself* repugnant—and that didn't make sense.

Yes.

He looked at me for a moment before he spoke: "Well, have a nice day," and then, as he started to turn away, I suddenly remembered the little packets I had with me.

"I have something for you, if you want it."

"What?"

I extended a packet to him. "It's for helping to keep your yarmulke on. You can have it if you want."

He took the little package from me, turned it over to read what it said, and then looked back up at me, considering the gift. He finally made up his mind: "Thanks."

"You're welcome."

As he started to walk away, I called after him, "What's your name?"

He turned around to say something but then stopped himself. After a moment he answered me: "Patrick."

I mulled that over and nodded. "That's a nice Jewish name."
He shrugged, and then turned and walked away.

The shadows were getting longer and I went inside and put
some more clothes on: my black pants, my tzitzis, and a white
shirt over them. I went back outside and continued to read
(*Jesus the Magician* by Morton Smith), occasionally glancing up
to watch the children playing next door, including Yaakov and
his older brother. One of the little boys, who was very good-
looking, kept showing off on his bicycle and his yarmulke kept
falling off.

"Excuse me," I called to him. "I've noticed that you keep
losing your yarmulke. I have something if you'd like. It helps
keep your yarmulke on." I extended the little packet to him.
"You can have it if you want."

I must have frightened him a little because he backed away.
"That's okay. My yarmulke stays on."

"All right," I said. "But I think you need it."

I continued to watch him, and a few minutes later his yarmulke fell off again. He was quite the little show-off. I guessed
him to be about twelve. When the boys had a race on their bicycles and he won, he threw his arms up in the air and shouted
exultantly, "And the winner is Sruli Perlman!"

I contemplated him.

One of these days Sruli Perlman is going to be a hot young
man.

Just before it got dark and I was about to go inside, I noticed
Meir walking up the street by himself. I still had one package of
Velcro left and I ran over to give it to him.

"Meir, how are you doing?"

He seemed a little nervous and shrugged his shoulders.

"When you were playing ball yesterday I noticed that your yarmulke kept falling off, and so I went to the store and got these for you," and I held the little package out to him.

"You bought this?" he asked.

"At Atara's," I told him.

"How many did you get?"

"Five."

He paused briefly, considering them; he seemed to really need or want them. Finally, taking the packet from me, he said, "Thank you very much."

"You're welcome," I told him. Then we abruptly parted from each other: he to continue on up the street and I to head back home.

A week later I was once again sitting outside, reading an article on Queer Nation in the *LA Weekly*, when Orestes stopped by to have sex.

I told him I was waiting for the boys to leave the school and go to the park. He said I should be careful, that an older man he knew once told him the worst thing you could possibly do was to move across the street from a school. I told him I didn't care and that I couldn't be threatened by jail because I had no vested interest in life.

Just then the boys started piling out of the yeshiva on their way to the park. A couple of them called out to me, and one of them asked where my binoculars were. I had them with me and raised them to show him. They said they were going to play a game. I pantomimed hitting a ball with a bat, and they said yes.

Orestes was surprised. "They like you."

I shrugged my shoulders, but I was really gratified by this

display. I told him I had to go. I put my director's chair back in the house, packed up my binoculars, and headed over to the park on my bicycle. The boys were just getting to the field when I arrived, and when one of them saw me he threw up his hands with the exasperated exclamation "Oh, man!"

I took my place up in the far corner of the bleachers facing the sun. I didn't use the binoculars so much this time and tried not to focus on any one boy, but it was hard not to pay attention to Mordecai on first base, especially since he had the easiest and sexiest manner of anyone on the field. It was especially interesting watching him now, as he always carefully kept one foot on the base whenever he reached out to catch a ball.

The only boy in the game I'd given some Velcro to was Meir, and not once while he was playing did his yarmulke come off. As I watched him I felt that he was imbued with a strange kind of inner strength, a certain implacability, and it made me feel as if his current youthful attractiveness was more ephemeral than I had previously thought. Near the end of the game, as he was walking by the wire-mesh fence that separated the field from the stands where I was sitting, he hawked some phlegm and wanted to spit it out. He turned toward me, took a step, and then spit through the fence onto the pavement at the foot of the bleachers: a simple expulsion of bodily fluid, *not* an audible show of contempt. Just before he turned back to the field, he looked up at me and our eyes caught for a moment, and in that acknowledgment was intimacy.

15 / brothers

Although I was mostly interested in the high school boys—their life-affirming testosterone in opposition to their ascetic upbringing—and followed their comings and goings with close attention, I couldn't help noticing the number of preadolescent boys who were increasingly taking an interest in me.

Whenever these little boys passed me, if our eyes met I would say hello. Sometimes I would get an answer and sometimes not, but my attendance in front of my apartment day after day had become a given of the environment, and I began to feel that my presence there offered them a certain kind of gratification.

The first of these boys I spoke to was the little boy next door, the day he and his younger brother taught me the blessing for the tzitzis. The day after that, when I saw them playing in the yard, I asked the older boy what his name was.

"Shmuel Dovid," he said.

Oh, brother! I thought. What a moniker for such a cute-looking kid. "Do you mean 'David,' " I asked, "like David and Goliath?"

He shook his head.

"How do you spell it?"

"D-o-v-i-d."

"Really?" and I tried that pronunciation, "Dovid," with a long "o."

"It's D*ah*vid," Shmuel Dovid said, slightly exasperated by my obtuseness.

"D*ah*vid," I said after him, getting the pronunciation right this time. "And who are you?" I asked his brother.

"My name's Yossi," he said.

"Hello, Yossi. My name's Rick."

After that I greeted Dovid and Yossi whenever they passed by. Sometimes I would practice the blessing for the tzitzis with them. And still other times I would just watch . . .

In the mornings they cross the street on their way to school and again in the afternoon when they come home. It is fascinating to observe them, especially Dovid. When crossing the street he is very conscientious, leaning his torso out beyond where he stands and looking both ways, a concerned expression on his face as he makes calculations for every moving object in either direction. After working these computations out to his satisfaction he gives an all-clear shout and then he and his brother run across the street. When Dovid and Yossi are with their younger siblings they all hold hands as they make a dash for the other side.

From their house, their mother presides over them at such times, an unseen presence just beyond the screen door, her voice irritably calling out commands and warnings if they aren't paying close enough attention to what they're doing.

On Saturdays and holidays the children are taken to services in various configurations but, more often than not, the father is with the two boys and the mother is never included. On these occasions, the father—who has a luxuriant dark brown beard— gets all dressed up in a long black coat and puts a blanket-like garment (a tallis) over his shoulders. As he walks down the street with his two sons he keeps his posture erect, proclaiming himself beyond reproach for all the world to see.

But then, during the day, when I am sitting outside and there aren't any services, I can hear him, with his horrible shrill voice, screaming at his kids—infuriated at their breaking some rule or "law" that might make the Creator of the universe even more angry than he already is.

Dovid and Yossi's house is actually the front apartment of a five-unit complex, each with two bedrooms. Upstairs and in the back is where Yaakov and his older and younger brothers live.

Like Dovid and Yossi, Yaakov and his older brother also cross the street when going to school, but with no mother there to watch them they are much more reckless, Yaakov impervious to danger while his brother, a slight scowl darkening his brows, often seems lost in thought.

One day, when the older brother was coming home from school by himself, I said hello to him and he said hi. He was about to walk on when he turned back to me. "Are you Jewish?" he asked.

"No. I'm studying the Jews, though."

He thought about this for a moment and then: "Well, bye."

"Are you Yaakov's brother?" I asked.

"Yes."

"What's your name?"

"Avraham."

"Oh, *Ab*raham—like in the Bible."

"No, *Av*raham. That's the way we say it in Hebrew."

I repeated the name with the soft "Av" instead of the hard "Ab," and discovered that it softened the "a" in "ham" as well. "*Avrahahm*. My name's Rick."

"Hi." I think this second hello embarrassed him a little, as it was almost immediately followed by a second farewell. "Well, bye."

"Bye."

After that I made a point of greeting Avraham whenever I saw him, always addressing him by name. Occasionally we would have short conversations, and I soon learned that his parents were from the Soviet Union and that both he and Yaakov were born in Israel. Although they had only been in the United States a few years, they both spoke English very well.

"Why did you leave Israel?" I asked.

"Because it's not religious," he replied.

I looked at him incredulously. "And Los Angeles is?"

Avraham shrugged.

Little Yaakov, seeing these friendly encounters between me and his brother, began to regard me a little less suspiciously. I might not be Jewish and I might be a faggot, but apparently I wasn't the devil incarnate, and his disdainful silences slowly turned into shy hellos and eventually he was hollering my name out with excited recognition whenever he saw me.

Late in the afternoons when all the other kids were inside or had gone home, I began to notice two little boys playing by themselves. Sometimes they would be playing in the deserted playground across the street, and other times they would just be wandering around together. The smaller of the two was the shy boy I'd noticed the other day, the one who'd defined for the others what I was doing: "He's pretending to be Jewish."

A few days after that, when they saw me sitting by myself, they came over to talk with me. The taller boy addressed me. "Is your name Rick?"

"Yes. What's yours?"

"My name's Moshe," he said.

God, I thought, it's too bad they only have ten names to choose from. I looked at the little boy standing beside him. "What's yours?"

"His name's Yitzchak," Moshe answered for him.

I tried to say the name, but I couldn't get my mouth around it.

"You can say Isaac," the little boy told me.

"No, I want to get it right," I said, and we went through several practice sessions until I could approximate the sound. There was something they did with the "ch" that I just couldn't get, however.

"Are you brothers?" I asked them.

"Yes," Moshe answered curtly, and then immediately turned the questioning back on me. "Are you Jewish?"

I shook my head and exchanged a look with Yitzchak.

"Then why are you wearing a yarmulke?"

"I'm pretending to be Jewish," I said, and when I looked at Yitzchak he smiled shyly at my quoting him.

Moshe was not to be so easily appeased. "Why?"

"Well, I'm writing a story about the Jews and I wanted to know what it feels like."

"So, how long are you going to be Jewish?"

"Well, I hope I'm done by September," I said. "That's when my first story is getting published. It's about the Jews, too."

Moshe thought about this for a moment, and then before he could ask me anything else, I asked him how old he was.

"Eleven," he said brusquely, obviously much less enthusiastic about answering questions than asking them. "All right, we have to go now. Bye."

He took off down the street, with his little brother trailing behind. Moshe was slim and had straight brown hair with just the slightest hint of red in it. There was a gap between his teeth, and he didn't seem anything like a blood relation to his dreamy-eyed little brother. I wondered if they had a different father or mother.

As the spring progressed and the days got longer, I found myself engaged in longer and longer conversations with Moshe and Yitzchak. Moshe would interrogate me about my life and motivations but would only reluctantly reciprocate with bits of biographical information. I did learn that there were seven kids in their family and that Moshe was the oldest. And while we spoke, little Yitzchak would sit still and watch us, some interior monologue dreamily but astutely taking place behind his eyes.

One day Avraham told me that Moshe and Yitzchak didn't have a father. When I asked them about this, they said he was in Israel, but it remained unclear to me if it was because he was working there or because their parents were separated.

Between the end of school and seven-thirty at night they didn't have anywhere to go or anything to do, and so they would come and see me and we would talk and it was very pleasant. Unlike Dovid and Yossi next door, and Avraham and Yaakov, whose parents I occasionally saw in passing, I began to perceive Moshe and Yitzchak as lonely children starved for affection, with a mother whose attention must be all taken up with their younger siblings and without a father altogether. I found myself feeling strangely paternalistic toward them and, instead of being a bit put out when they came around, I offered my undivided attention.

One afternoon some of the boys and I were sitting around and talking in front of my apartment when Moshe asked me how old I was.

"How old do you think?"

They started calculating. I nodded to Avraham, since he was the oldest. "How old do you think I am?"

"Twenty. Twenty-five."

"Moshe?"

"Thirty-three."

"Yitzchak?"

"Forty-two."

"Yaakov?"

"Thirty-seven."

"Forty," I told them, and pointed to Yitzchak. "He wins."

Avraham was really shocked. He thought I was much younger than I was. I don't know how much the differing ages meant to the others, but it was interesting that Yitzchak, who I assumed to be the youngest among them, had come closest to getting mine right.

"Why don't you become Jewish?" Moshe suddenly suggested.

I shrugged my shoulders. "I don't believe in God."

Yaakov was amazed. "How can you not believe in God?"

I shrugged my shoulders again.

"Do your parents believe in God?" Avraham asked.

I nodded. "And my sisters. One of them turned into a Mormon and the other one became a born-again Christian."

"Do you have any brothers?" Yitzchak asked.

I shook my head. "I wish I did, though. I envy you guys having each other."

The boys sat there quietly for a moment, this desire of mine for their life just as it was embarrassing them a little, and yet filling them with a strange kind of awe, that their relationships with each other were perceived by me to be something special.

"You have your sisters," Avraham said.

I shook my head. "It's not the same thing. My younger sister was born when I was ten, and I knew my parents would never have another baby, and I wanted a little brother so bad, and when it was a girl I hated her. I never forgave her for that."

"It wasn't her fault," Avraham said.

"I know, but whenever I saw her I just saw the little brother I'll never have."

"Do you see her very often?" Avraham asked.

I shook my head. "I haven't talked to anyone in my family in about five years."

"Why not?" Yaakov asked.

"Because they believe in God."

Yaakov was incredulous, and hit his chest with his hand. "*We* believe in God and you talk to us!"

"But you're not my family," I told him.

The boys were silent a moment as they tried to make sense of this.

"Well, actually my mother is dead. She died a couple of years ago, but I hadn't spoken to her in about five years. The last time I spoke to my parents I forgave them for the way they raised me, but I told them I could never forgive them for having had me in the first place."

Avraham was incredulous. "But if they didn't have you, you wouldn't be here!"

I looked at Avraham directly. "Exactly."

Yaakov couldn't comprehend what I'd said. "You wouldn't be here if you weren't born!"

"I know. And then I wouldn't have to pay rent, or go to work, or go to the bathroom . . ."

"You couldn't read, then," Moshe said, tempting me with what he knew I loved.

"That's okay. I'd sacrifice getting to read if I didn't have to be alive."

"Why don't you just kill yourself?" Avraham asked.

"I'm curious," I said. "You know, that's what the people who survived the concentration camps said, the ones who survived when they felt there was no reason to go on living—they said they were curious to see what was going to happen."

We sat quietly for a long moment, contemplating this meaning of life. I decided to pontificate.

"Everything that's wrong with the world today is because there are too many people. We're destroying this planet and it's all because there are just too many people. I feel sorry for you boys. I'm forty years old and I've had a pretty good life and I don't think it matters very much if I die or not, but I think you're going to see some really horrible things in your lives and I'm sorry for that. And every horrible thing you experience is going to be because there are too many people."

Yitzchak spoke up. "But the Torah says 'Be fruitful and multiply.' "

I looked at Yitzchak with his lovely dreamy eyes and their deep contemplative intelligence, and my heart went out to him.

"I know it does."

16 / the first day of shavuot

The conversations I had with the boys after school invariably ended up about God and Scripture. I had the Tanakh (the Old Testament), and I assumed the next important book to read was the Talmud, but the boys said before I read the entire Talmud, I needed to read just the Mishnah.

I had received my state tax refund, paid my rent and my union dues, and had sixty dollars left over, so I went to the Bodhi Tree, a local religious bookshop, and bought the Mishnah, translated by Jacob Neusner, for $37.45. I probably shouldn't have spent that much money on a book, but I really did want it, and I especially wanted it so I could show the boys I'd bought it.

I set myself up outside, in front of my apartment, with my chair, my binoculars, and a cup of coffee. I'd just started reading the introduction to the Mishnah when a service let out across the street. A few minutes later I noticed Moshe and Yitzchak playing together in the deserted compound.

They didn't seem to notice me at first, but after a while Moshe left the playground and crossed the street to me. Yitzchak didn't come with him as usual but remained behind, wandering around among the various jungle gyms by himself. I asked Moshe how it was going and he said okay. I showed him my Mishnah. He wasn't impressed and I was a little disappointed.

I asked him if today was something special, since everybody was all dressed up like it was the Sabbath. He said that this was the day when the Jews celebrated Moses giving them the Commandments on Mount Sinai.

Moshe suddenly changed the subject. "When did you get married?"

"I'm not married. Who told you that?"

"I know. I mean, why don't you want to get married?"

"I don't like women, and I don't want to have children. I think having children is awful, it's sadistic—"

"I know, I've heard this before," he said. "But I've never met anyone, not in my whole life, that didn't want to be alive."

"I didn't say that. I said I wish I hadn't been born; it's a different thing."

"Other people—*I* don't agree with that."

"I know you don't."

We continued talking and I asked him if he was going to the parade today, to "welcome home" the troops from the Persian Gulf. He didn't know about it. I told him they were going to have old airplanes fly in the parade, including some from World War II.

"You know," he said, "there are some people who say that World War II didn't happen."

"Those are stupid people," I told him; "they're not worth paying attention to. You can go up the street to the bookshop on La Brea and probably get a hundred books about World War II. I've got one whole bookshelf on World War II alone."

"You do? With pictures? Show me."

I went into the house and brought out two picture books, *Steichen at War* and *The Auschwitz Album*. I started with the

Steichen book, photographs of the war in the Pacific. I showed him my favorite pictures, the ones under the heading "Rest and Recreation." The first picture in that section is of a bunch of guys sitting on the deck of a carrier talking, reading, playing games, and sleeping.

"That's one of my favorites," I told him.

"Why?"

"Because I like to see them just sitting around and reading," I told him, and turned to the picture two pages later of four guys lying on deck with the ocean behind them: they are all leaning against one another, three of the men looking at a letter one of them is holding, while the fourth guy reads a book. "I love this picture."

Moshe was interested in my value judgments, and as I turned the pages, occasionally commenting on one picture or another, I showed him a photograph of Gerald Ford playing basketball and paused over another of two guys sitting next to each other, one of them closely examining the other's tattoos.

Then I opened *The Auschwitz Album*, a collection of photographs found after the war, the only pictures of Auschwitz while it was in operation, apparently taken with the permission of the SS, and showing the arrival of the Hungarian Jews in June 1944. We started at the beginning and went through every page. The first two pictures in the book were of old men with beards; one of them, the only "studio" shot in the book, was of two old men without any head covering. Moshe was really struck by these pictures, instantly recognizing these men as worthy of veneration and respect, and when I was about to continue turning the pages, he stopped me for a moment in order to look at them longer.

The next photograph is of the trains just before the unloading, and the only people in the picture are soldiers.

"Nazis!" Moshe exclaimed. I glanced at him and he explained, "I could tell by the uniforms."

We went through the rest of the book, and I added explanations where I remembered some particular detail. I pointed out Stefan Baretski, a notorious guard at Auschwitz (and minor character in my concentration camp story), and compared the pictures of one man who was photographed just after his arrival and then later in prison garments after his head had been shaved. I showed him which buildings were the crematoria and explained that the gas chambers were underground, while the ovens were on the main floor right behind the windows. In the final section, called "Birkenau," I pointed out one picture in particular: among a group of people in the little birch grove there is a woman who is reaching a hand across her breast in a kind of exhausted discomfort, while a little boy just in front of her is scratching himself, a painful distress in his features. I told Moshe I thought it was the saddest picture in the book.

"Why didn't the Jews fight back?" he asked.

"Because they didn't know what was going to happen," I told him. "They couldn't believe what would happen, and they didn't want to believe it. They'd just been in trains without food or water and they were hungry and thirsty. Their lives had been destroyed and they were depressed. They didn't know this was the last time they would ever have a chance of fighting back."

While we were talking we were joined by Dovid from next door, and Yossi, and then Avraham from in back. They took turns looking at the pictures in the books and we talked about them, and finally even Yitzchak joined us from across the street, ignoring the books and picking up my binoculars to look at the world from that point of view.

In the Steichen book I showed them what I think is an amazing photograph: a Japanese prisoner of war is bathing himself on the deck of the USS *New Jersey* before the watching eyes of hundreds of men. When Avraham first saw the picture he was appalled and said they were evil, thinking the naked prisoner a Jew and the soldiers Nazis. When I explained the soldiers were

Americans and the naked man a Japanese, he reversed his decision and said the soldiers were good and the prisoner was bad.

Apparently Moshe felt that our previous conversation had not been resolved properly, and while I was still talking to Avraham, he again asked me why I didn't want to be alive.

"I didn't say I didn't want to be alive," and I explained again, "I said I just wish I hadn't been born. And that doesn't mean I want to kill myself."

This frustrated Moshe; he couldn't see the distinction I was making.

"The Greeks used to say it: the best thing is never to have been born," and then I added, "It's in the Bible."

"We're not interested in that," Moshe said, emphatically discounting what he perceived as Christian lies.

I amended my assertion. "It's in the Tanakh."

"No it's not," he said; no such thing could be in the Tanakh. Avraham agreed, and said the Torah would never say that to be born was bad.

Okay, I thought. Where was it? Where had I just come across it? Where was it written down?

How could I find it?

"Born."

My concordance!

I ran in the house and got my *Cruden's Complete Concordance*, turned to "born," and found some references in the New Testament. But that didn't do me any good, not with these kids. I went through the Old Testament listings again, more carefully, and came across this under Jeremiah: "cursed be day wherein I was *b*. 20:14." I turned to the passage in my Tanakh: "Accursed be the day/That I was born! /Let not the day be blessed/When my mother bore me!"

I presented my evidence to the jury. Moshe, Avraham, and Dovid were shocked. Something was wrong. This couldn't be the real Tanakh. It wasn't right. Then they decided to check the real Scriptures, and in a flash the three boys were off—running across the street to the yeshiva, climbing over the fence, and racing inside.

Yossi returned to his yard to play with his sisters, but Yitzchak stayed, sitting quietly on the low wall across from me, the binoculars in his lap. I opened my book to read, but when I looked up I caught him staring at me with that dreamy look on his face.

"How old are you?" I asked him.

"Nine," he said.

That was a surprise. I thought he must be about six.

Although Yitzchak had explained me to the other boys, I don't think this explanation really made sense to him, and when I caught him watching me I think that's what he was trying to figure out.

The boys came running back with a Hebrew Tanakh, very excited and out of breath. Mine was wrong, and they opened theirs to show me, to compare and make sure, and then Avraham realized he'd been looking at chapter 21. He turned back a page and found the equivalent passage. Breathlessly, he read out the words in Hebrew, a few at a time, followed, in a real rush of excitement, by his own English translation.

When he finished the passage he looked at me in wonderment and said, "You're right!"

His exclamation was absolute: there was no sense that he had "lost" or that I had "won." What was exciting to him as he exclaimed "You're right!" was the thrill that there *was* an answer, and that he had found it.

But then, just as suddenly, there was an amazing consternation among the boys: *how* could such a thing be in the Tanakh! As I watched them it was amusing to me that the *context* of a thing was not any part of their consideration; for them the words had their own absolute meaning, and somehow it was unthinkable that these words should be in their holy book: it was against everything they believed in.

Once more the three boys took off, this time to get an explanation. I started taking my things inside, and Yitzchak watched me as I prepared to go.

A few minutes later they were back and even more out of breath; they had received their explanation. Dovid listened as Moshe started to tell me what they'd been told, and then Avraham began with his version. They were both greatly excited, but finally Moshe gave way to the older boy. "It's what a man says when he gets very mad," Avraham said. "It isn't the way things are, it isn't the truth, but something a man would say when he gets very mad."

"Well"—I smiled at Moshe—"I think your book is right."

Moshe knew I was teasing him, and he smiled back at me, but in his smile was the assertion that he didn't "agree" with me.

Okay.

But I *had* proved my knowledge: I had proved that there was something in their book which they couldn't believe existed. "Accursed be the day/That I was born! . . ."

And they were impressed.

I got my stuff together and locked my apartment, and when I was ready to go I noticed the boys had moved across the street and were playing a game: they were taking turns trying to bat a ball into a box on the ground several yards away. As I bicycled up the street, on my way to the parade for the returning troops, I waved to them and called out, "Bye."

They stopped for a moment to watch me ride past.

I felt great.

Victorious!

17 / the second day of shavuot

The next day I received my federal tax refund in the mail and I decided to go and check out the price of filing cabinets. I was on my bike and, as I rode past the school, I noticed Avraham and Dovid playing in the compound. They were excited when they saw me and called out to me, "We burnt you!"

"No you didn't," I said, riding up to them. "I burnt you."

"First you burnt us, then we burnt you, then you burnt us, then finally we burnt you best."

"I don't think so," I said.

When I got back (the filing cabinets were much too expensive), I set my things out in front of the apartment and prepared to read. I'd planned to spend the day finishing the introduction to the Mishnah, but I didn't get through it until nearly midnight. Since the holiday celebrating Moses receiving the law on Sinai lasts two days, it was like the Sabbath for the third day in a row: there was no school and everyone was dressed up.

Avraham came over to talk with me. I told him I had written about him, about yesterday. He asked to see it. I told him it was on the computer, and it would take several minutes to get it, but

I went inside and organized the entry for "The First Day of Shavuot" and printed it out.

When I finally got all the pages together, I came back outside; two boys I'd never seen before had joined Avraham and were sitting with him on one of the low walls bordering the walkway. The older boy wore one of the old-fashioned black dress hats which are reserved for special occasions.

I handed Avraham the pages, and while he started reading them, I talked with the boy in the black hat. He was in the eighth grade and he said he used to go to the yeshiva, the chabad, across the street. He explained that "yeshiva" just meant "school." "Chabad" was something more specific; he didn't say what. He told me he'd been kicked out of the school.

"Really?" I was very curious.

"They kicked me out because someone said I went to movies and somebody else said I was walking on Melrose."

Wow.

The other boy was his brother and said they were now going to another Jewish school on Pico Boulevard, one which wasn't a chabad. I didn't understand the distinction, and he explained that this school had a greater proportion of Hebrew versus English learning, while the school he was going to now placed a greater emphasis on English.

"Moshe didn't say that, I said that!" Avraham suddenly exclaimed, and pointed to a paragraph where I had written that Moshe had identified some American servicemen as Nazis.

I told Avraham I would change it right now, and I ran in the house and made the correction on the computer.

When I came outside again, I continued my talk with the boy in the black hat and we went through the basic preliminaries: no, I wasn't Jewish; no, I didn't believe in God . . .

"I know it's a cliché," I said, "but I really do think that everything is relative."

"But some things are bad—"

"I don't think so—unless *you* choose to call them bad. It's a value judgment, a subjective value judgment. For instance, I've had sex with about two thousand men, and I don't think that's bad."

"But don't you feel it's against nature?"

"No."

I think the concept overwhelmed him: what must it be like to do something bad and yet not think of it as bad! While we were talking I learned that he and his brother were here with their father for a service over at the school, but he didn't seem to care about it very much. What *did* interest him was my fascination with the boys and the fact that I was writing stories about them.

I sensed that he felt cut off from the world and that the world's incredible indifference to him and his way of life made him feel a little irrelevant. I think it amazed him that here was a forty-year-old homosexual atheist who was not only writing stories about the boys across the street but was wearing a yarmulke.

"I'm not wearing my tzitzis," I told him, "because I need to take them to the cleaners. I hear you can't put them in the washing machine because the strings will get messed up."

"You can put them in the washing machine if you put the strings in a pair of socks—that's what my mother does. And then that way they won't get tangled."

"That's great. Thanks a lot."

As Avraham finished reading the pages I'd written about him, he passed them on to the eighth-grader.

"Where did you get your hat?" I asked him.

"On Fairfax," he said. "In one of those stores."

I nodded. "It's really nice."

"Thanks."

He tried to read what I'd written but he never got very far because one or the other of us kept interrupting his reading to talk. He asked me for a copy of what I'd written, but I didn't make him one. I was suddenly a little nervous about my stories floating about, although later I was sorry I hadn't. I think he really needed some way to see his life from the outside.

While we were sitting there a boy I didn't recognize came over from the school and told them that the service was over. The eighth-grader and his brother stood up and prepared to go back to the yeshiva.

"Are you going to get in trouble?" I asked the boy in the hat.

He shrugged his shoulders: Yes, but so what?

"It's no big deal," his brother said.

We exchanged farewells, and I said it was nice meeting them.

When Avraham and I were left by ourselves, I asked him what he thought of the story. He said he really liked it and exclaimed, "There's so much in it!"

"In my stories I'm not sure how to spell 'Chassidic'—do you think I should spell it with an 'h' or 'c-h' and do you think I should use one 's' or two?"

"Two 's's, and 'c-h' definitely."

"Okay."

The kids next door were going to the park, and they asked Avraham if he wanted to come and play with them, but he said he didn't want to. "It's boring to play with them," he told me, and after they left we spent the rest of the afternoon talking about religion.

What most amazed and frustrated him was the fact that I didn't believe in God. "How do you think all this came to be?" and he swept his arm around in a circle.

"I don't know," I said, "but I certainly don't think there was some unified consciousness planning it."

Avraham shook his head. "You know, it's been proven that the first page of Torah is so perfect only God could have written it—no man could have written it."

I looked at him incredulously.

"It's true," he said. "The Hebrew letters are so perfect only God could have invented them."

"I think that's silly."

Avraham felt he must try some new tack. "You know about the war in the Persian Gulf? Those were miracles that show that the Messiah is very close. The Arabs aimed missiles at Israel and they didn't explode! That's a miracle!"

"Avraham, I think it's a pretty sad day when you have to call bad technology a miracle."

He looked at me and shook his head. "Someday you're going to believe in God, and then it's going to be so powerful—" and he threw his arms open in contemplation of the explosion that would happen in my mind.

I shrugged my shoulders.

"You're so hard to convince!" he said, impressed with my obstinacy. "Maybe only a great rabbi could convince you that God exists. There are bad people who, when they look into the eyes of certain very holy men, say they will never be bad again."

"But I don't believe in 'good' and 'bad,' " I told him.

While we were talking, some of the older boys had gathered in one of the rooms across the street, the room where Avi, the Catfish, lived. They shouted to Avraham not to talk to me, and among their admonishments I heard my epithet and name: "faygeleh Rick."

"The bochurs don't want me to talk to you," Avraham explained.

"What's a 'bochur'?" I asked.

"They're in the beit midrash."

"What's the—beit midrash?" I asked.

"They study the Talmud."

"Are they in high school?"

"No, they're out of high school."

I could see Avi in his room across the street, conferring with a group of guys and looking out the window.

"Is Avi a bochur?" I asked.

Avraham nodded. Hmm. I'd thought Avi was in high school. As I was looking over toward the school, Avraham suddenly interrupted my contemplation. "Why don't they want me to talk to you?"

"Well, first of all, I'm not Jewish," I said, "I'm an atheist, and I'm homosexual. The tzitzis you're wearing? One of the laws they represent says I should be killed for being homosexual." He asked me what I meant and I went into my apartment and brought out the Tanakh. I showed him Leviticus 20:13. He said he knew about that; they had told him all about it.

While we were talking, one of my neighbors in the building, Dan, "a Jew from Kentucky," as he facetiously describes himself in one of his songs, joined us. I had given him my story "The First Day of Shavuot" to read, and he was returning the pages to me. I introduced him to Avraham, one of the characters in that story, and Dan, easily projecting the transitions of story to publication to screenplay, asked him how he felt about becoming a character in a movie.

Dan's sense of humor has a kind of irony I am fairly sympathetic to, but Avraham is very literal—as anyone must be, I suppose, having moved to a new country—and the full meaning of Dan's remarks escaped him.

We were discussing the eternal dichotomy of life versus art when the guys who had been across the street in Avi's room, including Avi, came over. The first guy to cross the street was fat, had a slight beard, and spoke with a strong New York accent. As he neared us, Avraham rolled his eyes, and said this was "the Butt"—because he always butted in on everything.

As he came to the front of the steps he spread his arms and said, "This is the place to get sun, isn't it, the best place, right here?"

He was wearing his tzitzis without a shirt over them, and this caused a bit of consternation among his friends who were with him. Avi had positioned himself behind the others, so I had to shift around to see him and say hello. "You shaved," I said, noting his smooth cheeks. He just nodded.

The Butt turned to Avraham. "Why are you talking to this guy? Where do you live? You should go home."

Avraham, who lives next door, wasn't impressed and wouldn't tell him where he lived.

The Butt turned to me. "Do you consider yourself an intelligent fellow?" he asked.

"I like to read," I answered.

He didn't like this answer. "Don't be evasive—that's not what I asked. Why can't you answer a simple question? Do you consider yourself an intelligent fellow?"

I answered, "Yes."

"Then why don't you write a book like this?" and he picked up the Mishnah. "Why don't you write this?"

I picked up my story about Moshe and Avraham and handed it to him. "I wrote this."

He looked at the story, but couldn't be bothered to read it. One of the other men, dressed in a suit and hat and with a full beard, took the pages from him and began reading. The others read the opening paragraphs over his shoulder, and they all got a laugh about my buying the Mishnah to impress them. While the bearded man read the rest of the story, the Butt turned his attention to Dan, who was sitting on one of the low brick walls. "You're Jewish."

Dan admitted this was so.

"Where you from?"

"Chicago," Dan said. Dan had told me he was from Iowa.

"You were born in Chicago?"

"No, I was born in Iowa."

"You're lying. You were born in Russia."

Dan shrugged his shoulders and, speaking with a thick Eastern European accent, admitted his game had been seen through.

This dialogue was a little disconcerting to me. Dan was teasing the guy, bullshitting for the sake of bullshitting (not, I feel, a profitable mode of communication with these people), while the Butt was being belligerent. Underlying it all was an equality based on their mutual Jewishness which, rather than serving as some kind of bond, seemed to stimulate a nasty antagonism. A few minutes later Dan went back to his apartment.

The bearded man finished my story and handed it back to me. "What did you think?"

He was determined to be noncommittal. "You have a good prose style."

I thanked him.

When the Butt and his friends realized that Avraham had no real intention of bowing to their authority, they made a retreat across the street and gathered for a conference. I wondered what it was all about. The bearded guy was probably giving them the gist of what I'd written and, going over the pros and cons of my influence, they were probably trying to determine what the official line of action should be.

Increasingly I got the feeling that the purpose of their religion, and perhaps *any* religion, was to achieve power by *supposedly* protecting people from the chaos and meaninglessness of life—which is just what I must represent to them—and, after I looked through the Mishnah, it seemed to me that Orthodox Judaism, in particular, took pride in having an official answer for every eventuality.

What *are* the official plans of action for Gentiles who wear yarmulkes, for homosexual atheists? To avoid their company is undoubtedly the most primal directive. But what happens when your children like such a person?

Avraham and I watched the bochurs talking about us across the street. I almost got up and crossed the street to talk to them, but decided against it. Eventually the guys from the beit midrash went back into the school, and Avraham and I continued our talk for the rest of the afternoon.

Trying, once again, to convince me that there truly was a God, he pulled out, as a last resort, one of his most powerful salvos: the Messiah was coming *this year.*

"Really? You mean, a year from now, in May 1992, if we were sitting here talking, the Messiah would have come?"

"You'll see."

"Do you think any of the boys over at that school might be the Messiah?" I asked him.

This was clearly preposterous to Avraham. It was interesting that, on the one hand, he respected the school and the people there and yet, on the other, seemed to find it difficult to credit them with any kind of real holiness.

"Do you think I might be the Messiah?" I asked him.

For a moment this stopped Avraham completely, and he looked at me closely, rolling the question over in his mind. And then he laughed. "But you don't believe in God!"

There you go.

As the afternoon wore on, Avraham came up with a couple of interesting questions. "Is 'damn' a bad word?"

I had my dictionary right there and I opened it up to show him the definition so he could read it for himself. I told him that in 1939 it was against the Motion Picture Production Code to use that word in the movies, and when David O. Selznick wanted to use it in the movie *Gone With the Wind*, he had to pay a fine. I also told him that the head Catholic office at the time condemned the film and told Catholics not to see it.

We talked about movies for a while, and he said that when he was allowed to watch them on TV, "R" movies were the best. He told me about his friend Sruli Perlman (the knockout young man I'd seen win the bicycle race the other day), who snuck into a theater to see *Pretty Woman*.

"But that's such a terrible movie," I said.

"Did you see it?"

"Of course—otherwise, how would I know it was a terrible movie?"

"When you went to see it, did you see a boy there?"

"Avraham, that was a year ago, how would I remember?"

"That's when he saw it, about a year ago."

Avraham changed the subject again. "What's your favorite book, of all the books you've ever read?"

"That's a difficult question," I said. Even though I keep lists of all the books I read and choose my favorites at the end of each year, I really didn't know what my favorite book was. "I know what my favorite non-fiction book of last year was. It even won over the Bible. It's called *Let Us Now Praise Famous Men* by James Agee and Walker Evans."

As I thought about it, I was stymied when it came to fiction, non-fiction, and poetry, but I suddenly realized that I *did* have a favorite play, and that was *Hamlet* by William Shakespeare.

"We're not allowed to read Shakespeare because he's anti-Semitic."

"Really?"

I went into my apartment and got *The Merchant of Venice*. "Have you heard of this play? I'll show you the most famous speech in it and you tell me if you think it's anti-Semitic or not. The man speaking is named Shylock and he's a Jew." I found the right page and handed it to Avraham.

Shy. To bait fish withal: if it will feed nothing else, it will feed my revenge. He hath disgraced me, and hind'red me half a million; laughed at my losses, mocked at my gains, scorned my nation, thwarted my bargains, cooled my friends, heated mine enemies; and what's his reason? I am a Jew. Hath not a Jew eyes? hath not a Jew hands, organs, dimensions, senses, affections, passions? fed with the same food, hurt with the same weapons, subject to the same diseases, healed by the same means, warmed and cooled by the same winter and summer, as a Christian is? If you prick us, do we not bleed? if you tickle us, do we not laugh? If you poison us, do we not die? and if you wrong us, shall we not revenge? If we are like you in the rest, we will resemble you in that. If a Jew wrong a Christian, what is his humility? Revenge. If a Christian wrong a Jew, what should his sufferance be by Christian example? Why, revenge. The villainy you teach me I will execute, and it shall go hard but I will better the instruction.

When he had finished reading I asked him if he thought it was anti-Semitic. He thought about it for a moment, and said he didn't think so. And then he asked me what "anti-Semitic" meant.

"Let's look it up."

I looked up "Semite" first:

Sem'ite, Shem'ite, *n.* a member of any of the peoples whose language is Semitic, including the Hebrews, Arabs, Assyrians, Phoenicians, Babylonians, etc.; not, specifically, a Jew.

This definition didn't seem to please Avraham very much. I looked up "anti-Semitic":

an'ti-Sem'it'ic, *a.* 1. having or showing prejudice against Jews: disliking or fearing Jews and Jewish things.
2. discriminating against or persecuting Jews.
3. of or caused by anti-Semitism.

Here was a definition that Avraham accepted. As for myself, I found it strange that while "Semite" designates a wide range of peoples (as I had so believed), "anti-Semitic"—according to an official dictionary definition—has an exclusively Jewish connotation.

I'd thought "anti-Semitic" was an exclusively racial term: I didn't realize it could be ideological as well.

18 / anti-semanticism

When I told my friend Josh about my conundrum concerning "Semite" and "anti-Semitic," he said I still hadn't got it right—that "anti-Semitic" was *not* an ideological as well as a racial term: it was *only* an ideological term.

According to *Webster's New Twentieth Century Dictionary of the English Language*/Unabridged/Second Edition:

> an'ti-Sem'i·tism, *n*.   1. prejudice against Jews; dislike or fear of Jews and Jewish things.
>   2. discrimination against or persecution of Jews.

So, is it a racial or an ideological term?
I guess that depends on how you define "Jew."

> Jew (ju), *n*. [ME, *Jew*, *Giw*; OFr. *jeu*, *geu*; L. *Judaeus*; Gr. *Ioudaios*, a Jew, an inhabitant of Judea, from *Ioudaia*, Judea, from Heb. *yehudhah*, Judah.]
>   1. a person descended, or regarded as descended, from the ancient Hebrews of Biblical times.

2. a person whose religion is Judaism.

Ju'da·ism, *n.* [LL. *Judaismus*; Gr. *Ioudaismos*, Judaism, from *Ioudaizein*, to Judaize.]
1. the Jewish religion.
2. conformity to the Jewish rites, ceremonies, customs, rules, etc.

Well, "a person descended, or regarded as descended, from the ancient Hebrews of Biblical times" sure sounds like a racial term to me.

But is it? Just what exactly does "racial" mean?

ra'cial (=shal), *a.* of or pertaining to race, family, or descent; of or pertaining to the races of mankind; ethnological.

race, *n.* [Fr. race; It. *razza*, race, family; perh. from L. *generatio*, a begetting.]
1. (a) any of the major biological divisions of mankind, distinguished by color and texture of hair, color of skin and eyes, stature, bodily proportions, etc.: many ethnologists now consider that there are only three primary divisions, the Caucasian (loosely, *white race*), Negroid (loosely, *black race*), and Mongoloid (loosely, *yellow race*), each with various subdivisions: the term has acquired so many unscientific connotations that in this sense it is often replaced in scientific usage by *ethnic stock* or *group*; (b) mankind.
2. a population that differs from others in the relative frequency of some gene or genes: a modern scientific use.
3. any geographical, national, or tribal ethnic grouping.
4. (a) the state of belonging to a certain ethnic stock, group, etc.; (b) the qualities, traits, etc. belonging, or supposedly belonging, to such a division.

5. any group of people having the same activities, habits, ideas, etc.; as, the *race* of dramatists.

6. a group of people having a common parentage; the descendants collectively of a common ancestry; family; clan.

7. (a) a breed; a stock; a large division or class, the species and genera of which are traceable to a common origin; (b) in zoology, a subspecies or variety.

8. characteristic strength or flavor indicating the origin of some natural product; as, the *race* of a wine. [Rare.]

Syn.—breed, family, nation, people, tribe.

According to the Encyclopaedia Judaica (second printing, 1973), "anti-Semitism" is a term coined in 1879 by "the German agitator Wilhelm Marr to designate the then-current anti-Jewish campaigns in Europe." The encyclopedia goes on to say: "It is often qualified by an adjective denoting the specific cause, nature, or rationale of a manifestation of anti-Jewish passion or action: e.g., 'economic anti-Semitism,' 'social anti-Semitism,' 'racial anti-Semitism,' etc."

As far as the word "Jew" is concerned, according to the encyclopedia it was "originally applied to members of the tribe of Judah . . ." After the destruction of the Northern Kingdom of Israel the term lost its specific connection with the Southern Kingdom (Judah) and first began to be used as a religious term.

With Christianity began a series of negative connotations for the word and, as the encyclopedia points out, "Many attempts to root out these derogatory meanings by having the dictionary definitions revised have been made in the United States, England, and Europe but have, however, met with little success, since the problem is not one of ill-will on the part of the lexicographers, but rather of semantics and popular usage."

The Encyclopaedia Judaica goes on to state that the definition of "Jew" is very controversial, with the rabbinical courts
standing behind the "Halakhic Definition":

A child born of Jewish parents or a convert to Judaism
are considered Jews, possessing both the sanctity of the
Jewish people (Ex. 19:6) and the obligation to observe
the commandments. The status of children from inter-
marriage is designated by the Mishnah and Talmud as
following that of the mother (Kid. 3:12; Yad, Issurei
Bi'ah 15:3–4). "The son by an Israelite woman is called
thy son, but thy son by a heathen woman is not called
thy son" (Kid. 68b). A child born of a non-Jewish
mother must therefore undergo ritual conversion, even
though his father is Jewish. The halakhic definition was
accepted for centuries. However, in modern times and
particularly since the establishment of the State of Israel,
the definition has been more and more questioned. The
act of conversion is of course a religious act and thus any
candidate for conversion is required to subscribe to the
principles of Judaism and practice all the *mitzvot*, something which the majority of born Jews do not do. Thus it
is felt in wide circles that identification with the Jewish
people and its fate should constitute sufficient grounds
for being considered a Jew, particularly since during the
Holocaust tens—even hundreds—of thousands of Jews,
who were not halakhically so considered, perished
because the Nazis had considered them Jews . . .

On my way to the store one afternoon I passed a man wearing a
yarmulke and said, "Shalom." He answered me and then asked
if I was Jewish.

I cycled back around to him, explaining that I wasn't, and that I actually only knew a few Hebrew words. He said he was here in Los Angeles to study with a certain rabbi in order to "squeeze knowledge out of him, like juice from an orange."

During our brief talk, the question of the definition of "Jew"came up, and when he said it was not a racial term, I pointed out to him some of the definitions of the word "race."

He conceded my point and said, "It's all right to call the Jews a 'race,' as long as you don't say it with any negative connotations."

I nodded my head.

Gotcha.

19 / the hat

Now that I had some money, I thought it might be time to get one of those black dress hats the boys wore on special occasions. I drove around the Fairfax area and asked at a few clothes shops if they had any hats and was surprised to learn that you could get them at Atara's, the store where I'd bought my tzitzis and yarmulke. They were kept in the very back of the store, behind the books.

While I was waiting for the old man who ran the store to finish helping an Orthodox Jewish boy I didn't recognize, a young man with a beard came in, the guy who'd read my story the other day and told me I had a good prose style.

"I wrote about you," I told him, "and what you said."

"You write down the compliments people tell you?" he asked.

And then he asked me what I was doing there, and I told him I was looking for some books. I was hesitant somehow to tell him I was looking for a hat. The old man overheard part of our conversation and was surprised to learn that I wasn't Jewish. I was wondering if he might then tell me I couldn't buy the hat, or to get out of his store. I felt bad because, while I wasn't actually saying I was Jewish (even though I had a week or so of stubble and was wearing a yarmulke), I didn't want to have a conflict of ideology with an old man. And this bearded guy was taking advantage of my precarious position.

"So why do you have all this interest in Jewish things?"

I reached in my pocket and pulled out a quarter. "See this," I said, and pointed to the words next to the embossed portrait of George Washington: " 'In God We Trust'—those words are on my money. All the money I make, every penny I spend, has those words on it: 'In God We Trust.' The Jews invented God—how could I *not* be interested in Jewish things?"

"The Jews didn't invent God," the bearded young man said, rather hesitantly.

I shrugged my shoulders: Whatever you say—it's all semantics.

We looked at one another for a long moment, and then the bearded young man said he had to go and we wished each other a good day.

After the old man had finished waiting on the Orthodox boy, he helped me pick out a hat, size 7¾, which cost $55. It was very cool. I also bought a couple of books, *Hasidic Tales of the Holocaust* and a prayer book, *The Artscroll Weekday Siddur*. He didn't seem to be bothered by the fact that I wasn't Jewish, and I wondered if that was because the relationship between a merchant and his customer is more primal than that between a Jew and a Gentile.

It was almost three-thirty when I got home, too hot to justifiably get into the full outfit with my new hat, so I went outside and sunned a little. My landlord stopped by and I told him that two months' rent was in the mail, and then I just had to show him my hat. George is Jewish and speaks with a Hungarian accent, but he is also an atheistic heterosexual Republican, and I thought he might be amused at this new demonstration of my cause. I went into the apartment and put the hat on. George was impressed and we talked for a while. He said he was doing some large painting about the Holocaust, and so I showed him *The Auschwitz Album*. He went through it carefully, and although he was torn between wanting to look at it and not wanting to, I think he was a bit disappointed that there weren't any conventional atrocity pictures.

When George had finished looking at the book he went to check on one of the empty apartments. It was getting on in the afternoon and, what with the overcast weather we'd been having—like June although it was still May—I felt it wouldn't be that inappropriate if I went ahead and got all dressed up. I put on my black pants, coat, and shoes, the tzitzis under a white shirt, and my new dress hat and checked myself out in the mirror: yes indeed—all dressed up and with my scruffy-looking face I looked like a real Jew. I moved my chair into the shade and sat down with my newspapers.

When George came back from his inspection of the apartment, he was impressed by my appearance and said he was sure I was going to become Jewish. We talked for a few minutes and he told me a story about the Jews I'd never heard before: the reason lineal descent is on the mother's side is because, in the centuries after the fall of the Temple, so many Jewish women were raped by marauding bands that it became impossible to determine patriarchal descent and it was determined that if the line had continued through the father's side, there soon would have been no more Jews.

I asked George what he felt about the possibility of my actually telling people I was Jewish. He said he thought I should. I told him I wasn't really comfortable lying, but was wondering if this was something I should do to follow through on this project of mine. (An imagined bit of repartee: "Are you Jewish?" "No, it's just a stage I'm going through.")

After George left I noticed that there were some boys in Avi's room looking out at me. I stood up and held out my arms to show off my outfit. "Good?"

No response.

Several minutes later two boys came over, Avi's friend the Nondescript Boy and a bespectacled fellow who told me his name was Jerry, but whose real name was Vladimir. He was from the Ukraine and said he couldn't give out his last name for security reasons. I didn't care.

The Nondescript Boy sat opposite me and we discussed morals, the concept of good and bad, and the value of life and property. I expounded:

"When I first came to Hollywood I had a roommate who threw my diaries away one day. I don't think he meant to, I think it was just an act of extreme inconsideration. But those diaries were the most important things I had in the world. Every other material thing I owned could be replaced, but all those pages, all those notebooks I'd written in as a teenager—those things could never be replaced. And I felt really bad, but I made up my mind then that I was never going to be attached to material objects again. So, if you took all my stuff—yes, I guess I'd feel bad, but I'd feel even worse that I felt bad at all. 'Property is theft'—that's what the anarchists used to say."

"So do you think it's a sin to kill someone?"

"Of course not. I don't think there's any such thing as 'sin.' If *you* think there's sin, then there's sin for you, but it's a completely subjective experience."

"You don't think it's bad to kill someone?"

"No. Not unless *you* think so. Then it is. It's bad for the person getting killed if they want to be alive, but it's not bad for the person doing the killing unless they *think* it's bad."

"So why don't you kill someone?"

"I don't want to kill anyone," I said. "Besides, I don't want to have to deal with the law and that whole process of courts and jail and all that stuff."

"What if one of the boys wanted to kill you, you don't think that would be a bad thing?"

"It would be bad for me if I wanted to be alive, but it wouldn't be bad for him unless he thought it was bad," I reiterated. "But you know what really interests me? If one of the boys tried to kill me, would he think he was doing it just for himself, or would he think he was doing God's will?"

I'm not sure if they thought this was too theoretical or not, but they didn't answer me. The Nondescript Boy brought the conversation back to tangibles. "Would you feel bad if I put this cigarette out on your pants?"

I shrugged. He moved his hand with the burning stub toward me, and I moved my leg away.

I was a little embarrassed, and they smiled at this victory.

The Nondescript Boy brought up my homosexuality. He'd obviously told the Russian guy about me and was showing me off, as it were. I dutifully went through my paces. Vladimir asked me if I found his friend attractive. I said I didn't.

"I think *he's* attractive," I said, and I motioned toward Avi, who was standing in his window, looking over at us.

"It's Avi's birthday today."

"Really?" I brought the date into focus. "May twenty-third."

"We had a party for him last night."

"I should get him a present."

"If you give us some money we'll get some cigarettes for him."

"I'm not going to buy Avi cigarettes. They're stupid."

"It won't make any difference, he'll still smoke just as much whether you give him an extra carton or not."

I shook my head.

When they got up to go they made some reference about me to an old woman standing in the driveway. I'd seen her before: she is noticeable because of a very large sole on one of her shoes

to balance her disproportionate legs. I think she is Dovid and
Yossi's grandmother. After the boys left we spoke briefly.

"You go into a store and buy ham with the tzitzis?" she
asked me. "You shouldn't do that. Pretending to be a Jew. It's
not kosher."

"No, I don't usually eat ham. I mostly eat oatmeal. I don't
like to cook. I eat spaghetti."

"That's okay," she said.

"I know that a rabbi has to approve the food to make something kosher, but do you eat everything kosher?"

She seemed to hedge on this a bit. She said whatever I bought
should have an "O" and a "U" on it, that in a store I shouldn't
buy food that wasn't kosher with tzitzis on, but oatmeal was all
right.

Dovid and Yossi's mother came out of the house and
retrieved the old woman from her conversation with me, and I
went back to reading. I remembered I'd eaten a pepperoni pizza
the night before with my yarmulke on.

Kimberly, my next-door neighbor, stopped by my chair on
her way to the store. She laughed at my new getup, and when
she mentioned she'd got back her most recent school papers
with A's, I asked to read them. She brought them out and I
started on her paper about Asian stereotypes in the media.

While I was reading, some of the kids came over from the
school where they'd been playing: the two sets of brothers,
Avraham and Yaakov, and Moshe and Yitzchak, and, on a bicycle, their good-looking friend Sruli Perlman. They came toward
me with a great deal of excitement.

"When you stop being a Jew in September," Moshe said,
"can I have your hat and suit?"

I explained that the suit was just some old clothes I had, but
the hat had cost me $55 and I thought it was probably the most
beautiful piece of clothing I owned.

The boy on the bicycle was doing some wheelies in the street and, in the style of a sports announcer, I proclaimed, "The one! The only! The famous—Sruli Perlman!"

"Sruli Perlman! That's me!" and he made a fast victorious turn on his bicycle before coming back over by the curb. "How did you know my name?"

I showed my palms to the sky: How could anyone not know the great Sruli Perlman?

The kids were all strangely excited, running about and shouting. Avraham wanted to finish reading what I'd written about him, so I went into my apartment to find it. When I came out with the story I handed it to Avraham, and then I noticed two men walking toward us from across the street. Chris, my Pynchon-loving wispy-haired neighbor, was just about to stop and chat awhile, but after a quick look at me and the gathering storm he hurried on his way, no time to talk.

The shorter, and younger, of the two men had red hair, a fair complexion, and wire-rimmed glasses and was all business. The taller, older man with him had a long straggly beard. The younger man did the talking.

"Not fair," he said. "Not fair."

"What?"

And he immediately started trying to get the kids to go home—where did they live, anyway? Avraham wouldn't tell him. How funny, I thought, that they don't know he lives right next door. I had my stories with me and offered the man with the straggly beard a couple of them to look at. "These are two stories I wrote about my conversations with the boys."

He took the papers in his hand and idly glanced at them. The younger man was still trying to shoo the boys away.

"We don't want the kids talking to you," he said, "and unless you stop it, we'll have to call the authorities."

"I'm in front of my own house. I'm not asking the kids to talk to me."

"We don't want the kids to talk to you. It's your responsibility to tell them to go away and not talk to you. Otherwise, it won't be friendly. Okay?"

The man with the straggly beard handed me my stories and then the two of them started back across the street.

I called after them, "It's *my* responsibility to keep the kids from talking to me?"

Boys had gathered at the windows and in the compound and watched as the two (self-imposed?) deputies corralled my little fan club back to the school. I went back to my reading and tried to concentrate.

Not fair.

A half-eaten apple came flying from the direction of the school and smashed onto the pavement across from me. It had been thrown with real force, but this physical threat was a very small thing.

Not fair.

He'd been talking about my suit and hat! Was he talking about magic? It was getting chilly, but there was still a lot of light, and I resolved not to go in until I couldn't read anymore, whether I was reading or not.

When Kimberly came back from the store she was surprised I hadn't finished reading her two short reports. I told her about the confrontation and said I would bring the papers to her when I was done.

When Chris came back from the liquor store I told him about the altercation and suggested I might be going to jail. "Little men," he said, indicating another alternative, "white coats, long sleeves . . ." and he moved on away from me, shaking his head.

Did it make any sense? Was it *my* responsibility to keep the kids from talking to me? What kind of law would that be?

After a while Avraham and Yaakov and Moshe and Yitzchak came back. Yitzchak was on a bicycle this time. The famous Sruli Perlman was nowhere to be seen.

"What did they say to you?" I asked.

"Nothing."

"They didn't tell you why they didn't want you to talk to me?"

"They just told us to believe them."

"Really?"

Now *I* was offended. God, I hated that in school, that "Because I said so!" crap.

"They really didn't tell you why they don't want you talking to me?"

They shook their heads.

"You know why, don't you?"

They just looked at me.

"It's because I'm not Jewish, I'm an atheist, and I'm homosexual. You know that, don't you?"

I wasn't getting a very responsive reaction. I don't think they cared.

I got up and went across the street. Avi's window was open, and even though I hadn't noticed him there during the altercation, I was sure he knew what was going on.

"Avi? Avi!"

He came to the window. He had his tzitzis on over his lanky frame and was slim and dark and attractive—and I felt like he might never really know it.

"Avi, those guys came over and told me not to talk to those kids. Well, no one told those kids why they're not supposed to talk to me. You guys have got to tell them. *I* told them, I'm not Jewish, I'm an atheist, and I'm homosexual. But that isn't my responsibility. If those guys don't want those kids talking to me, they have to tell them why."

Avi obviously hated being the go-between. "I don't know. Their parents wouldn't like it."

Well, I had said what I had to say. "Avi, I hear it's your birthday."

"Who told you that?"

"Some kids. Happy birthday. How old are you?"

"Twenty-three."

I was a little taken aback: I thought he was only about eighteen. "Well, I hope you have a wonderful day, and a wonderful life. I hope you get whatever you want."

"Thanks."

"Would you like some money? The guys said I could give you some money."

"It's all right."

"Okay. Happy birthday."

I went back across the street. Avraham and Moshe were spying on the kids with my binoculars, very undercover agent time, hiding behind trees, below walls, and whispering warnings back and forth.

"He said your parents wouldn't like it," I told Avraham. "Your parents know I'm not Jewish, don't they?"

Avraham shrugged.

"Well, I'll tell them," I said.

They think I'm Jewish? I'd exchanged hellos with both of them, and I'd assumed they knew what was going on. That old woman knew what was going on. I felt it was a very small community, where one word spoken here is known there at the same time. But maybe that wasn't the case.

It was too dark to read, and I put my chair, the papers, and the Mishnah back in the house.

After Avraham and Yaakov went home, Moshe and Yitzchak were still playing outside. And I suddenly did wonder—where *were* their parents, where *did* they live? It must have been about eight.

I walked out to the end of one of the walls bordering the walkway, which at the sidewalk is about four feet high. Yitzchak brought my binoculars back and then headed on down the street. Moshe was now on the bicycle and making circles below me. I wondered if I was very imposing from down there. In my suit, with my beautiful new black hat on, did I have the stature of a rabbi?

"They really didn't tell you anything? They didn't say why they don't want you to talk to me?"

Moshe brought the bike to a halt on the sidewalk and, still straddling it, looked up at me. "They said something about a sickness, and if you spit . . ." and then his voice trailed off indefinitely.

I wilted.

God, it was depressing.

I didn't want to have to explain homosexuality to this lovely eleven-year-old boy; I didn't want to talk to him about AIDS.

"You know why they don't want you to talk to me, don't you?" I repeated. And then trying to make it emphatically clear: "It's because I'm not Jewish, I'm an atheist—I don't believe in God—and I'm homosexual."

"Ay-thee . . ." Moshe was trying to get his mouth around the word. "But how can you not believe in God?" And he swung his arms around.

"I know, I know, but apart from that—*that's* why they don't want you to talk to me."

Moshe started cycling in circles again, occasionally looking up at me. He wanted to prove to me that there really was a God.

"There's this disease," I started to explain to him, "AIDS . . ."

But I couldn't finish the sentence, the explanation. It was too depressing. My despair telegraphed itself to him as finality.

He started driving his bicycle down the block.

Not fair.

"I'm sorry, Moshe."

20 / unfinished business

I had just set myself up outside with my director's chair, a cup of coffee, my binoculars, and my unread newspapers when Avraham and Yaakov's mother came walking down the driveway with her three-year-old.

Sometimes, in the afternoons, she takes her three-year-old over to the yeshiva and sits with him under the trees in the playground area. When the other women are outside with the nursery-school children I've seen her talking with them, but more often than not she sits by herself, placidly amusing her little son while she takes in the quiet and thinks.

I was only dressed in my shorts and yarmulke, and felt a little hesitant about approaching her—after all, I'd been told my nakedness, my lack of modesty, offended the women—but just as she started to cross the street I got up and went over to her.

"Hi, are you Avraham's mother? My name is Rick, I live here, and I just wanted to tell you that yesterday some of the boys at the school got very upset that I was talking to Avraham . . ."

She made a gesture indicating height—boys?

"No, the older boys, right over there"—and I pointed toward the school—"and I just wanted you to know that I'm not Jewish, I don't believe in God . . ."

She indicated to me that she didn't care.

". . . and I'm homosexual. I'm usually sitting here when Avraham comes back from school, and we talk sometimes, about the Mishnah and the Tanakh, and our conversations have been really nice, and I don't think there's anything wrong, but that's your decision, and I won't talk to him if you don't want me to. I just wanted you to know. I think Avraham is a very nice boy . . ."

She smiled at the compliment.

". . . and my name is Rick, and I live right here."

She nodded that she understood and continued on across the street. I returned to my chair, and as I settled down to read I noticed a boy watching me from one of the windows in the dormitory.

Several minutes later Avraham's mother came back with Yaakov. He was walking ahead of her, and she was following him, speaking in Hebrew and apparently mad about something. As he passed I said hello to him, but he didn't answer me.

Early in the afternoon, Shaul, the plumber for our building, came by to work on some pipes in the back. His truck was parked in front of the building, and whenever he passed me we would acknowledge each other. I tried to engage him in conversation, but he didn't speak English very well and, apart from his very thick accent, he seemed to have some kind of speech impediment as well.

My friend Josh called. I told him about buying my new hat

so that I would look like a real Chassid, and how I was threatened, and about the little old lady next door and what she had
said about the "O" and "U" being on food containers.

"A lot of foods have that sign," he said.

"An 'O' and a 'U'?"

"It's on your oatmeal."

"Really? *Quaker* Oats?" and I emphasized its brand name.

"Uh-huh. Go get it."

I put the phone down and went into the kitchen and came
back with my box of Quaker Oats.

"See it?" he asked. "It should be next to the name."

I turned the container over in my hand, and then I saw it.
Right there, just above the "NET WT," was a small circle with a
"U" inside it.

I had kosher food in my house!

Josh tried to explain it to me. "It doesn't mean that a rabbi
has approved it. I'm not quite sure how it works."

"But you've always known about it?"

"Sure."

I felt very strange: *I* hadn't always known about it.

When I got off the phone I started going through all the
products in my kitchen and found that circled "U" on several of
my cereal boxes and even on my Morton salt.

How weird: that there is this symbol, just for Jews, on
products which are sold all over this country! And according
to my figuring (based on statistics in my 1990 almanac) only
3.8 percent of the population of the United States are Jews,
and probably only a small proportion of them are Orthodox.

Very strange.

I was still looking through the products in my kitchen when
I heard raised voices outside. I went to the window in my living
room and saw the Big Ugly Boy talking to Shaul by his truck. I

didn't know if he could see me through the glass, but he was pointing toward my window.

"I want to kill him, I just want to kill him," he was practically yelling. "I hate him, he's a faggot . . ."

I'd never seen any of the boys in such a virulent rage before and I wondered if I had, in fact, gone too far. Had the confrontation with the elders been a signal of some kind? Had I now been deemed an acceptable object for all of their pent-up hate? Watching the Big Ugly Boy gesticulate against me, I could just imagine him doing some stupid, violent thing and I began to feel a little uneasy.

Otherwise, it won't be friendly.

Later in the afternoon, when I went back outside to read some more, I left my yarmulke inside. While I was sitting there, three of the older boys stopped to talk to me on their way to the store. I recognized one of them, a tall willowy boy with a goofy grin. I'd asked Avraham what his name was and he said the boys called him Sea Horse.

"So where's your yarmulke?" they asked. "And the tzitzis? Aren't you going to become Jewish?"

I shrugged my shoulders. "I'm thinking about it."

They thought that was very funny and laughed at the idea of my being a Jew.

I was feeling a little defensive, but since they weren't in too antagonistic a mood, I asked the tall boy, "Is your name really Sea Horse?"

He smiled at me, his goofy grin looking even goofier than usual. "That's what they call me," he said.

His friends laughed and patted him on the back.

"I think it's great," I said, and then I asked them if they were in high school, or if they were bochurs in this thing called beit midrash. They laughed and said they were in high school. And then they wanted to know about my "morals"—they'd obviously heard about my conversation of the previous day.

"You don't think it's bad to kill someone?"

"No. I mean, I think it's subjective."

"If I stole your binoculars right now, what would you do?"

"I guess I'd ask for them back. But I'd be embarrassed that it was important to me."

"Would you be embarrassed if someone stole your car?"

"I don't have a car."

"What happened to it?"

"Nothing. I never had one. I don't know how to drive."

The boys were slightly incredulous at this. "Then how do you get around?"

"Bicycle. Walk. Bus. Friends."

"Don't you want a car?"

I shook my head. "I don't like modern things. I don't have a TV either."

"You don't? Why not?"

"I think it's stupid, and besides—if I had a TV I'd watch it. I'm hypnotized by the media. Two years ago I saw more than four hundred movies in a theater in one year, so you can imagine what would happen if I had a TV . . ."

Looking at their faces, I suddenly wasn't sure that they could.

"If I had a TV, the first thing that would happen is I'd stop reading, and I don't want to do that because that's one of the main things that make my life worth living. Not counting sex, it's what I love doing most, and so I have to protect it."

And so we went through an inventory of my things—my books, my bike, my computer—and they asked me if I'd be upset if this or that thing was stolen, and as they did, it was embarrassing to feel in myself the fact that I really did place a value on things, on material objects.

I was not as free as I pretended.

The late afternoon twilight was just ending when Moshe came over to see me. He was all dressed up in a gray suit, in preparation for the Sabbath.

"Where's your yarmulke?" he asked.

I looked at him for a moment, wondering how to answer him. "I forgot to put it on," I said, answering his accusation with guilt, and I ran into the house and grabbed my kepa, pressing it and the Velcro onto my hair as I came back outside. After I sat back down, Moshe looked at me as if he was waiting for me to finish talking—as if it wasn't *he* who had come over to see me.

"I spoke to Avraham's mother this morning, and I told her that I wasn't Jewish, and didn't believe in God, and was homosexual."

"What did she say?"

I shrugged my shoulders. "She didn't seem to care."

"What's AIDS?"

I took a deep breath.

How amazing: he realized as much as I did how unresolved all this was.

"AIDS is a disease that lowers your body's immune system, and its ability . . ." I began, and gave it up. "AIDS is a disease that doesn't have a cure. You can get it in three ways. You can get it from having sex, you can get it from sharing needles if you do drugs, and you can get it from blood transfusions—that's very rare—and there's a fourth way, a mother who has it can give it to her child if she's pregnant. When the disease first started, mostly homosexual men got it: *I'm* homosexual—"

"Do you have AIDS?"

"No."

"But if you had it, you could give it to another man if you had sex?"

"If I had it, I could. You can't get it from talking, or anything."

"What's a 'faggot'?"

"A 'faggot' is a 'faygeleh.' It's a name for a man who's homosexual—a man who has sex with other men. It's a slang term. Like some people might call a Jew a 'kike.' "

"A 'kike'? What's that?"

"It's a name people used to call Jews." I suddenly realized I *didn't* know what it meant.

Moshe scrutinized me for a moment, as if professionally assessing my words and performance, and then he gave his verdict: "Fine. Well, I have to go. Bye."

I watched him walk back across the street.

Something had gone unspoken between us the night before, and Moshe knew I wanted to make up for that as much as he wanted to hear from me what it was all about.

As I watched him disappear around the corner at the end of the block, I was humbly in awe at *our* understanding.

21 / tailing sea horse

When I went back into the house I looked up "kike" in my *Slang and Euphemism* dictionary:

kike 1. a highly derogatory term for an uncouth Jewish merchant.
2. a highly derogatory term for any Jewish man or woman. From Yiddish *kikel,* the "circle" which was used by illiterate Jewish immigrants in place of a cross (X) as a signature. [both senses, U.S. slang, early 1900s–pres.]

That was interesting.
I looked up "sheeny":

sheeny (also sheen, sheenie, sheney) a derogatory nickname for a Jewish man or woman. Considered to be a strongly derisive epithet. [slang, early 1800s–pres.]

Not so interesting.
I was just about to turn my computer on and start writing

about my day when I saw a police car drive slowly by. I went outside and saw them park just up the street and then two officers got out and walked down the adjacent driveway toward where Avraham and Yaakov lived. According to my neighbor Chris—whose windows were opposite the stairwell of the building next door—there was always a lot of shouting going on. Avraham's family lived in an apartment across from two lesbians, and apparently the two groups of tenants didn't get along: either the dykes were fighting or Avraham's siblings were screaming or else the two households were yelling at one another, and now, apparently, someone had called the police.

When the officers returned to their car about fifteen minutes later I went over and spoke to them. I asked them if there was any law that prevented me talking to some children, twelve years of age and younger. I told them that I had been threatened by some people at the school who told me that it was *my* responsibility not to talk to the children. The policemen said there was no law against it and that it was a school problem.

Good.

I was about to go back home when I remembered something else I wanted to ask. Was there a law against looking at people with binoculars when you were on your own property? I was surprised when they said there was—that it was an invasion of privacy.

They said it was a misdemeanor.

When I had finished reconstructing my day on the computer I didn't feel like going to bed, so I decided to take a walk. It was the Sabbath, I knew people would be dressed up and walking around, and so I got dressed up myself: white shirt, black pants, black coat, and hat.

I started walking south down Alta Vista. Two men, all

dressed up, were briskly walking away before me. At Waring I stopped and looked over toward the entrance of the yeshiva. No one seemed to be about, so I turned west and headed toward the minimart on Melrose, two blocks away.

I turned south on Fuller and was almost to the store when I saw a tall boy in black pants and a white shirt standing on the corner. He was very tall, and although I couldn't tell if he had a yarmulke on, it looked like Sea Horse.

Hmm.

I thought I might go up to him and say, "I thought you weren't supposed to be on Melrose."

I started walking toward him.

He was mostly facing the street, watching the people passing by, the weekend revelers cruising the street and showing themselves off to one another. As I looked at him standing there like that, all by himself, I remembered when I first came to Hollywood more than twenty years ago and how, night after night, I would walk up and down the boulevard all by myself, looking at the marquees and the stores and the lights and the people . . .

I felt such aching loneliness coming from him, so many desires: to become one with the flow of humanity so close and yet so far away—

Suddenly he stepped out onto the sidewalk among the people and started walking east on Melrose.

I was about fifty yards away from him, and even though I didn't particularly get the feeling that he was aware of me— Orthodox apparition that I was—I suddenly wondered if he *had* caught sight of me and knew who it was or whether he suspected I might be some admonishing authority. Or . . .

I stopped and was about to cross over to the minimart and forget the whole thing when I suddenly decided: no, this was too interesting. I started walking again, a little faster now so as not to lose him: just see where he went.

A crowd was getting out of the Groundling Theatre, and he

moved through them rather briskly. I followed at a nice pace about a half block behind him. I decided I wouldn't hurry, or run after him, or anything like that. I would just follow after him, and if I lost him, so be it.

He crossed Poinsettia, still going east, and made his way through another group of people in front of a nightclub. Beyond that was our street, Alta Vista, and I thought he might turn up there, but he didn't. As I crossed the street after him I passed two queer fellows and looked into the eyes of one of them matter-of-factly. He looked back at me: I was a foreigner, I could sense that in his eyes, but what else—did he wonder if I was queer, if I'd thought about it, or what?

Sea Horse was moving easily down the next block, and there were no more people now. Just him, and about half a block behind him, me. Now he *knew* I was there, and every so often he looked back to see if maybe he had been mistaken, but no— I was there every time, whoever I was, and I was watching and following him.

He paused for a long moment when he got to Alta Vista. If he turned up there, he would be right back at the yeshiva. I think he was wondering what to do, and then, when I was just a couple of store-widths away, he stepped out into the street and continued walking east.

So did I.

There were only two more streets before La Brea and he cruised over them without breaking stride. He was walking faster now.

Melrose and La Brea is a major intersection, and there's a traffic light there. When he got to the corner, the light for La Brea was red, so he turned and crossed Melrose, heading south. I arrived at the corner just as the light changed.

While I was standing there I wondered if I should really continue doing this. Up to now I could pretend to myself (and him) that I wasn't following him, but if I crossed Melrose any pretense that I wasn't tailing him would be gone. When the light turned green I crossed the street and leisurely started down La Brea, watching him as he looked in windows as an excuse to see if I was coming after him.

I was.

At the first street below Melrose on La Brea there is another light. Here he stopped for a moment and, after some brief consideration, crossed La Brea. I thought he might actually go in a Jewish building of some kind on the southeast corner, but instead he turned and headed back up the street, toward Melrose.

Now, with this second light between us, he was getting farther away from me, but I didn't hurry myself. I just pushed the button to change the light and stood at the corner, waiting patiently. When it finally turned green I crossed La Brea and started on up the street after him.

Now there was absolutely no way I could *not* be following him. I could sense him getting nervous, his looks a little more furtive, a little more desperate. At the big intersection he crossed *back* across La Brea, and then *back* across Melrose, heading north, past Pink's hot dog stand.

I was quite a way behind him now, but with each passing moment I could feel my power increasing, myself becoming a dark and inexorable force, casually shadowing his every move.

I had just started back across Melrose, and could see him in front of me half a block away, when suddenly he turned aside into some doorway or driveway and disappeared. For a moment I deliberated going after him, but then I lost my nerve.

After all, what *was* I doing?

An image of him jumping out and attacking me briefly crossed my mind.

I turned down Melrose and headed home.

I'd gone about a block when I noticed three individuals approaching me on the sidewalk, a man and two women. The women were conservatively dressed and the man was in classic

Orthodox attire: a black suit with a black dress hat. As we neared one another the man said, "Shalom."

I burst into a big grin.

We passed one another, and I caught an inquiring look from one of the women.

I couldn't say anything: I was too overwhelmed.

I just hoped my big, truly happy grin was enough.

Suddenly everything was okay: they thought I was one of them!

I wanted to dance in the streets.

They thought I was a Jew!

22 / levi

Moshe and Yitzchak stopped by the next day. Because it was still the Sabbath they were all dressed up. While we were talking, my neighbor Dan left to go teach a tennis lesson. We exchanged pleasantries and then, after he'd gone, Moshe turned to me. "Did you fag him?"

"No, I think Dan's straight. He has a girlfriend."

Moshe mulled this over, and I tried to take in what he had said: "Did you *fag* him?"

"Fag" had become a verb. How fascinating the mental process whereby the act that defined "faggot" had become "fag." And I wondered: could "God" become a verb just as easily?

Did you *God* him? How funny—a *proper* verb. Maybe that was it—"God" could become a euphemism for "fuck," for the ultimate experience we have as human beings. He *God* me in the ass. They *God* their brains out.

Of course, "God" should be the same for each tense. They had *God* one another. They *God* one another. They will *God* one another.

God you!

While I was contemplating these semantic possibilities one of the guys in the beit midrash approached us. It was the man I'd seen in Atara's the day I bought my hat, the guy who'd read one of my stories. All dressed in black, with his hat and dark beard, he really did look quite imposing and I wondered if he was going to give me any trouble. As he passed by I nodded to him and there was a moment when I thought he might say something, but he just continued on walking.

I turned to Moshe. "Are you going to get in trouble for talking to me?" I asked.

"Show me some pictures."

"Are the bochurs going to get mad at you?" I insisted.

"I don't care."

I shrugged my shoulders: All right, *fine*.

"Show us some pictures!"

I went in the house and brought out Don Bachardy's *Last Drawings of Christopher Isherwood*, the pictures he drew during the final six months of Isherwood's life. Some of the drawings were of Chris without any clothes on, and Yitzchak was amazed at this: "He doesn't have any clothes on!"

Moshe didn't understand it either. "Why didn't he put any clothes on?"

"Well, he was very sick, and sometimes it was easier to not have to get dressed, and the artist wanted to draw his whole body, not just his face."

As the boys continued turning the pages I became aware of the bearded man approaching us again, this time from the other direction. When he was beside us I looked at him and said hello.

He answered me formally. "Hello."

"How's it going?"

"What are you doing?" he asked, gesturing toward the book.

"I'm showing them some pictures a friend of mine did of his lover just before he died."

"He's dead?" he asked.

I nodded. "The man in the pictures is dead. The artist is still alive. They lived togcther for thirty years. They met on the beach when Chris was forty-eight and Don was eighteen. Don is the artist. Chris was a writer; he was really famous. Have you ever heard of the movie *Cabaret*?"

The bearded man barely shook his head.

"It was based on one of his books. He went to Berlin in 1929 and wrote about it, just before Hitler came to power."

"You know him?" he asked.

"I knew him before he died. I know the artist, he's a friend of mine—we go to movies together."

The boys had looked up at the bearded man when we started talking, but after a moment or two they went back to looking at the pictures in the book.

"Your name's Rick?" the guy asked.

"Uh-huh. What's yours?"

"Levi." He said the name under his breath, pronouncing it "Lay-vee."

"Like one of the twelve tribes," I proposed, making my connections. "The priestly class, right?"

He nodded a begrudging assent, and then spoke to the boys. "What are you doing here? You should go home. Where do you live?"

The two boys stood up and moved away across the yard, resentful at being ordered around and yet somehow still respectful of this elder of theirs, but a moment later they were back.

"Are you going to talk about sex?" Moshe asked. "I know all about that."

"Go away for a minute," Levi said, and when they didn't he asked them their names.

Moshe and Yitzchak didn't answer him and walked away

across the street, apparently feeling that obeying a command was less onerous than giving away their identity. Were they afraid he might tell on them?

When they were out of hearing, Levi turned back to me. "Are you a homosexual?"

I nodded. "Are you?"

"We don't believe in that," he said.

I shrugged my shoulders and sighed.

"How old are you?" he asked.

"Forty. How old are you?"

"Twenty-four."

"Really? You're only twenty-four? You look so much older, with the beard and everything. Are you a bochur?"

He nodded his head.

"That means you're in the beit midrash, right? And you study the Talmud?"

He nodded assent to these questions, and I indicated the book he was holding. "What are you reading?"

"A book about the Rebbe."

"It's in Hebrew?"

He nodded again.

I raised the book I was reading. "I'm doing *The Varieties of Religious Experience* by William James. Do you know it?"

"I've heard of it," he said.

"It doesn't say very much about the Jews, though. Is your book about a specific rabbi?" I asked.

"It's about *the Rebbe*, Rabbi Schneerson."

I shook my head. "Who's he?"

"He's our leader."

"Does he teach at the school?" I asked.

Levi shook his head. "He's the leader of all Lubavitch. He lives in Brooklyn."

"What's 'Lubavitch'?"

"That's our kind of Judaism."

"I thought you were Chassidic."

"We are, but there's many kinds of Chassidim. We're Luba-vitch, and Rabbi Schneerson is our Rebbe."

That was interesting and I said the name Schneerson over again in my mind several times so as not to forget it. "Do you think there's an English version of that book you're reading?" I asked.

"Why?"

"I'm interested. I'd like to read about your religion. I've already read the Tanakh and a couple of parts of the Mishnah. What would you recommend?"

"A book about us? Have you ever heard of Elie Wiesel?"

"He won the Nobel Peace Prize a couple of years ago. I have *Night*, one of his books about the concentration camps."

"He wrote a book about the beginning of our religion called *Souls on Fire*. You should read that."

"*Souls on Fire* by Elie Wiesel," and I noted the title down on one of the back pages of my James book. When I looked back up at Levi, I changed the subject. "Are you a virgin?"

He didn't seem particularly offended by my question and I could sense a certain curiosity about my motivation in asking it. Maintaining his eye contact with me, he barely nodded his head.

"I'm sorry," I told him. "You know, your sexual peak was at eighteen, and that's already six years ago."

"We don't believe in sex before marriage," he said.

"Is your marriage going to be arranged?" I asked. "I mean, will you have any say in the matter about who you get married to?"

"I'll have complete say."

"Hmm," I mused, and then I thought I might as well see if I could get to the bottom of the threat I had received. "The other day two of the guys came over here and told me I shouldn't talk to the kids. They said it was my responsibility not to talk to them, but they didn't tell the kids why they weren't supposed to talk to me. And so I told them that it was because I wasn't Jewish, I was an atheist, and I was homosexual."

"There's nothing wrong about the children speaking to you on the first two grounds. It doesn't matter that you're not Jewish or an atheist. The problem is your homosexuality—it's a sickness, a disease, and when it's acted on, it becomes a criminal act."

A sickness. A disease. A criminal act.

"What about my wearing tzitzis or a yarmulke or this hat? Since I'm not Jewish, what does that mean?"

"Nothing. They don't mean anything, for you. You're not a Jew."

"Really? Leviticus, the laws of Moses—they don't apply to me?"

"You're not one of the chosen people."

That was the first time I had ever actually heard one of them use that term.

The Chosen People. The Master Race.

"Do you think your homosexuality is right?" he asked.

"I don't believe in 'right' and 'wrong,' " I told him. "I think those things—'good' and 'bad' and 'right' and 'wrong'—are just arbitrary value judgments. Something that you might think is 'right' I might think is 'wrong.' It's completely subjective."

Levi thought about this for a moment. The more I talked to him, and the more I was able to look at him, the more he became an individual. Underneath those clothes and that beard was a young man. He had a straight nose and a white but slightly oily complexion, and buried somewhere deep within his clear eyes was a human being petrified by existence.

"Do you believe in things you can't see?" he asked.

"Well, I don't know how the phone works, but when I'm talking to a friend I believe he's talking to me on the other end of the line."

"That's not belief."

"I'm sorry, then—what is your question again?"

"Do you believe in something that is beyond everything, something that you can't see, like God?"

"I guess I would have to say no."

"What was your religion when you were growing up?"

"Protestant. American. Middle-class. During my most formative years I went to a Congregational church, and then we moved and my parents went to whatever Protestant church was closest to the house." I suddenly gave Levi a big smile. "You know what I was trained to do when I was a kid?"

He shook his head.

"I was taught to worship a Jew. We sang songs about him and we even prayed to him." I paused a moment to let this information sink in. "I think that's one of the reasons why I'm so attracted to you guys. Even though I'm an atheist now, I still have this need inside me to worship a Jew, and so when I see you—"

"Did you ever believe in God?" he interrupted me.

"Oh, yeah, when I was a kid. And then when I was twelve I read this book called *Elmer Gantry* by Sinclair Lewis—have you read it?"

He shook his head.

"It's a book about an evangelist, and in it he doesn't believe in God, and that was the first time I had ever come across the concept that you could doubt God's existence, and so for me at twelve it was like—well, if you could even *doubt* that God existed, then—then 'He' didn't exist."

"Is your family religious?"

"Oh, yeah, they're a mess. My mother was an organist in her church, and one of my sisters turned into a Mormon and the other one became a born-again Christian."

Levi thought about this for a moment, and then he asked me, "Is your father very religious?"

"Well, I don't really know my father. When I was growing up I didn't see him very much. When I woke up in the morning for school he'd already gone to work, and I was in bed before he came home at night."

"What did he do?"

"When I was a little kid he worked in restaurants, and then later he worked in a casino at Lake Tahoe—that's where I went to high school."

"So you were never religious again?"

I shook my head. "When I was twenty, though, I became a born-again Christian for a year. It was pretty pathetic. I hitchhiked around the western United States with a Bible. And then one day I realized I was unhappy. I came back to Hollywood, and I met this boy I really liked, and one day we were going past that big Catholic church—up on Sunset? And we went in and this boy said he was an atheist, that he didn't believe in God, and I loved him, or thought I did, so I said: I'm an atheist, too. I've been one ever since."

Levi just looked at me for a moment. I felt he was trying to use my answers to reach some preconceived notion he had, but I wasn't sure what it was.

I suddenly thought of something else. "Oh, and that boy? That boy I was in love with? Well, he was raised Catholic, but he was adopted and I think he was really Jewish. He had curly brown hair and a big nose, and it's because of him that I've always been attracted to Jewish boys. You know: big noses, big cocks."

I could sense a war going on within Levi. He was being torn by his contempt, on the one hand, and his curiosity, on the other. I was just about to ask him if he had a big cock when he suddenly spoke up. "So you think of us as sex objects?"

"Some of you. There's a boy named Mendel who I think is cute, and there's a beautiful boy named Mordecai—"

"What do you find attractive about men?"

"Basically, I think the most beautiful thing there is in the world, the most amazing thing, is an erect penis ejaculating, and every time I've been around one I've felt honored. I've felt that I was close . . ." and I paused to think what I was saying. "I have felt that I was—*God*, so to speak."

Somehow that wasn't quite right.

"When was the first time you had sex with a man?" Levi asked.

"When I was sixteen, when I was visiting my grandmother in Phoenix. I was sitting out by the pool at her apartment building, and I was getting red, and this guy asked me if I had some lotion for my skin and I said no, and so we went up to his apartment and he said—what?—oh, I remember, he said, 'I'll give you a blow job if you give me one.' "

"And you liked that?"

"Well, I had never had sex before. And I'd never jacked off before—I didn't start jacking off until I was seventeen, I started late—I'm retarded."

"What do you mean—'retarded'?"

"I'm just being facetious. I'm not really retarded, although I still don't shave on my cheeks. But I had never had an ejaculation, and so it was a little frightening to me, I didn't know what was happening. When I came I remember he asked me, 'Is that it?' And then when I went down on him and *he* came, I thought that he had cancer: I didn't know what his sperm was. Later, when I went home, I thought about it and suddenly everything I knew and had heard about sex all came together with my experience—and then I wanted to have sex again, over and over. But he didn't want to."

"Did you like it—did you like having sex?"

"Well, it was a little scary at first. I mean, at first I didn't really like the taste of semen, so you know what I did? When I jacked off I started eating my own cum, and after a while I really came to love it, and now I'm obsessed with it—I love the taste and texture of semen more than almost anything else in the world."

Levi glanced over his shoulder, back toward the school, as if he was afraid someone might see us talking together or overhear us. "When was the next time you had sex?"

I thought for a moment. "The next time I had sex was, let's see, the next summer—when I ran away from home and went to Hawaii. I stayed at the YMCA and had sex with some guys there. And then the next year I came to Hollywood and that's when I really started having sex a lot. It's just a rough guess, but I think I've had sex with more than two thousand men."

Levi's expression was absolutely unreadable. After twenty-four years in that Jewish environment he had mastered the ability to present a totally inscrutable face to the world.

"Have you ever had sex with a woman?" he asked.

I shook my head. "No. I've never had sex with a woman, I've never driven a car, I've never smoked a cigarette, I've never had a checking account or a credit card, and I haven't seen TV since 1969: I'm very pure."

"What do you do?"

"I'm an extra. I'm a stand-in on a TV show."

"No, I mean, what do you do when—"

"When I have sex? Well, I'm a cocksucker, and I like to get fucked. I don't like to fuck. I think sex is a power game and I like to be the one in the powerful position—"

"So men fuck you?"

I nodded. "You wanna see?"

Before he could answer I got up and ran into the house and found the magazine with the interview of me and the pictures from my porno films. When I handed the magazine to Levi he held it in his hands very gravely as I turned the pages for him. He looked at the photographs with a magnificent impassivity. I could only glean his response by the questions he asked me.

"What about—what about the shit?"

"Well, if I know I'm going to have sex, I usually douche—you know, like an enema—so it's not usually a problem."

"Aren't you afraid of getting AIDS?"

I shrugged my shoulders. "I'm forty years old. I've had a really good life—"

"Aren't you afraid of dying?"

I shrugged my shoulders again. "Levi, I just can't go around being afraid all the time. It's boring. It's different for you, you're twenty-four, you have your whole life before you—you've never even had sex, so I can imagine, you'd be afraid of dying. You want to live. You want something in the future. I don't. I don't believe in the future. I just want to have fun. I want to have as many cocks ejaculating around me as I can. Unless I'm kidding myself, and I may be, I'm more afraid of getting old than I am of dying. One of my best friends got AIDS, and he died, but the day he was diagnosed and he found out he had it—you know what he said? He said, *'You don't know what this feels like.'* And that's true—I don't."

Levi thought about this for a long moment, and then handed my porno magazine back to me. I couldn't tell what he was thinking. And then he asked, "Are you happy?"

"Well, I think it's stupid, but—I took the Scientology personality test and I scored a hundred percent on happiness. It freaked the guy out who was giving me the test. He tried to sell me some of their classes because I didn't get a hundred in one of the other categories, but I told him I'd be afraid to take one of those classes because then I might jeopardize my happiness."

"Does your family know you're gay?"

I nodded my head. "They read my diary when I was seventeen. And you know the man I told you about, that I first had sex with? Years later, when I was talking to my grandmother, she told me she thought she knew what was going on, and she said if she had been sure, she would have had him arrested. Can you imagine?"

"Do you see your family very much?"

I shook my head. "I haven't seen them in about five years. I told them that either they could have a son or they could have God, but they couldn't have both. They chose God."

"So you don't speak to your parents? You don't see them?"

I shook my head.

"Don't you think you're acting immature?"

I looked at Levi incredulously. "Levi, look at you! You're twenty-four years old—you're in the very bloom of your youth—and you're throwing it all away! Look at the way you dress and that beard! You look like an old man. You should be going out and having fun—having sex. If I'm being immature, I'd say you're being *too* mature."

I suddenly remembered something I'd read in Ecclesiastes, and I excused myself and ran into the house and got my Tanakh. A moment later I came back outside and opened it to a passage I'd marked, and read aloud: " 'O youth, enjoy yourself while you are young! Let your heart lead you to enjoyment in the days of your youth. Follow the desires of your heart and the glances of your eyes—' " and I concluded with that, not reading on.

Levi asked to see the book and I handed it to him. He looked down at what I'd read, and then back up at me. "You didn't finish," he said, and read the next little portion: " '—but know well that God will call you to account for all such things . . . ' "

Levi handed the book back to me, and with that turned and started across the street.

"But there is no God!" I called after him.

He didn't respond but just continued on walking.

"It was nice talking to you!"

He mumbled something, but I couldn't hear what.

Although I'd clearly lost our little scriptural confrontation, on some deeper level I felt I'd won. Even though he'd asked many more questions than he answered, the intensity with which he'd pursued his questioning had revealed an interest that *wasn't* impassive, and I think he knew it.

Moshe and Yitzchak had been playing in the playground of

the school yard, and when they saw Levi walking away they climbed over the fence and ran back across the street to me. I slipped the porno magazine into the book of drawings of Christopher Isherwood.

"So did you talk about sex?" Moshe asked.

I nodded.

"Do you want to fag him?" he asked.

I watched Levi turning the corner at the end of the street, and reflected on that. I nodded my head. "Yes, I think I would. I *would* like to fag him."

Moshe laughed at the incredible picture of me fagging one of the bochurs, and little dreamy-eyed Yitzchak squealed with delight.

23 / "wouldn't it be funny . . . ?"

I was talking to my neighbor Dan about the problem of italicizing foreign words in stories, specifically "tzitzis," "yarmulke," and "yeshiva." *The Chicago Manual of Style* suggests italicizing words not found in a standard dictionary. Of the words that I was concerned with, only "yeshiva" was in my dictionary. Dan was just about to tell me what he thought when I saw the boys, a big group of them, going up the street to play in the park.

I told Dan I had to go and he said he understood. I hurried into my apartment to get my things. I made sure I had my binoculars and books in my backpack and then I headed out. I was almost to the park when an ice cream truck tinkled by and I stopped it to get a Popsicle.

I bought a very phallic "Super-Pop" and was just on my way over to the game when a woman suddenly stopped me.

"Excuse me. Hello."

"Hi."

Now that she had my attention she seemed unsure how to proceed. "There's some people making a movie, they were just here, they were looking for people," and she sized me up (all I had on was some shorts and sneakers). "They were looking for beach types."

"Well, I'm on my way to see a baseball game."

"Oh, you're . . ." She indicated my yarmulke.

"No, I'm not Jewish. I live across the street from a Chassidic school, though. As a matter of fact, I'm on my way to go and watch them play a baseball game right now."

"I was adopted," she said, "but I just found out I was born in Russia and I'm part Jewish. Isn't that amazing? I'm part Russian, part American Indian, and part German."

This woman was in her forties, I'd guess, she was moderately attractive, she had red hair, and she was wearing white pants with a pink "Caesars Tahoe" T-shirt.

I asked her about the shirt. "Are you from there? That's where I grew up, Tahoe."

"No, I was just visiting. I'm traveling around the country, seeing things."

"Oh. Well. I've got to go."

"My name's Jean."

"I'm Rick."

It seemed like she wanted to follow me.

"Would you like to come and watch the game with me? It's just around the corner."

"Sure. I love baseball."

And we were off. We walked over to the park, passed the tennis courts, and made our way to the baseball diamond, where the boys were already playing. As we neared the bleachers I heard my name called out several times, as well as a few cries of exasperation. I could also sense the boys' curiosity regarding my female companion.

I didn't hear the word "faggot" all afternoon.

I sat back and tried to size up the situation: who was playing, how the teams were divided up, who were the captains. Since Jean and I were sitting immediately adjacent to first base, we really got to focus on the boys playing that position. Patrick, the Serious Young Man, was there now and he looked over at us. "The yarmulke," he said. "You're not Jewish."

And I thought: God—aren't we over that yet?

As soon as we were settled in the bleachers, Jean started talking to me. In a way I wanted her to be quiet so I could concentrate on the game, but she didn't seem to require any particular response from me and the only time she actually asked me to pay attention to her was when she showed me two pictures of her children. One was a black-and-white shot of an adorable baby that looked like it could sell baby food, and the other was of a nice-looking boy with glasses, who looked like he might be in junior high school.

"That's Adam. I don't know where he is. He'd be about eighteen now; we figured it out on a computer. I'm going to inherit five million dollars, and then I'll get my children back. That's all I want. Of course, all the papers are tied up in court, but as soon as we get them all signed—you see, I just found out who my real parents were . . ."

Something amazing was happening on the field. The boys were making some real hits, nice catches, and good throws. Compared with the other games I'd watched, today's seemed pretty good. Most of the boys were familiar to me from before and I wondered: Were they really better, or was today just lucky?

". . . a limousine was following me, and a woman got out and ran up to me and said, 'Your name is Fisher.' That's what she said my real name was, Sarah Fisher. Sarah's a funny name—"

"It was the name of Abraham's wife in the Old Testament."

"I could go to the press with it, but I don't want to cause waves. You see, my mother is Elizabeth Taylor. Isn't that amazing? When she was married to Eddie Fisher she gave me up for adoption . . ."

It was then I realized she was crazy. She didn't seem like a bag lady, she wasn't unkempt, and her speech was clear.

"When I get my birth certificate I'm going to send her a registered letter so her staff won't see it. I used to have hair, jet black hair, and then it turned auburn, and now it's red. But that's how I found out I was Jewish."

"Elizabeth Taylor's not Jewish. She only became Jewish when she married Mike Todd."

"No, she was adopted. Her real name was Nidur."

The teams switched sides. When Patrick, the Serious Young Man, got to bat he struck out. One of the other boys started yelling at him, calling him Mordy. *So!* Proof! His name wasn't Patrick—it was Mordy. Another Mordecai!

I took a piece of paper out of my backpack and wrote on it: "Mordy—Patrick—the Serious Young Man."

"What are you writing?" Jean asked, and there was a note of apprehension in her voice.

"I'm just trying to get all the boys' names, and that was the first time I'd actually heard one of the other boys call him by name."

She looked at what I'd written and seemed mollified, but I suddenly sensed a certain awareness about "the word" ("In the beginning was the Word . . ."): I think Jean felt that in writing there was the actual possibility of identity being created, or transferred, or even stolen.

"I had eight children. And I lost them all. I just hope they're alive, I don't really care about anything else. There was always some confusion at the births. I was married each time, though. I think they switched babies on me. They do that, you know."

This whole question of identity seemed so futile to me, and I tried to put my thoughts on the matter as clearly as possible. "I don't think about the past," I told her; "I think it's best to just think about what's happening *now*."

I leaned forward and really started to pay attention to the game, not following it so much as focusing on the boys and their interactions with one another. I hoped my concentration might help Jean to get out of herself a bit, and finally she *did* begin to notice the action on the field.

"What are those strings hanging down?" she suddenly asked.

"Those are tzitzis," I explained. "They're part of something like a shirt they wear, they have an intricate set of knots, and they represent the six hundred and thirteen laws of Moses."

Jean pondered this for a moment. "See that boy," she said, indicating a tall boy with glasses, who had reddish hair and seemed rather geeky. "Doesn't that boy look like me? He *moves* like me. Isn't he funny? What if he was my son?"

I looked at the boy that reminded her of herself, a boy I'd never really paid attention to before, and I wondered what he'd think if he found out that this woman watching this baseball game thought he was her son.

"Most of these boys come from a long line of Orthodox Jews, and their parents and grandparents are mostly from Eastern Europe."

I felt it was incumbent on me to somehow mellow Jean's impending excitement. I didn't think any of these boys was quite ready for a reunion with a long-lost mother right now.

Jean contemplated the boys on the field. "A stranger said my son would end up in Israel."

"This—isn't Israel," I ventured.

"I know," she said, and then as the condescension of my remark sank in, "I *know* that."

I noticed a Chassidic boy, not part of the game, standing on our side of the fence, watching his friends play.

"Seven different strangers, with seven different religions, said they would protect my children. All my children had the Mogen David sign carved on their heads. If you ever see a boy with marks on his face, that's my son, marks like scratches. That's what a Mormon woman did to him."

The boy who was watching the game started to walk away, crossing in front of us on his way out of the park.

"Hello, how are you?" Jean greeted him.

He was obviously surprised by this sudden address and glanced our way, sizing us up and acknowledging Jean with a little smile.

When he was past us, Jean asked me if I'd seen the marks on his face. She didn't give me a chance to respond. "It's Andy. Look, look, did you see him look back at me? He can feel it. He knows it's me."

I watched the boy walk out of the park.

"Where's he going?" Jean asked.

"I assume he's going to the store. Some of the boys go there after the game, the drugstore."

"Do you think he'll be okay? That's him, that's my son. I knew I would find him."

The idea of a baseball game suddenly seemed to take hold of her, and she started yelling encouragements and reprimands, not a lot but just enough to make her presence felt. These loud interjections surprised the boys and (which was surprising to me) also seemed to gratify them somehow. But her cheering was never quite right—it often came, inappropriately, a beat too late, or else the cheering she was emulating from past experiences wouldn't quite mean anything, since she obviously didn't have any sense of the big picture: which team was which, what the score was, or even what the rules were.

One of the pitchers was a little awkward, and was throwing his balls short of the plate. "Throw the ball!" Jean yelled. "I'll get out there and show you!"

No one seemed to pay any attention to this remark, but she suddenly spoke to me in a quieter voice. "What would I do if they asked me? I haven't played ball in years."

Then, returning her attention to the game, she responded to another of the pitcher's efforts by calling out to him, "That's just like me! You're probably my son!"

Well, this was too much, and I burst out laughing. Jean was

surprised at that, but pleased she had been able to elicit such a response, and she started laughing, too. The pitcher in question didn't seem to hear, and I wondered if any of the boys who *did* hear could possibly have believed *what* they heard. Luckily, the game required most of their attention.

A few moments later there was the sound of sirens coming from Santa Monica Boulevard.

Jean tensed as she defined the sound. "The police."

"There's a fire station just down the street."

This seemed to reassure her a bit. "I see my son trying to buy food, and there's someone there with a gun trying to kill him. It's a dream I have, I've always had it."

I could almost see it: the Chassidic boy standing at the counter of the drugstore, trying to buy a Coke or some candy, and being brutally gunned down. What if that *was* why we were hearing the police sirens?

Someone threw a ball to first base, Mordy missed it, and it went bouncing behind us toward the tennis courts. There was a pause on the field as to who should go get it, and then Jean was up and running after the ball. She threw a grounder back to the field and Mordy caught it.

"Thank you very much. It is greatly appreciated," he said. *Very* much? *Greatly* appreciated?

When he had thrown the ball back to the pitcher I called out to him, "Nice catch, *Mordy!*"

He swung around to me and seemed about to protest, but I interrupted him with my smile, and he turned his attention back to the game.

When Jean returned to me she was very excited and, as an initiated participant, she began paying closer attention to the game. Suddenly she yelled out to a boy who was making a play, "Grab that yarmulke and run!"

One of the boys slid into first, and as he did he yelled back at someone about something, "Suck my cock!"

I was impressed. Mordy looked at me, our eyes met for a moment, and I think each of us could have said something, but Jean was here, so we both remained on good behavior.

"Such a mouth on that one!" she said, and a moment later, about another boy, "See that one? He has such a mouth! Just like me. All the ones with mouths are probably mine," and then she turned to me. "Wouldn't it be funny if they were *all* mine?"

The official game ended at three-twenty, but since there was still time they played an extra inning. And then it was over and they started back, one of the boys staying behind to pick up the bases and return them to the recreation department offices.

I told Jean I was off to see a movie, but that it was nice meeting her. I think she sensed my brusqueness (I didn't want her following me, and I didn't want her to know where I lived) because she said, "I'm just a good Christian woman."

As I was walking out of the park, the boy who had left earlier was just coming back. As I neared him I said, "Be careful. That woman thinks you're her son."

The boy stopped. "What?"

"Be careful. That woman"—and I indicated Jean, who was now standing by the bleachers looking in her purse—"thinks you're her son."

I left it at that and went on my way. I had started crossing the street behind a truck that blocked my view of the field when I realized I should go back and see what happened when they met.

Jean was still so busy rooting around in her purse that when her "son" passed by a few feet from where she was standing, walking slowly and staring at her, she didn't even notice.

24 / the shooting

I wondered if it was a spider.

It looked big. But it was strange, exotic, and white in the morning light. I stood up from my desk and stepped nearer to the window, to see if it was inside or outside, and suddenly realized that the strange brightness was not an insect at all but shattered glass surrounding a small hole.

The boys had thrown (or shot!) something at my window.

But *was* it them?

Could it be an accident?

I didn't think so.

Instinctively I felt I knew who did it, and I could just imagine him: the Big Ugly Boy, with his pimply face and his mincing imitations, the one who hated me so much, the one who told the plumber he wanted to kill me: picking something up off the ground and throwing it at my window—yes, I could just see him doing that.

This was obviously a breach that shifted the whole conflict up onto a higher (lower?) level: the destruction of property.

I went outside and looked around. There was a lot of loose material on the ground in front of my window, making it impossible to guess what might have been thrown. There were three large pieces of rock on the sidewalk, weapons just waiting to be thrown, so I picked them up and took them into the backyard and threw them away.

When I came back inside I worked on my story about the crazy lady. It was getting close to the time when the boys went to the park, and I was curious to see just what kind of reaction I would get, I was moving along with my writing, and . . .

Zmackt.

What?

An impact: some small object had pierced the screen and broken the glass, making a new hole in my window.

I immediately got up and looked across toward the school: little kids were playing in the compound next to the dormitories, the women overseeing them were sitting under the trees, and it was all very quiet.

And then I saw him, the Big Ugly Boy—he was walking across the yard where the kids were playing. How perfect. A moment later he was coming across the street. I got my binoculars and stood behind my bookcase so he wouldn't be able to see me, although I doubt he could with the reflections in the glass. He walked past my apartment, and then back. A moment later one of the other boys, Sea Horse of the goofy grin, joined him and also surveyed my window. After several lingering passes they headed on up the street.

Pretty soon more of the guys were coming from the school, crossing and walking up the street. I decided to go outside. I had on my jeans, a Bruce Springsteen T-shirt, and my new black hat. I'd been wearing it while I was writing and I wanted to show my lack of repentance.

I came out and sat on one of the "stoops," two blocks of

stone fronting the apartment building. As they filed past, some of the boys looked over at me: "What's with the hat?" "How much did it cost?" "Are you Jewish?"

"Yes."

I'd never said that before. If you ask enough times, do you eventually get a different answer?

"Why are you growing a beard?"

"I'm showing my respect to God," I said, only slightly sarcastic.

An aggressive little kid with glasses who looked like a beaver came up the walk toward me. "You're a faggot. Jews aren't faggots," he said.

"Do you fuck other men? Then you can't be a Jew," one of the other boys said.

"Why are you shooting BB guns at my house?" I asked them.

This was a cue for the aggressive little beaver. "I did it, my name's Harry Newman, so why don't you go and call the police?"

Little liar. It was interesting that I actually had a name and a confession, though.

They called me "faggot" a few more times and then went on up to the park.

After they were gone I decided I wasn't going to just sit there and take it, and I got up and headed across to the school, my hat still very much in place. Various boys and men watched my resolve with interest as I went down the street and around the corner to the main entrance of the building. Just to the left of the front door was an office. I turned in to the little waiting area there and knocked on the door. Through some sliding office windows I could see a woman in the next room talking on the phone. When she didn't answer, I waited a little longer and then knocked again, but she didn't seem inclined to relinquish her conversation.

A lot of guys were gathering around, including Avi and the

guy with the wire-rimmed glasses, the one who had told me several days earlier not to talk to the kids. I asked to speak to someone, and a few minutes later a black man came out and introduced himself to me. His name was Leo. He said he was the maintenance man and he asked if he could help me.

I told him what had happened and that I suspected the boys had used a BB gun. He said the boys weren't allowed to have anything like that, even assuring me that their luggage was searched. He asked to see the damage and, as we walked over to my apartment, I explained that the reason they'd done it was because of the hat I was wearing.

That didn't really make sense to him, but then he asked me if I was Jewish. When I told him I wasn't, he laughed and said, "Uh-oh." I told him that one of the boys had said he did it, but I thought he was lying. Leo said he knew who most of the troublemakers were.

He looked at my window, ascertaining the damage, and then we walked back to the yeshiva together. Nothing was resolved, but there was a vague sense that he would get back to me. When we got to the office, a lot of the boys were hanging around and looking at me with interest, to see what I would do. I saw Catfish standing in a corner and said hello, but I must have spooked him because he turned and ran up some nearby steps to the second floor.

When I got home I called my friend Josh. With the excuse that I didn't want him to think that things were boring over here on Alta Vista, I told him the latest. He was impressed: levels had indeed shifted.

I was inside my apartment when the boys started straggling back from the park. The Big Ugly Boy was the first one back. He sauntered by fairly slowly and then let himself into the school's compound, where a class of nursery school children were running around and playing on the jungle gyms.

Once inside the gate he did not continue on into the building as usual but walked back and forth, occasionally trying to make small talk with some of the little kids. It was so odd that I wondered if he were setting up some sort of alibi. At one point he sat beneath Avi's window.

I stayed in my apartment while the boys returned from the park, but when they were all back, I went outside and sat on one of the stoops. I didn't take my chair, or a book, or even my binoculars. I just sat there and waited and watched.

I thought I might go over and talk to a rabbi if I saw one, or—

Ow!

Hot: force striking my neck.

Those little bastards!

Heat throbbing.

Where?

I looked around and noticed a movement of blinds in one of the second-story windows.

I jumped up and strode across the street and around the corner to the office. When I got there the door was open and I saw Mordy, the Serious Young Man, talking to a woman inside.

She turned and asked if she could help me, and I told her that one of the boys had just shot me, with a BB gun, I assumed, and I reached up to show her and—there was blood! I was shocked. For some reason I didn't think I was really hurt. I hadn't thought I might actually have proof that I was shot.

The boys who saw me went off to tell their friends, and within moments there was quite a little crowd, looking into the area where I was standing and then backing out again. The woman asked me who did it, and I said I didn't know, but that I suspected it was a boy I thought of as the "Big Ugly Boy." I explained in which window I'd seen the shade move, and when I said that, there was a sudden commotion: the threat of possible accusation spread like wildfire. One boy asked me who I was, and when I told him, he defined me to myself: "the famous Rick."

I repeated the phrase—"the Famous Rick"—as verification. I liked it. I stood there and told my story about what had happened to whoever asked. The secretary finally had me come in the office, where she took my name, address, and phone number. She asked me when this occurred. I asked her the time. She said it was three thirty-five, and I told her it happened five minutes ago: three-thirty. She wrote that figure down and then told me to go see about my neck and said they would get in touch with me later.

I went back to my apartment and tried to decide what to do. I called 911, the emergency number, and asked the woman who answered what I should do. She said that would have to be my decision. I looked in the mirror at the blood on my neck, and went down to Chris's apartment to show him. I knocked on his door, but there wasn't any answer. On my way back to my apartment, I saw him coming toward me, just back from a walk. I told him the boys had shot me and showed him my neck. He was interested in the drama of it, but his attitude was basically "I told you so."

I asked him what he thought I should do, and he said I should probably wash it. I went in the bathroom and cleaned off the blood where it had dripped down my neck; where the blood was coagulating I pressed lightly with my fingers. It was swollen and I wondered if there might be something actually imbedded there. I came back out to Chris and he looked at it in the sunlight. He said he couldn't really tell if there was anything there or not, so I decided to go to the hospital.

While we were talking, two boys came up to speak to me: Mordy, who'd been in the office a few minutes earlier, and the Nondescript Boy, who'd tried putting out a cigarette on my pants the other day.

"Hey, Rick, how's it going?"

"Are you all right?"

I shrugged my shoulders.

"What happened?"

"One of the boys shot me."

"You think one of the boys at the school shot you?"

"Who else would want to shoot me?"

"With what?"

"I don't know, a BB gun, I guess."

"A BB gun can't shoot that far away—"

Chris was listening to this conversation with interest and interjected that a BB gun certainly *could* shoot that far away, that he had one as a kid, and he went on to describe two different kinds of BB gun, one with a spring action and another that used a CO_2 cartridge which could really shoot far.

"So what are you going to do?"

I shrugged my shoulders. "I don't know."

After they had gone, Chris turned to me and said, "They're lying." He said they obviously knew who did it and were just trying to find out how serious it was, to see if they might get charged with murder or something.

That was interesting.

When I went back in my apartment I called Josh to tell him what had happened and see if he might give me a ride to the hospital. He wasn't there, so I left a cryptic message on his machine, for the sake of its suspense and entertainment value: "I've been shot in the neck and I'm bleeding. I guess I'll go to the hospital."

I got my backpack, put in a book to read, and headed out on my bicycle. I wore my hat.

I was almost to the corner when one of the smaller boys flagged me down. He was all dressed up in a suit and wore wire-rimmed glasses, which sat on the very thick bridge of his nose. He looked like a little businessman. His self-confidence suggested he must be at least thirteen years old, although he looked younger.

"Hey, Rick, where are you going?"

"To the hospital."

"Are you hurt very bad?"

"I don't know. That's why I'm going to the hospital."

"You think one of the yeshiva boys shot you?"

I just looked at him: What do you think?

"These are religious boys, they don't have guns. It's not possible that a yeshiva boy would shoot you."

This was a pointless conversation.

"I have to go." I tried to steer away, but he grabbed my hands on the handlebars of the bike and held me there.

"Rick, people want to kill you."

"So?" and I tried to explain to him the freedom of having nothing left to lose: "I don't care. I'm forty years old and forty of my friends have died of AIDS—so what difference does it make to me if somebody wants to kill me? Who cares?"

"Rick, nobody wants to kill you," he said, reversing his previous position, idly experimenting with different modes of procedure. "So are you mad at the boys?"

"*I—don't—care*," I said, ridiculously raising my voice. And then, quietly, I tried to explain my feelings to him as carefully as I could. "I'm embarrassed it makes any difference to me at all. Okay? Now I've got to go."

I managed to get my bike across the street, but he wouldn't let go of it, staying with me, holding fast to the handlebars and blocking my way.

"Rick, Rick, you want to know who shot you? You want to know who did it? It was the *schvartzers*. You know who that is?"

I just looked at him. It was strange to see that kind of ugly self-righteousness in such a little boy.

"The *schvartzers*," he said. "The niggers. It was the niggers. They're the ones who did it."

I thought of their maintenance man whom I'd met that afternoon. "You mean Leo?" I asked.

He deflated in exasperation and disgust. "No, not Leo," he said.

I pried myself and my bike from his cold little hands, and finally got cycling on down the street.

I had the weird feeling of being an insect prior to dissection: there was such a sense of superiority in his tone, such disdain, such an incredible feeling of inconsideration toward anything non-Jewish.

He had no responsibility to me whatsoever as a fellow human being.

I was beneath contempt.

25 / the police

At the hospital, Cedars-Sinai, they took three X rays, determined there were no fragments embedded in my neck, cleaned my wound, and gave me a tetanus shot. They told me to come back in two days. I received treatment by virtue of a health plan I was eligible for through the Screen Actors Guild.

The woman in charge of admittance I spoke to was shocked when I told her what happened. She said that she attended temple herself, but that my wearing the hat was no reason for anyone to shoot me. She told me I should very definitely make a police report.

I bicycled home, and as I rode up Alta Vista, I noticed Josh in front of my apartment. He was sitting on one of the little walls bordering the walkway and smoking a cigarette. He was hunched over, his elbows resting on his knees, in what I have defined for myself as the classical male heterosexual position (in the sauna at the gym I feel you can always tell which men are heterosexual because they usually sit that way—looking down at their hands, as if they were resigned to some overwhelming defeat and as if to say, "I did what I could—now what more do you want?").

As I rode my bike up on the sidewalk I called out to him and he looked up.

"My God, are you all right?" he asked, standing up and flipping his cigarette away as he came toward me.

I reassured him. "I'm fine. I went to the hospital and they gave me a tetanus shot. Did you see the holes in my window?"

I brought my bike up the steps onto the walkway and parked it, then took Josh over in front of my window, where we examined the glass.

"I talked to them," Josh said.

"Who?"

"The boys."

I turned around and looked at him. "You did? You talked to the boys? What did they say?"

Josh went back to the walkway and as he sat on one of the little walls he lit another cigarette. "When I got your message, I called you right back, but you were already gone. I was really mad, so I got in my car and drove over here."

I began to feel a little queasy—that somebody would get really mad because of something that had happened to *me*.

"You still weren't here, so I looked around and saw one of the old men with a yarmulke, so I went up to him and told him that one of the boys in the school had shot a friend of mine."

"Who was it?"

Josh shook his head. "I don't know, I don't even know if he had anything to do with the school."

"What did he say?"

"He said a yeshiva boy would never use a gun and told me to go talk to a rabbi. So I went over to the school and looked around, but I couldn't find anyone. That place is a dump, by the way, it's a real pigsty—"

"You went in the school?" I asked. "And nobody stopped you? Did you go in the main entrance?"

Josh shook his head and pointed toward the building. "No, I went in the side entrance around the corner."

I knew which one he meant—it faced Waring and led into the dormitory part of the school.

"So I wandered around, I even went upstairs, but I couldn't find anybody. I finally went outside in the back and found some of them playing basketball."

Josh took a deep drag on his cigarette before going on with his story. " 'I'm a friend of the guy that lives across the street,' I said and pointed over here. 'This is America,' I said. 'And just as you have the right to wear funny clothes, so does anybody else, and you don't just go around shooting people if you don't like them.' "

"What did they say?"

"They said you didn't have any proof who did it, and I said, 'Don't give me that. He saw you.' "

"You know," I said, "I *didn't* actually see who did it."

Josh shrugged. "You know it was them . . ."

I nodded, and then we both said, "Who else?" together and laughed.

"So what did they say?"

"One little kid said to me, 'Well, some of us don't like him,' and I said, 'That doesn't give you the right to shoot somebody!' And then I got really mad and I told them that this was America and that here you're innocent until proven guilty—'I don't want to ever hear that you shot at him again.' "

How weird—it had never really occurred to me that I might have a friend who would stick up for me in a confrontation.

"What did they say?"

Josh shrugged. "Nothing. No, that's not true—it was really strange, they started saying, 'We respect your opinion,' and they kept repeating that: 'We respect your opinion,' almost like a chant."

"So what happened?"

Josh shrugged. "Nothing. They just kept saying, 'We respect your opinion,' and then I came back over here."

We sat in silence for a few minutes.

"I think that's really amazing," I said, finally. "I'm really humbled. I don't think anyone has ever done anything like that for me before. It seems like some—ultimate definition of friendship. It seems like something worth writing about."

After Josh had gone home, I went into my apartment and played back my messages. There was this: "Hi, Rick, this is Josh. I mean, that's some message you left . . . uh . . . How? With a BB, with a bullet, what? Uh, if I'm not here, please leave a message and tell me—if you come back. I mean, *when* you come back. Okay. Bye."

I sat at my desk wondering what I should do and then, after several minutes, I picked up the phone and called 911. They transferred me to a police department that gave me another number to call. However, that office was closed, and they referred me to the Hollywood Division, which briefly put me on hold, transferred me somewhere else, and finally took down my information, saying they would send a police car over.

After I hung up I went outside to wait for the police. The typical spring overcast had made the sky particularly gray in the early evening. I walked out to the end of one of the walls bordering the walkway and looked over toward the school. I still had the hat on and I stood there with my arms folded across my chest. The hospital bandage was prominent on my neck.

Some boys were out in the compound across the street, and in a moment they were joined by others. Pretty soon there was quite a little gathering, and they began standing up on their wall and holding on to the fence that surmounted it. A few boys called my name, but I didn't say anything.

"What's he doing?"

The boys who were arriving were unsure just what the occasion was, and I wondered if my solitary self, standing still on the end of a wall, was the whole show.

There was a tension between us: they had hurt me, and in that action had become the aggressors. Their gathering together was instinctive, to wait and watch for some action from me that would comfortably allow them to perceive themselves as victims once again. Their sense of victory was palpable, but it contained a taint of dishonor, a dishonor that could be eradicated only by some act of craziness or violence on my part that would retroactively justify their attack.

But I didn't feel like giving them that satisfaction: let them stew in their guilt. And besides, when the police arrived, that would be all the answer they would need.

After a while some of the boys, including the big ugly one, came across the street toward me.

"Hey, Rick, what are you doing?"

"I'm waiting for the police."

"You think one of the boys shot you?"

"Who else hates me enough to shoot me?"

"Who do you think did it?"

Standing at the end of one of the walls above the sidewalk, I was looking down at the boys who were standing in the street. Like God I pronounced my verdict and, without saying anything, pointed my finger straight at the Big Ugly Boy.

He put his hand up to his chest incredulously. "You think *I* did it?"

"You're the only person I ever heard threaten to kill me."

"What are you talking about?"

"Several days ago, when you were talking to Shaul, our

plumber, I heard you, right here on these steps: 'I want to kill him. I just want to kill him.' "

He sputtered some denial and I wondered if, in his general hatred of me, he could actually remember one particular instance of it.

"No one has ever called me worse names than you," I told him. "No one has been more abusive to me than you have."

The Big Ugly Boy and his friends went back across the street, and I paced back and forth on the wall.

Among the boys congregating across the street I noticed Mordecai in particular, the beautiful Arabic-looking boy: he was pantomiming shooting me. The boy I think of as "passing"—the one who mooned me—was particularly concentrated on my actions, standing on the low cement wall and leaning forward against the fence, staring at me with a fascinated intensity.

And then they started yelling things at me. My position as a victim was intolerable to them, and any means to make me reveal myself as a genuine threat was now deemed acceptable.

"Hey, Rick! We hear you can't pay your rent and your landlord wants to evict you."

I had always imagined that there would eventually be a meeting of some kind, in an office with a presiding rabbi and his charges, or a school assembly perhaps, where I would be asked to speak and state my position clearly. That would be the beginning of a meaningful dialogue between me and the school. I would be asked to join them in their study of the holy Scriptures and, ultimately, I would either successfully refute their belief in God's existence or make them admit their "religion" is a front for a social organization that wants to claim a tax-free status.

"Hey, Rick, we think it's about time you moved out of this neighborhood!"

But this fantasy was apparently never to be. The only forum

I would ever be given was this one, atop a four-foot-high wall, from which I would have to shout to be heard, and with my audience not much more than a mob, across a street and behind a fence.

"I was here before you," I yelled back at them, and with this first answer to their noise, I felt myself starting to sink into an ugly, name-calling world.

The disturbing thing about the situation—as I imagined my landlord in cahoots with them—was their sense of invincibility, and it was more than knowing I didn't have any proof who shot me: it had something to do with an assurance they had been given from above that, not only were they being vindicated, they were right.

It was getting cold, and I went back into my apartment, as if I were through with them, but a moment later I returned with my police jacket on. Suddenly they all scattered and I thought a teacher must be coming, that they were going to get into trouble, but a cautious moment later they were all back in their places.

"Hey, Rick, you got a gun? Huh? You got a gun?"

And then I saw the man with the wire-rimmed glasses who had threatened me the other day. He came out into the compound and tried to disperse the boys but to little effect, answering their inquiries and suppositions in a let's-put-an-end-to-this-now manner: "I shot him, okay? *I* shot him."

They didn't pay him much attention and continued to taunt me, yelling across the street, and finally letting go with their most powerful weapon, the ultimate accusation: "Racist!"

Some other boys took it up, once it had been uttered. "Racist!" and it was on its way to becoming a chant when I stepped down off the wall and walked across the yard in front of my home.

"I am *not* a racist," I shouted back at them, as clearly and definitely as I could. "But I *do* have *absolute contempt* for your *religion. Not* your 'race.' I think Judaism is the worst thing that has ever happened to this planet, and I think your belief system, your belief in God, is not only stupid and a lie but offensive and dangerous. But I would fight anybody to defend your *right* to believe in whatever you want."

I was marshaling all my thoughts, all my feelings, and making every effort to present my position as clearly as possible, and yet I knew that by condemning their religion I was, as far as they were concerned, condemning them. But I was *not* condemning them *genetically*, and their lack of a unified response to my statements underscored this distinction. They were and are, in my eyes, a declension: animals first and foremost, human beings second, and, third (gloriously!), males. Only much more insignificantly are they "Jews."

A dialogue of sorts began, questions were shouted across the street, answers attempted, but the communication was a gabble of hopeless passions and assertions. Ultimately, however, they *had* made me angry.

"Are you embarrassed?" one of the boys called out to me.

Do I care about my windows being broken? Do I care about being shot at? *Do* I care about material objects? *Do* I care about my physical person?

Do I care about being alive?

Is that what being angry means?

"Yes."

And I wondered . . .

Was that my real defeat?

Was that affirmation their final victory?

When the police arrived I stepped down to the sidewalk and approached their car, but they waved me away, and I went back to the steps and waited. Most of the boys cleared out, but I noticed Meir, the exotically dark-skinned boy with the large straight-lined nose, standing across the street with a friend of his.

The police parked down the street, just across from the school. After a few moments they got out of the car, their movements vested with authority, in anticipation of whatever this encounter might bring. They walked back up the sidewalk toward me and we made our introductions.

They asked me what happened. I explained that three BB's had been shot through my window and that I had later been shot in the neck.

"How do you know they were BB's?"

"I don't. I was just making that assumption. I don't even know what BB's are."

"But you assumed that since you were still alive, it probably wasn't a bullet."

I laughed. "Right."

They went over to my window and looked at the three holes. The officer who signed the report later, Alistair, placed his hand against one of the panes, and four cracks went splintering away across the glass. When I made some kind of protesting sound he said, "It's going to have to be replaced anyway."

Yes, well . . .

They asked me where I'd been sitting, and I showed them, sitting on the stone block as I had been, and facing out. The wound was on the left side of my neck, and the officer with Alistair, Nieman, pointed up the street away from the school. "So the shot came from over there?"

"Well, I think I was turned this way," I said, surprised at the possibility that the shot might not have come from the school. The officer made no further note of the discrepancy.

Then they accompanied me into my apartment. Books were in neat stacks on the floor and the bed was made, but dirty clothes were piled on top of it, and I suddenly wondered what they must think of all this. Did they notice the gun belts hung over one bookcase? Did they notice the picture of me as a Nazi on the back of the front door?

It was twilight, and Nieman turned his flashlight on.

"Oh, I'm sorry," I said and, stepping over the books on the floor, turned the overhead light on. For the most part they stood forward of the bookcase projecting from the wall near the door, Nieman nearer the window.

Alistair studied my collection of the Norton Critical Editions. "Lot of books."

I laughed. "That's what I do."

"Did you see who shot you?"

"No. The street was quiet. When I looked around, I saw the shade fluttering on the window facing the street, upstairs and nearest us."

"Do you know who did it?"

"I have a pretty good idea. I think it's a big ugly boy who hates me and calls me names."

"But you didn't see him do it?"

"No. But right after they had fired this shot"—and I pointed to the hole in the window nearest my desk—"I looked out and saw the Big Ugly Boy across the street."

"When was this?"

"Just before the guys go to play ball in the park, probably between two and two-thirty."

"Why do you think they'd want to hurt you?"

"Because of this." I indicated my hat.

"Why is that?"

"I'm not sure. I guess it's because it's what the rabbis wear."

"Why are you wearing it?"

And here it was, the big question: *Why?*

"I'm not really sure. I guess it's because I want to see what it means to them. I mean, I've read their Bible, and now I'm on the Mishnah, which is the second of their holy books, and we've had some great discussions, me and some of the kids."

Bullshit, bullshit. I could practically read it in their eyes. But was it *crazy* bullshit?

"They know I'm not Jewish, and that I'm an atheist, and that I'm homosexual, and some of them don't like it. They threatened me a few days ago, two of the older guys, they said they didn't want me talking to the kids, and I asked the kids if they told them why, and they didn't, and so I told them, and then I told the mother of the kids next door— 'I'm not Jewish, I'm an atheist, and I'm homosexual.' "

I was much too excited, I was running on, it didn't make any sense, and even as the words were still pouring out of my mouth, I felt that the gist of it, for *them*, was that there was (although perhaps legally insufficient) definite provocation.

"What do you do for a living?" Alistair asked me, beginning to fill out the report.

"I'm an extra," I said, and, indicating the jacket I was wearing, "Sometimes I'm a cop."

There was the barest of acknowledgments: we all wear costumes.

As I was going on, justifying myself, I began sizing up the two of them, and Nieman (Jewish?) seemed particularly cute: short and lean, with close black hair and wide pretty eyes. Ultimately, I think they felt I was harmless, and when Alistair finished filling out the report he told me they would list it as Assault with a Deadly Weapon.

As they were leaving they gave me a copy of the report. Nieman handed me the wrong (pink) copy at first and then, as he gave me the proper (yellow) one, said he was spaced out. They told me they would give the case to a detective who would probably call on me within a couple of days.

LOS ANGELES POLICE DEPARTMENT
PRELIMINARY INVESTIGATION OF ADW/VANDALISM

INVEST. DIV.:   HWD   DR: 9106
LAST NAME, FIRST, MIDDLE: SANDFORD, RICK STEVEN
SEX: M   DESC.:   W   AGE: 40   DOB: 12-31-50
PREMISES (SPECIFIC TYPE):   1-STORY APT
DR. LIC. NO. (IF NONE, OTHER ID & NO.):   EO443881 I.D.
OCCUPATION: STUDIO EXTRA   R.D.:   674
PRINTS BY PREL. INV./ATTEMPT: N
DATE & TIME OF OCCURRENCE: 5-29-91   15:30
DATE & TIME REPORTED TO PD: 19:45
TYPE PROPERTY STOLEN/LOST/DAMAGED: BROKEN WINDOW
EST. DAMAGED ARSON/VAND.: $100 *ea*
MOTIVATED BY HATRED/PREJUDICE: X
REPORTING EMPLOYEE(S):   P. ALISTAIR
SERIAL NO.:   3546
DIV./DETAIL: HWD X42

After they left I stayed in my apartment. I watched Meir and his friend across the street. All the time the police had been here they had stood there, looking across toward my apartment. Meir was impassive. I remembered the evening I'd given him some Velcro for his yarmulke. I wondered what he was thinking now.

I sat down at my computer and started to write about the day and what had happened. Parts of it were difficult to think about and sometimes I would skip ahead so as not to have to go through it again, but then later I would go back and try to fill in the blanks.

And the most difficult question of all was: Why?

I called a couple of friends to tell them what had happened, including Tom, the boy who had given me my first *yarmulke*, and I tried talking my way through my motivations:

Why was I wearing a yarmulke and tzitzis? *Why* did I spend $55 on a hat?

I didn't really know.

No, that wasn't true.

I didn't really *want* to know.

What I *wanted* was Understanding—I wanted it to thrust itself suddenly upon me and reveal its inner workings.

What I *wanted* was for one of them to renounce his religion and tell me he loved me.

What I *really* wanted was for something—*anything*—to happen.

And now it had.

But: *why?*

A detective was going to be here within a couple of days and that same question would come up again: *Why* was I wearing these clothes, the hat or a yarmulke and tzitzis?

Okay.

I didn't really know what the hat meant.

The yarmulke was a way of showing one's respect to God.

Tzitzis represented the 613 laws of Moses.

And . . .

One of the 613 laws of Moses is Leviticus 20:13: "If a man lies with a male as one lies with a woman, the two of them have done an abhorrent thing; they shall be put to death—their bloodguilt is upon them."

I had it!

One simple reason, the solid bottom line on which was erected this whole strange relationship that had culminated in my being shot in the neck with a BB gun.

They wear clothes that say I should be killed!

It's the same as it would be for them if I wore a swastika.

It's offensive.

And *that's* why I'm wearing these clothes!

It's a way of invalidating their meaning.

Yes!

26 / the detective

I couldn't sleep. I woke up about four o'clock in the morning, tormented by an equation without a resolution: someone had shot me. I couldn't resolve the issue in my mind, but even though my dreams and consciousness were all a part of one another and the distinctions wouldn't clarify themselves, I was uncomfortably aware of one ineluctable fact: *I* made a difference. And somebody didn't like that. I kept my eyes closed and stayed under the covers, hot in my dark little cave, very aware of my cracked windows with the holes in them, cognizant of the big hospital bandages, one over the place on my neck where I'd been wounded and the other over the place on my arm where they'd given me the tetanus shot. At about six-thirty, dirty gray dulling the dark outside, I heard the thump as the newspaper landed outside my door. I began to hear people coming and going, but I didn't want to get up, I felt weirdly depressed, and I just wanted to stay in the dark until everything was okay.

There was a strong knock on the door.

Okay, so I wouldn't be able to resolve all this before I woke up. I stepped to the door naked and opened it a crack. A man in his fifties was standing there, neat and trim, with dress pants on, a white shirt, and tie.

"I'm Detective Bucher of the Los Angeles Police Department," he introduced himself, showing me his badge.

"Oh. Uh—just a minute, let me put something on," and I grabbed the big blue robe off my bed which I'd been using as a blanket, stepped back to the door, and asked him in.

The room was a mess. All the stuff that had been on my bed the night before was now on the floor, and to get a seat for the detective I had to climb over my bed and retrieve my director's chair from the kitchen and then shift my bicycle over so there'd be some place for me to set down the chair. With these preliminaries taken care of, I sat cross-legged on the bed facing him.

He handed me his card, an off-white color: "Los Angeles Police Department" and a "Detective" insignia were embossed in gold, with the other information—his name, ID number, and the precinct address and phone—in black.

He asked me what happened, and as I started to tell him about the shooting, I saw Avraham walking across the street, on his way to school, and I pointed him out to the detective. "That's Avraham, he's a great kid, he's twelve. He just moved here from Israel with his family. They live next door. The other day I was talking to him when two of the older guys, the ones who are in something called the beit midrash, came over and threatened me. They told me to stop talking to the kids and said it was my responsibility not to talk to them. Then the other night I saw two cops up the street, and I asked them if I was doing anything wrong in talking to the kids—I mean, I'm not initiating these conversations and it's not like I'm trespassing or anything—and they said there was nothing wrong about it. I use binoculars sometimes, and I asked them if there was anything wrong in using binoculars to look at people across the street, and they said it was, in fact, an invasion of privacy, and since then I haven't used them to look at the boys . . ."

I talk fast anyway, but I felt like I had to tell the story of my life in thirty seconds, and was hurrying as fast as possible to get out as much information as I could.

Detective Bucher interrupted my spiel. "Where were you when you were shot?"

"I was sitting outside on one of the stoops in front of the building."

"Could you show me?"

"Sure," and I led the detective outside and showed him where I was sitting, angling myself toward the school so there wouldn't be a repeat of that embarrassing situation with the policemen when one of them pointed up the street *away* from the school and suggested that the shot had come from there.

Detective Bucher then walked over to the window, and I had a sudden premonition of him touching the glass and it breaking out and then having to come up with money I could not afford in order to replace it. He looked at the holes in the glass and, in particular, at the one that had pierced the screen.

He looked at how the screen was attached to the window frame and then lifted it off, and began looking in the sill grooves. After a moment he lifted up a small copper-colored pellet.

"Is that a BB?" I asked.

He said it was, pocketing the evidence and then replacing the screen. "You can tell the shot came from over there." He pointed toward the school.

"You can?" I asked. "How?"

"By the way the glass is shattered."

I was impressed.

We went back into the house and I continued my account of the shooting. "I think I know who shot me, although I can't be sure. I think it was this one boy who calls me names all the time; a few days ago he told our plumber that he wanted to kill me . . ."

Detective Bucher was a pleasant man, very responsive, and his professional demeanor, for the sake of gathering information, was as engaging as possible, and I felt I just couldn't let that engagement down. At the same time I wondered about his own prejudices: religious, political, sexual.

"The reason they shot me was because of this hat," and I got up and retrieved the hat from my desk, and put it on.

"Why? Is it German?"

"I'm not sure. It's a 'Fléchet.' One of the boys said it's what their rabbi wears."

"Why are you wearing it?"

"Well, to tell the truth, I don't really know. But I've been thinking about it and I think, although this is only part of it, the bottom line, in terms of wearing clothes, is that this is my way of protesting their wearing tzitzis. Do you know what tzitzis are?"

Detective Bucher shook his head.

I dug around among the dirty clothes on the floor and found my tzitzis, and I lifted them up to show him. "These are tzitzis: they wear these over their undershirts and under their regular shirts most of the time, but it varies, and these four sets of strings with the knots in them? These just hang at their sides, and they represent the six hundred and thirteen laws of Moses, and one of those laws says that if you have sex with another man you should be killed. That's a statement they are making with the clothes they are actually wearing, and so I think that is the bottom line about why I'm wearing these clothes: I am trying to destigmatize them. Because I really do despise their religion, and their belief in God, and—"

"Do you hate Christianity, too?"

"Oh, sure, and Mormonism, and Islam, they all come out of Judaism. I've read the Koran—"

"So you hate all religions?"

"Well, I mean, I hate those religions because I know about them, I don't really know about the other religions, Hinduism and Buddhism and stuff, but the ones I do know about I despise, but I like the kids. And, you know, it's funny. I mean, when I grew up I knew that Jesus' being Jewish was downplayed, but I just found out that it works the other way, too. I told two of the kids, 'You know what I did the first twelve years of my life? I worshipped a Jew.' And one of them said, 'Jesus wasn't a Jew,' and his friend said to him, 'Yes he was.' And this boy said, 'Well, he wasn't a Jew when he died,' and his friend said, 'Yes he was.' It was very funny. They're really smart, though, they're smarter than most kids I know. I mean, take any ten kids from that school and compare them to kids from Fairfax, or even Beverly Hills High, and I bet they'd be smarter. So it is really fun to talk with them, because they'll talk to you, about ideas and about God and what life is all about, and we've had some great talks—I've written most of them down. Some of the guys don't like me and get abusive and call me faggot, but most of them are good kids. Oh, yeah, once I said to one of them, one of the ones who's always calling me names, 'If you worshipped the penis instead of God you wouldn't be so bitter'—"

Detective Bucher blanched slightly at what I said and interrupted me. "So they know you're gay?"

It was rather sweet watching him deal with his own understanding of diplomacy and I appreciated his effort: when he asked his question he was careful about using politically correct terminology ("gay").

"Oh, yeah, and they know I'm not Jewish and I don't believe in God, and in fact, when they told me not to talk to the kids, that's exactly what I told the kids, so they'd know why they weren't supposed to talk to me: 'I'm not Jewish, I'm an atheist, and I'm a homosexual,' and I told that to Avraham's mother, too, so she'd know. I don't want there to be any confusion, other than the fact that I'm wearing Jewish clothes. You see, I'm writing a blasphemous, homoerotic version of the Christ story in the style of the 1611 King James Version of the Bible, and since that's all about Judaism I thought I'd be Jewish until I'm done. That's all I've been reading about for the last couple of years, I think it's the most important thing that's ever happened to this planet, in terms of ideas—I think it's awful but I think it's worth studying, and now I'm reading the Mishnah, which is their second major holy book, after the Tanakh . . ."

When I told him I'd written about the shooting the day before, he asked if he could have a copy of it, and so I turned on my computer, went into the proper file, and, after spacing the entry down so it was even, printed the five pages out, numbered them with a pen, and handed the account over to him. He said no one else would read it, that it was just for himself. I told him I'd tried to write down everything that happened. And I wondered, as I watched him holding the pages in his hands, just what *did* I write? It wasn't finished, I hadn't reread it, and it had never occurred to me that it might actually become evidence.

He asked me if I thought he should go over there and speak to them.

"I don't know. It might be interesting for you, you'll certainly find out what they think about me."

"Does anybody else have trouble with them in the neighborhood?" he asked.

I smiled. "Well, when the school first opened they made a lot of noise and there was a mini-riot and one of the rabbis was arrested. The JDL left threats around the neighborhood saying that anyone who interfered with them would pay in blood, but other than that I haven't been aware of any trouble. About a week ago the police came next door because someone complained about the noise in the back. There's a family back there with four kids, and the three-year-old screams all the time. The man next door has seven kids—it's really shameful. I feel so sorry for the kids. Dovid is eleven and he's really nice, but I feel so sorry for him."

As he was leaving, Detective Bucher said he thought he would go over to the school, and he told me to contact him if there was any further trouble. As soon as he was gone I printed out another copy of the five pages I'd given him and read them over to see how I might have incriminated myself. It seemed all right, except that in the last two paragraphs I revealed that I only discovered my motivation *after* the fact:

> I've just been going over this and trying to piece my thoughts together. I called a couple of friends and spoke to them, and then while I was talking to Tom I suddenly felt like I found the hook, the solid objective reason *why* I was wearing a hat and tzitzis.
>
> The tzitzis stand for the 613 laws of Moses. One of those laws says that men should not lie with men, that they should be killed. That is offensive to me. And that is what their clothing says.

I stayed in the house the rest of the day, reading and writing. When the boys went to the park I watched them from inside my apartment. They all looked over here, but I don't think they saw me, what with the reflections on the glass.

Later in the afternoon, after they had returned from the park, I decided to go outside and see if I could find any of the BB's that had been shot at me.

I looked at the window. It consisted of two panes of glass, one of which could slide open and was covered with a screen. As I examined the hole in the glass behind the screen, and the tear in the screen itself, I suddenly realized that *I* could deduce something of the angle of the bullet that hit the window.

The BB had to go through the screen before it hit the glass, and as I looked at the window I noted that the incision in the screen was considerably farther to the left, facing the building, than the hole in the glass, pretty clearly indicating a direction compatible with the school across the street.

I was surveying the ground when my landlord stopped by. I told George what had happened and asked him about replacing the windows.

"We shouldn't replace them too quick," he said. "They might try and shoot you again."

I laughed: well, that was a practical way of approaching the matter.

After George left I went back to looking for the missing BB's. George had hated having to pay for the upkeep of a lawn and so had paved over our yard with bricks. The more I looked around, the less likely it seemed that I might find a small copper-colored pellet on the brick-covered ground. There was all sorts of debris—gravel, loose mortar, and dust. I tried examining the yard systematically, combing one small area after another, but it was very frustrating and then suddenly I found one of them: a little shiny copper ball. It was a couple of yards from where I'd been sitting when they shot me.

I had just picked it up when I heard someone calling me from across the street. "Rick!"

I turned around and saw Avraham over at the school. He was inside the compound, but he had climbed up on the wall and was holding on to the fence that surmounted it.

"What?"

"Did you see a little kid go by here just now?"

"No, I didn't," and I gave him an explanation. "But I wasn't really looking."

He nodded to me and then got down and went away.

Holding the little pellet in my hand, I watched as Avraham disappeared between two of the school buildings. I suddenly felt as if a hand had been extended to me across an abyss, and I thought how sweet that Avraham should make such a gesture. That, to him at least, I was not a pariah . . .

I had to blink away the tears.

27 / after the fact

The next day when I took a shower, my first since going to the hospital, I took off my two bandages, the one on my neck and the other on my arm where I'd received the tetanus shot. Both wounds were practically invisible. I also shaved for the first time in a couple of months: I wasn't going to be a catfish with peyos anymore.

I was just finishing reading the paper when Orestes stopped by. He'd just bought a new motorcycle he wanted to show me.

What he really wanted was sex.

An hour or so later (no crystal), I walked Orestes outside. He'd parked his motorcycle under the eucalyptus tree and it was quite the gleaming, stream-lined machine. He asked me if I wanted to get on it and I said sure. I straddled the machine, reaching out and grasping the handlebars, and I felt like I looked very cool— what with my shades, my tzitzis, my black dress hat, and my tanned bare legs.

Several moments later I heard the boys, and then saw them as they appeared between the two school buildings, passing through the playground area and making their way toward the gate. As they became aware of me, the noise they had been making diminished into silence.

Astride the motorcycle, I regarded them as they began to cross the street beside me. They were not talking and shouting together as usual, and it was curious to see them so quiet and subdued.

"Nice hat."

I wasn't sure which one had spoken to me, but what I heard was a simple affirmation and I responded with genuine gratitude for the acknowledgment that I could wear whatever I wanted to: "Thanks."

It was strange. They knew they shot me, *I* knew they shot me, and yet this knowledge could not be spoken between us because of possible legal ramifications: my emergency room visit and the price of my window.

They are the aggressors. *I* am the victim.

Whereas before it could be seen the other way around—myself the aggressor, and they the victims—now, with the roles reversed, I think we were all a little uneasy with our new definitions: I'd been attacked, and what they did had been officially classified as "motivated by hatred/prejudice."

My attack—the wearing of their "holy" garments—was symbolic.

Their attack was physical.

I wasn't sure how many baby ravens were in the nest at the top of the eucalyptus tree, but at least one of them was out and clinging to a branch. While I was reading ("Self-Reliance" in Emerson's *Essays*) I would occasionally look up to see it with my binoculars. The parents would fly away and bring back food. As soon as the baby was aware of them, it would start crying, and after some suitable interval—to see if everything was safe?—they would come and feed it, sticking their beaks down its gaping gullet.

I got the feeling, however, that the parents were getting a little tired of this routine, and their cawing seemed to be impatiently imperative: "If you think you're going to sit there the rest of your life while I fly around getting you food, you've got another think coming. Look at me! Open your wings and let the air support you! I *know* you can't see it, but you can feel it, can't you? You're not going to catch any worms just sitting on that branch."

Sometimes I answered their calls with a "Caw!" of my own, a loud high-pitched noise with a slight trill from the back of my throat.

"You sound just like a bird."

I turned around and saw Avraham in the driveway behind me. Yaakov was standing just beside him.

I shrugged. "I like to talk to them."

We looked at one another for a moment. I imagined that Avraham felt a wrong had been committed against me and somehow he wanted to make it right.

"One of the baby ravens is out of its nest," I told them. "You want to see?" and I offered them my binoculars.

Yaakov came forward and took the glasses. He looked up into the tree. "Where?"

I was used to looking up and being able to see it for myself, but now trying to point out the little black speck in that mass of foliage was very difficult. Yaakov couldn't find it, so I showed him the nest instead, a dark mass at the top of the tree.

While we were looking up at the birds I noticed Moshe and Yitzchak approaching us from across the street.

I greeted Moshe, with a personal allusion to my stories. "My hero!"

As he came up to me, he skipped over the preliminaries. "Do you have a gun?"

"What do you mean? No."

"Not even a BB gun?"

I shook my head. "Who told you that?"

"Some of the boys."

"They think I have a gun?" I asked. And then I remembered standing there that day, the boys all gathered in the compound across from me, and I remembered that strange moment when they all scattered. At the time I'd thought one of their teachers was coming and they were afraid of getting into trouble, but it wasn't that at all: somebody had said I had a gun, and they'd all ducked for cover. How strange.

"Where did you get hit?" Yitzchak asked, looking up at me with curiosity—his beautiful dreamy eyes filled with what world of considerations?

I turned my neck so they could see the welt.

"Did it hurt?" Yaakov asked.

"It was like a very hot sting. I didn't even know I was bleeding at first."

"Do you think one of the boys shot you?" Moshe asked.

"I think so."

"Do you know who?"

I shook my head. "I didn't see. I think it was somebody on the second floor over there."

We all looked over toward the school. I could see a couple of boys at the windows.

Yaakov turned back to me. "All the boys say you're crazy. Are you crazy?"

He was so endearingly bull-headed in his pursuit of the facts. I shrugged my shoulders. "Maybe just a little—around the edges."

Avraham suddenly shifted his position so that the eucalyptus tree was between him and the school. "Is he looking?" he asked the other boys.

"Yes," Moshe answered.

I looked at them. "You're not supposed to be talking to me, are you?"

Moshe shrugged his shoulders: he didn't care.

"What did the police say?" Avraham asked.

"They just made a report. Do you want to see it?"

They did and I went in the house and brought my yellow copy out to them. Avraham recognized the paper from some previous experience.

"I even found the BB that hit me," I said.

"What's a BB?"

"You want to see? I'll show you," and I went in the house and came out with my notebook, and I turned to the last page where there was the entry about the day I was shot, and where I'd taped onto the paper the little copper-colored pellet. They examined it.

"Moshe!"

It was a voice from across the street. I could see the guy with the short curly hair calling from the room next to Avi's.

"Are you going to get in trouble for talking to me?" I asked them. "Do those guys have authority over you?

"Do you have to do what they say?"

"They spoke to our parents," Avraham said.

"Well, I talked to your mother," I told him. "I told her what they said, and that I wasn't Jewish and that I was an atheist and homosexual."

"Moshe! Come here."

It was the guy with the short curly hair again. The boys were a bit undecided about what to do. They clearly didn't want to return across the street.

"Follow me!"

Avraham had spoken with absolute decisiveness and, taking the initiative, he led the boys after him as he walked away. My chair was facing the sun, and since I didn't turn around to watch them go, I wasn't sure if they went down the driveway to Avraham's home or just continued on up the street.

222 / rick sandford

A little later I saw the four of them walking back to the school on the opposite sidewalk. Once they were in the compound, the guy with the short curly hair stopped them and spoke to them from his window. I lifted up my binoculars to see what this conversation consisted of.

"Put your binoculars away, Rick," the guy called over to me, but I didn't, not until his conversation with the boys had ended and they had disappeared back into the recesses of the school.

I spent the rest of the day outside reading. The baby raven was out on a branch most of the day. The parents both cawed at him with particular emphasis and occasionally he flapped his wings, but he still wouldn't let loose and actually try them out.

I was reading the Mishnah. I wondered if there might not be something in it about this whole situation—after all, it was practically a lawbook: *was* there some policy about attacking Gentiles who were dressed up as rabbis?

There was an extensive index in the back of the Mishnah and it was easy to look things up. In the section called *Baba Qamma* I found something:

Baba Qamma 8:1
A. He who injures his fellow is liable to compensate him on five counts:
B. (1) injury, (2) pain, (3) medical costs, (4) loss of income [lit.: loss of time], and (5) indignity.
I. *Medical costs*:
J. [If] he hit him, he is liable to pay for his medical care.

That was interesting. But it still begged the question of whether it applied to the relations of all people or just Jews.

While I was going through the book, the man next door

started screaming at his kids. It was hard to concentrate as I could so clearly see in my mind Dovid and Yossi and their sisters receiving the brunt of their father's rage. As I listened to the high-pitched inarticulate sounds, the process of interpretation seemed similar to the one I had applied to the ravens, only this was uglier: "Oh, my God, what are you doing! I set that book there for a reason! Don't you understand! Can't you look where you're going? What if the Messiah were just about to come back and save us and then he saw you and decided it wasn't worth it? How would you like that? And it would all be your fault!"

I couldn't stand it any longer and turned to look over toward their house to see if I could distinguish what he was actually saying by paying stricter attention.

Avraham was standing in the driveway, and our eyes locked on one another as the screaming continued.

After a long moment Avraham finally spoke. "He's always yelling."

"I know," I said. "I feel sorry for Dovid."

We continued looking at each other and then Avraham, having done his part in identifying the disturbance, went down the driveway and into the street, on his way to the school.

I felt as if I'd found as much as I was going to in the Mishnah, so I went and got my Tanakh and my concordance, and started looking for applicable quotations in the Torah.

I found a couple:

Exodus 21:18–19: When men quarrel and one strikes the other with stone or fist, and he does not die but has to take to his bed—if he then gets up and walks outdoors upon his staff, the assailant shall go unpunished, except that he must pay for his idleness and his cure.

Leviticus 19:33–34: When a stranger resides with you in your land, you shall not wrong him. The stranger who resides with you shall be to you as one of your citizens; you shall love him as yourself, for you were strangers in the land of Egypt: I the LORD am your God.

Late in the afternoon I saw Avi leave the compound and start walking up the street. I called out to him and said hello, but he didn't answer me.

I watched him walk away with his awkward gangly stride, the tzitzis hanging down beneath his shirt, and I thought to myself: Maybe I should sue the school. It would be worth it just to see Avi take the stand and explain what he thought about me for the court record.

Orestes said he thought I should definitely take legal action and at least demand compensation for my hospital visit and my broken window. I told him I would think about it.

Even though I didn't have the money to pay for the damage (the estimated $200 for the broken glass and who-knows-what for the hospital visit), in a way I didn't really want to pursue this thing. If I did, they could get into their defensive "You can't prove it" mode, and that was definitely not a place where I wanted them to be.

I wanted them to be ashamed of themselves, I wanted them to be sorry, I wanted them to apologize.

I *didn't* want to force them.

I wanted them to have to deal, inside themselves, with their own immorality.

I just wanted to be friends.

I wanted to hold Avi in my arms, and I wanted him to tell me he loved me, and I wanted him to come in my mouth, and I wanted him to see his God—in me.

28 / the sacrifice

There were only a few weeks of school left, and during that time the baby raven finally left his home in the eucalyptus tree and never came back. I wasn't there when it happened—I didn't get to see that initial victorious flight—but for a while I continued to see the parent birds around the neighborhood, and when I heard them I would answer their loud raven cries with one of my own.

My encounters with the boys were considerably more reserved. I continued to sit outside during the day, but I never dressed up in my full rabbi regalia again, although I still wore the hat most of the time, and sometimes the tzitzis.

When the boys came out of the school and started up the street to go to the park they would glance over at me, but there were no more greetings or flirtations or mincing imitations. They would look at me to see what I was doing, as if to somehow get a better fix on me, but the days of our being friends seemed to be over. Occasionally one of them would surreptitiously give me the finger.

One day Mendel and the Fat Redhead left the school after the main group of boys and I thought I would try to mend some of the broken bridges. I felt that Mendel liked me, even if I was some sort of bug under glass.

"Hey, Mendel!"

He stopped and turned back to me: "Next time it'll be in the head, bud."

He waited a second to see if I had anything to say, and when I didn't, he and his fat friend turned and continued on up the street.

That took me off guard. I guess Mendel must have been in the compound that day when I was yelling how much I hated their religion. I don't remember him there. Mendel is too cute to be religious, and even worse than the ugly tone he'd directed toward me, it was sad to hear him defending their ideology.

If he ever becomes a rabbi, maybe he'll say it was all because of me.

When I received my hospital bill I was shocked: my little visit, plus the X rays, came out to $512 and even though I had insurance, I was still responsible for $288. That was money I just didn't have.

I started making a more concerted effort to get work, calling in to Central Casting every day to see if anything was going. I was using a headset so I had my hands free, and while the phone rang and rang *and* rang in my ear (waiting for them to pick up and give me a job or tell me to call back), I worked on my stories.

One day, when I saw the boys start heading up the street toward the park, I went outside to sit on one of the stoops and watch them pass. In addition to my black pants and a white T-shirt, I had on my black dress hat.

When they saw me, two of the boys crossed the street to talk to me: the Big Ugly Boy, the one I had first thought shot me, and Harry Newman, the little beaver who claimed he shot the BB's through my windows.

Harry was in a jocular mood. "So are you going to miss us? Wednesday's the last day."

"Of course I'll miss you. Spring break was terrible. I was very lonely without you boys running up and down the street."

"So you still think I shot you?" the Big Ugly Boy asked.

"I did at first, but I don't anymore. Now I think it was that guy with the wire-rimmed glasses in the beit midrash."

"So are you going to sue the school?" Harry asked.

"Why?" I was incredulous. "You did me a favor. You gave me an ending for my stories. I didn't have an ending. So you shot me. That's an incredible ending."

Harry started to protest, but I interrupted him. "No, no: I think we understand each other very well—underneath, subconsciously, I mean, it wasn't *my* ending. *My* ending was that one of you boys would renounce your religion and come over and we'd have great sex."

"Like Avi?"

"Well, Avi. I mean, he's so sweet. Of course Avi. My fantasy with Avi is that he'd come to me and we'd have sex and then afterward he'd get over his speech impediment and it would all be because of me, because I loved him."

They just looked at me.

Apparently there wasn't anything to say to that.

And then they turned around and walked away.

I watched them until they were out of sight.

And then wondered at what I'd said . . .

Could I ever "love" anyone?

Did saying it make it so?
Arbitrarily . . .
Avi?

During the next couple of days I could sense the school year ending. On Tuesday the boys didn't go to the park in the afternoon as usual, and I noticed a large number of them returning to the school with their dress clothes wrapped in the clear plastic of a dry cleaner's.

And some of them seemed to be moving.

One afternoon while I was inside writing at my desk, I noticed Avi cross in front of my apartment several times with bags and boxes and load them into a car. The Nondescript Boy was helping him. I saved what was on my computer and went outside. I was wearing black pants with my tzitzis and hat.

"Avi!"

He didn't respond.

I tried again. "Avi!"

He turned to me, put upon and exasperated, his eyes glowering in his catfish face. "What!?"

"Are you guys leaving?"

"No."

I felt like he was lying to me, so I stayed outside and watched them.

They made one more trip, and then the two boys went to get in the car. Apparently the front passenger door was locked, because Avi had to stand beside the car while the Nondescript Boy got in on the driver's side and then reached across to open it. While he was standing there, he turned to look back at me. I raised my hand to him and he looked away.

Once they were both inside, there was some delay in getting the car started and then there was a very sloppy pullout, a feeble attempt at burning rubber, and finally an awkward business of having to slow down because of an oncoming car.

I never saw Avi again.

Wednesday was the last day of school. I made a point of being home and sitting outside that day to see how the school year was going to resolve itself, to see if, perhaps, I might get an apology or some special goodbye. I was wearing my hat and long black pants, but no shirt, and I was browsing through *The Artscroll Weekday Siddur*, my Jewish prayer book. I was amused to find that in the morning prayers they thanked God for "not having made me a gentile" and for "not having made me a woman."

Late in the afternoon some of the boys started leaving the school. They were in an exuberant mood that suggested they might not be doing this again this year, and as I watched them leave in their various groupings, I wondered about them in the outside world. When they were in airports, dressed like that and with everyone looking at them, what did they think?

As I sat there, lost in contemplation of them, two boys came out of the compound through the gate. I guessed them to be about twelve. The taller of the two was wearing a bright yellow shirt. The other boy had on a red shirt and I recognized him: he was the boy I had spoken to a long time ago, the one who had said that sex was like "a beautiful rare jewel."

When they saw me looking at them, they started toward me, just stopping at the edge of the curb across the street. We considered one another for a moment, and then the taller boy suddenly put an arm around his friend and, bending down to put his other arm under his legs, lifted the boy with the red shirt up off the ground. It was just a bit of a struggle.

And then the boy in the yellow shirt set out across the street, walking straight toward me, the "beautiful rare jewel" docilely watching me as his friend carried him to . . .

To what?

It was like Abraham bringing his son Isaac as a sacrifice to God.

And I was God!

I was grinning at them in absolute, profound delight.

When they reached my side of the street the boy in the yellow shirt put his friend down and spoke to me. "Rick, how's it going?"

"Absolutely wonderful," I told them, and then, after a brief and awkward pause, they continued on up the street together. I was too overwhelmed to turn around and watch them walk away, but as I looked down at the book in my hands, it seemed incredible to me.

What *were* they doing?

It was certainly a joke. But what exactly *was* the joke?

Was the joke that *I* was God? *A* God?

Was the fact of one of them carrying the other associated in their minds as a *sacrifice*?

Whose idea was it? Somehow, on some level, they had made a mutual decision. Was it spontaneous or had they planned it? Was it based on some previous associations: Rick is a homosexual, he likes boys, therefore: we'll bring him a boy?

My sacrifice, my "Isaac," was adorable. He looked at me with a matter-of-factness that just hinted at a sense of bemusement. I felt in him a willingness to play this part in the ritual, to be offered up as a "beautiful rare jewel," and this acceptance of his, as he gazed on me, was lovely almost beyond words.

And I wondered: Was it a game?

Okay, I'll be Rick and you be the sacrifice. I was Isaac last time. Okay, you be Abraham, and we'll let Yitzchak play the sacrifice this time . . .

29 / summertime

When the school year ended, most of the boys went away, but some of the bochurs stayed and new ones arrived, in order to study the Talmud over the summer. The smaller boys who lived in the neighborhood went to various camps during the day, but in the late afternoons and early evenings, before they had to be home, we spent a lot of time together.

A new boy moved into the room just across from me, where Avi used to live. His name was Dimitri, he was fifteen, and he played the violin. Avraham told me he was a child prodigy and had played concerts all over the world. In the afternoons, while I sat outside reading, he would practice his music and I would find myself looking up from my books and staring off into space as he made his strings vibrate with the most exquisite melodies.

I finally finished my two big projects, going through my unread newspapers for the last two years and cataloguing Christopher Isherwood's library onto my computer, and with that done I started doing more research on the Jews across the street.

Originally, Chassidism was a movement that sprang up in

Poland in the eighteenth century among impoverished Jews reacting against scholarly Judaism. The leader of this movement was a man called the Baal Shem Tov. After he died, Chassidism splintered into various groups centering on different rabbis. One of them, Rabbi Schneur Zalman, developed a system of "spiritual growth" called Chabad, an acronymic abbreviation of the Hebrew words for wisdom (*chochmah*), understanding (*binah*), and knowledge (*da'at*), Chabad later became based in Lubavitch (a town about three hundred miles west of Moscow), with the two terms "Chabad" and "Lubavitch" becoming synonymous.

The head of Chabad that summer was a man named Menachem Mendel Schneerson, and he was called the Rebbe. He was the seventh leader of the Lubavitch and had been their Rebbe since 1950, the year I was born.

One afternoon, while I was reading, I saw Levi walking by across the street. He was the only bochur I had ever really spoken to and I wanted to ask him about a book called the *Tanya*—it was written by the first Rebbe, Schneur Zalman, and was apparently very important for Lubavitchers.

I got up and ran across the street to him, calling his name.

"I can't talk now," he said, waving me away with his hand.

"I just wanted to ask—"

"I'm sorry—I really can't talk now—I'm sorry," and he hurried on away from me. I watched him go and then slowly turned around and came back to my place in the sun.

Avraham was standing by my chair. Apparently he'd seen my brief encounter with Levi.

"He's not supposed to talk," he said. "He's *davenen*."

"What's that?"

"*Davenen*—praying. You're not supposed to talk when you *daven*."

I looked back up the street where Levi was just turning the corner. I liked that—the idea of praying and walking at the same time—and I liked that word: *daven*.

Twice a day, once in the morning and once in the afternoon, I would see Levi walk by. If he happened to glance over at me I would say hello, but he never answered my greetings and so I stopped doing even that.

But then I had an idea. I took a piece of paper and wrote on it, with a thick black ink pen, in big block letters: "HELLO, LEVI." When I was finished, I walked to the corner and taped it to a light pole, so that he would have to see it as he walked past.

I don't know if he saw it the next morning because I wasn't up when he took his walk, but that afternoon, as he passed by on the opposite sidewalk, he turned and stared at me. I had imposed myself on his wisdom, understanding, and knowledge . . .

I waved.

He didn't respond, but he didn't look away either.

Dovid and Yossi, the two little boys next door, stopped speaking to me. For a while I still greeted them, but then it just began to feel too strange. Yossi did a better job of ignoring me because we didn't really have a relationship in the first place, but when I spoke to Dovid he would turn his head just slightly to the side and, without answering, look at me as if trying to divine my purpose beneath the strange foreign language I was speaking.

And I would look back at him and wonder what his parents had told him.

In the afternoons, Dovid and Yossi would ride their bikes up and down the sidewalk. Leaves and seeds from the eucalyptus tree in front of my apartment had covered the ground, and when the boys sped down the walk, the wheels on their bikes would invariably skid whenever they passed by. One day, after watching this happen several times and once seeing Dovid nearly fall and hurt himself, I went in my house and got a broom.

For the next hour or so I worked up a real sweat, sweeping all the detritus from the sidewalk and pulling up the weeds that had grown in the cracks. While I was doing this, Dovid and Yossi left off cycling on my stretch of the walk. Occasionally they would stop and watch me working, but then they'd get back on their bikes and go riding up and down the block.

When I was finally finished, and they were momentarily poised in the adjacent driveway, I looked over at them. "I think it'll be better now."

They didn't say anything, but Dovid cocked his head to the side and looked at me with that deep consideration of his, a small furrow of concentration between his brows.

"Well, have fun," I said, and I took the broom back in the house. When I came back outside to read some more, they were racing up and down the sidewalk again, almost as if I hadn't cleared it just for them.

When I was working inside during the summer I usually kept my door open, even though I didn't have a screen, and one afternoon, while I was writing, Yaakov and Yitzchak suddenly appeared in the doorway.

"Rick, can we have some money?" Yaakov asked.

I turned toward them. "What do you need money for?"

Yaakov shrugged. "We want to get some candy at La Brea Kosher."

"I don't really have any money. I'm just collecting unemployment."

Yitzchak saw something on the floor. "Here's a penny," and he came in the room and picked it up. "Can I have it?"

Sometimes when I get undressed my change falls on the floor and usually I just leave it there. I liked the idea of having money on my floor. Need some money? Then just reach down and pick it up.

"Any money you find on the floor you can have," I told them, and with that pronouncement they started scurrying about the room, looking for coins.

There was something gratifying in the idea of these little boys searching my room for pennies.

"I found a quarter!" Yaakov suddenly yelled, and then he looked up at me to make sure it was all right. "Can I have it?"

I nodded my head.

Yitzchak bent down and started looking under my bed, while Yaakov headed for the kitchen.

"There's lots of money in here!" Yaakov shouted, and I turned to see him looking in the drawer of a desk I had in my kitchen. Yitzchak ran to join him, and turned back to me. "Can we have this money?"

I shrugged: Why not?

They started going through the drawers of the desk and then, when they had finished searching around in the kitchen, came back into my living/bedroom to count their loot. They had the change spread out on my bed when Yaakov noticed a large jar of pennies on one of my filing cabinets.

"Can we have those?" he asked, standing up on the bed to see it better.

I shook my head. "That's my desperation money—for when I don't have any money left. You've gotta leave me that."

Yaakov turned back to Yitzchak who was counting the change. "Oh, no! You mixed it up! Now we won't know which is mine and which is yours!"

I suggested that they split it evenly. They went through a careful process of counting the money and separating the coins into two piles. When they were done they each had several dollars. After pocketing the coins, they turned and offered me a brief "Thanks, Rick!" and then sped out of the apartment on their way to the store.

"Show me some pictures!"

Moshe and Yitzchak were sitting on one of the low brick walls beside me. Yitzchak was looking through my binoculars, but Moshe was bored.

"Do you want to see some pictures of me when I was a little boy?" I asked.

Moshe said he did, so I went into the house and got out a small basket in which I kept all my photographs. I brought it outside and opened it up. I had some representative pictures of myself from when I was a baby until fairly recently, but most of them were from a time when I took my camera to the sets of the movies and TV shows I worked on, and I showed Moshe photographs of me variously dressed as soldiers or policemen or aliens.

At first I went through the pictures myself and, whenever I found one that I thought might be interesting, handed it to Moshe or Yitzchak and explained it. But after a few minutes they were both rooting through the basket, holding up one photograph or another for me to identify.

"Who's this!?" Moshe suddenly exclaimed.

He had come across a few pictures of me and some friends hiking up at Lake Tahoe. We had taken photographs of one another on top of Mount Tallac without our clothes on.

"That's my sister," I explained, "and that's her first husband's sister."

Yitzchak reached across and grabbed one of the photographs from his brother. It was of me, naked, standing on top of the mountain with Lake Tahoe in the background.

"You're naked!" he shrieked.

The boys couldn't get over these pictures, and I wondered if it had been such a good idea to bring the whole basket of photographs outside. Moshe put the pictures he had found aside and started digging through the rest of the basket to see if he could find any other photographs of naked people, while Yitzchak held on to the picture of me with both hands, as if he were afraid it might escape his grasp.

"You're naked outside!" he exclaimed again.

"When you and your family go up in the mountains together, don't you take pictures of each other without your clothes on?" I asked.

"Never!" Moshe stated definitely.

"You should," I told them. "It's fun."

Yitzchak continued staring in wonderment at the picture of me without any clothes on. I reached over to take it from him, but he held it tight and wouldn't release it.

"Can I have this picture, *please*," he begged me.

"It's my only copy," I told him.

"But you can get another one," he pleaded.

"I don't have the negatives," I said, and wasn't sure if I was lying or not. I held my hand out for the photograph, but Yitzchak jumped up and ran a couple of yards away, where he stood—staring still at the picture.

"Yitzchak!" I said, a little exasperated, holding my hand out toward him.

After looking at me naked on the mountaintop for a few more moments, almost as if committing the image to memory, he reluctantly walked over to me and handed it back. I enjoyed the fact that I could trust these two boys, that there was a basic sense of propriety we all understood and respected.

I took the pictures of me naked and held on to them as we continued to look through the rest of the photographs. I found several other naked pictures before Moshe or Yitzchak did, and appropriated them as well.

"Please let me see," Moshe begged.

I shook my head.

"We've already seen you naked," Moshe reasoned. "What difference would it make?"

I shook my head again and stood up, planning to put these particular photographs in a hiding place. I started back toward my apartment. Yitzchak stayed behind, looking through the rest of the pictures, but Moshe followed me. "Let me see! *Please!*"

I put the pictures up on one of my bookshelves where little boys couldn't reach them without a chair.

"Why?" he asked. "Do you have a boner?"

I laughed. "No."

"Then *why?*"

Some friends of mine had told me that it was against the law to show kids certain pictures, that it was contributing to the delinquency of a minor or something, and ever since then I'd been very discreet about showing any naked pictures of myself to the boys. I hated not being honest with Moshe. I hated being trapped into being a dreary old grownup.

"I talked to some people," I said, deciding to be forthright about my reasoning, "and they said I shouldn't show any naked pictures to kids, because I could get in trouble."

"I won't tell anyone!"

I looked at Moshe, standing in the doorway, looking up at me. He was so earnest in his desire to get his own way, to see my pictures.

"Okay," I said, giving in and handing him the pictures. They were just some amateur shots of me standing around in my apartment. I watched Moshe as he went through them.

After he was finished, he looked up at me with a little frown on his face. "Why didn't you want me to look at them?"

He obviously didn't believe I could get into trouble for showing them to him. I shrugged my shoulders. "I don't like the way I look in them."

That was true as well, and this time he believed me.

One day, promising that I would buy them some candy, I accompanied Avraham and Yaakov to the store. I had never actually been abroad with the boys before and it was exciting. We walked down Waring, past the front of the school, and over to La Brea.

The store, La Brea Kosher, was about four blocks south of Melrose, and on the way there we passed a number of Jewish schools and synagogues. It was a Friday and we arrived just after four o'clock, when the store closed, and so had to make our way home empty-handed.

On the way back, I asked Avraham what his father did for a living.

"He's a mortician."

"He has to stay with dead bodies at night," Yaakov said.

I wondered how much procedure this entailed. From what I'd read in the Mishnah, there were tons of laws concerning corpses and what was clean and unclean.

I looked at Yaakov. "Do you remember when we first met and you told me a black man had attacked your father, and you said your father jumped over ten benches—was that at the mortuary?"

A big grin spread across Yaakov's face at hearing his story repeated.

Avraham shook his head. "He's always telling stories. He gets in trouble for it."

There was a gas station at the corner of Melrose and La Brea that sold candy, and I asked Avraham and Yaakov if they wanted me to get them any. They shook their heads.

"What would happen if you ate non-kosher candy?" I asked.

"God would get mad," Avraham said.

"He'd get *very* mad," Yaakov confirmed.

"How would you know?" I asked.

"He'd keep Moshiach from coming."

How horrible to convince little kids that the coming of the Messiah was dependent on their smallest actions!

"I'll bet you anything in the world the Messiah never comes."

Both Avraham and Yaakov burst out laughing.

"He'll come, you'll see," Avraham said.

"And then he's going to kick ass!" Yaakov yelled, going into some kind of kick-boxing mode.

As we walked along, Yaakov began attacking me. He would come upon me from different angles, practicing some kick-boxing moves, and otherwise jumping on my back. It was a little difficult for me to figure out exactly what the intentions behind these assaults were, but at the same time it was very enjoyable being a physical object for Yaakov's energy.

We'd just turned back onto Waring when Avraham suddenly said, "You'd be a good father. Why don't you have children?"

"I'm queer. Besides, I couldn't afford it. I can barely afford to support myself now," I told him. "If I had to be responsible for other people, then I probably couldn't do the things I want to do. When I work, I have a very easy job, I only have to work three or four days a week, and in my spare time I can write. If I had to be responsible for some little kids, I don't know what I'd do—"

Yaakov jumped up on my back, and I spun him around. "How would you like it if I was your father, Yaakov?"

He jumped off my back and stood apart from us, taking stock of whatever figure I was presenting. He looked to Avraham, widening his eyes in disbelief, and then he burst out laughing and went running down the street yelling, "I already have a father!"

"I think you'd be a good father," Avraham repeated as we continued on together. "You know how to talk to kids."

"Avraham, your parents had children because of their religion, but I think most people who have children just do it as an excuse to express their feelings toward other human beings. They're too frightened or egotistical or embarrassed to admit the way they feel, and so they have to have kids to justify their own—what?—love of species. And there's, what, five *billion* people in the world—it's so sad. I think that's why queers are so important: they have the courage to love other people without making more of them."

Yaakov had met up with Yitzchak at the corner and they started playing together, running around and then chasing each other across the street.

"Be careful when you cross the street!" Avraham yelled after his little brother, and then more quietly to me, "Stupid kids."

"You know, in a way," I said, "I do think it would be nice to be Moshe and Yitzchak's father, since they don't have one. I mean, I really do like them and they need a father, they need *somebody*, but I just couldn't do it."

We were almost to Alta Vista when Avraham suddenly asked me about my homosexuality. "When you do it with another man, do you put your cock in their ass or do they put their cock in yours?"

"Usually they put their cock in my ass," I told him.

"Doesn't it hurt?"

I shrugged my shoulders. "Sometimes. It did at first, when I first had sex. It doesn't anymore."

We walked on in silence for a bit, Avraham thinking all this over. As we turned up Alta Vista, we could hear Dimitri playing his violin, its music blessing the street with beauty.

"You're not like other grownups," Avraham said, making a definite distinction. "You tell me everything."

I shrugged my shoulders: I didn't know what to say.

When we got to my apartment we sat outside and listened to Dimitri practicing in his room. Looking over toward his window, we could see him walking back and forth as he played.

And then I thought of something.

"Avraham, by any chance, does your father work at the mortuary up on Santa Monica Boulevard?"

Avraham said he did.

"Really? The one near Fairfax?"

"Yes, so?"

"Do you know what that building used to be?"

He shook his head.

"When I was eighteen and first came to Hollywood, the place where the mortuary is used to be a gay bar called the Stampede. It was the first gay bar I ever went in. Isn't that amazing?"

I looked around us and everything suddenly seemed so beautiful: the afternoon light all amber and glowing, Dimitri's music resonating the air, Yaakov and Yitzchak playing together down the street, and here beside me Avraham, with his dark inquiring eyes.

I contemplated the vicissitudes of time . . .

"When I got drafted to go in the army I told them I was homosexual, and they made me go see a psychiatrist to make sure I wasn't lying. He only asked me one question. He said, 'Where do you hang out?' and when I told him the Stampede, he went ahead and filled out my papers. And so I didn't have to go to Vietnam. And now the Stampede is a Jewish mortuary and your father works there."

I looked at Avraham, contemplating his beauty, and he smiled back at me.

"It's a strange world, isn't it?"

30 / yitzchak

On Independence Day I was supposed to go see a film with Josh, but he got invited to a party and so instead I sat outside all day reading. I had gone back to Fairfax and discovered a bookstore I hadn't noticed before, the Mid-City Chabad, and there I found *Despite All Odds: The Story of Lubavitch* by Edward Hoffman, a book that gives a simple overview of the movement.

As I sat there reading about the Lubavitchers, and watching their occasional comings and goings, I found it interesting that as far as they were concerned this was just another day for them: there were no holidays but Jewish holidays. I wasn't quite sure how I felt about that. On the one hand, I resented the tacit "Fuck you!" it implied while, on the other, I respected them for not kowtowing to the majority.

In the middle of the afternoon, when it was hottest and all activity seemed to cease, Yitzchak came over to see me. Unlike Moshe, Yitzchak didn't appear to have any particular agenda in his life—nothing he needed to know or find out. Maybe it was in deference to his older brother that he was so quiet: watching, listening, assimilating.

After we exchanged greetings, I didn't know what to say to him—we didn't really have any grounds for our relationship—and so we sat there together in silence. While I read, he picked up my binoculars and looked through them. I tried to concentrate, but invariably I would be drawn to look at this little human being sitting near me, with his dirty shirt on, the strings of his tzitzis hanging down beneath it, little yarmulke crowning his light brown hair, and peyos curving back around his ears. He was beautiful and shy and charming, and in his presence I simply wanted to melt into him.

We didn't say anything for quite a while. Occasionally, when I looked up from my book, our eyes would meet and we would consider each other for a moment or two. I felt as if I could look into his eyes forever and, in a way, I think that's what he wanted me to do. I could feel some process going on, in and behind his eyes, but I couldn't define it and, conversely, as he gazed on me and into *my* eyes, I wondered if he knew what he was seeing . . .

It was only conventional politeness that made me look away, or maybe I was frightened, of what he could or did see, and then of what *I* might see.

And so I went back to my book, making a pretense of my autonomy.

"Do you want to know who shot you?"

I looked up, and little Yitzchak was just sitting there, watching me, holding my binoculars in his lap as he straddled the low brick wall.

I was *very* interested, but I answered him as casually as I could. "Yeah, sure."

"It's the boy who lives over there," and he pointed toward the dormitory across the street.

"Which window?"

"The one in the middle."

"On the ground floor?"

Yitzchak nodded.

That was the room next to Avi's, where the guy with the short curly hair lived. "Do you know what his name is?" I asked.

Yitzchak shook his head. "I'm not sure. Maybe it's Levi."

Another Levi!

I tried to think back. I knew who he meant. I hadn't had too many dealings with him, but I knew he deeply disliked me. I remembered his imperious tone of voice once when he told me to put the binoculars down, and another time when he told me to go away or he would call the police.

If I were to bring suit against the school, and if the question came up of who shot me, what would I say? Would I tell them that Yitzchak had told me it was the curly-haired boy named Levi?

I looked at little Yitzchak sitting there and I knew I could never do that. I could never put him in that position. And I wondered what it meant: Had he found out? Did everyone know? Was it a secret?

Well, whatever it was, it had suddenly become more than just a secret between us—it had become an expression of trust.

Or maybe it was just curiosity: If I tell Rick who shot him, what will he do?

A little later Moshe came over and joined us with one of his sisters, a girl named Rachel who looked to be younger than Moshe but older than Yitzchak. And then we were joined by some other kids, including Sruli Perlman and two of his younger brothers, Mendy and Mooki, and finally Yaakov from next door.

I had never really talked to Sruli before, and I asked him how old he was.

"Twelve."

"Are you excited about your bar mitzvah?"

"No. I don't really want to do it. It's too much work."

"But you get lots of money, don't you?"

Sruli shrugged his shoulders, and then he suddenly asked, "Are you a homosexual?"

I nodded.

Yaakov came over to me then. "What's a homosexual?"

This was very strange, having to explain sexuality to a ten-year-old. "Well, it means I have sex with other men, that makes me homosexual, and your parents, for example, they're *hetero*sexual."

Yaakov was indignant. "They are not!"

I was startled by Yaakov's vehemence. "I mean," I tried to explain, "your father's a man and your mother's a woman, and since they have sex with each other that means that they're *hetero*sexual. I have sex with other men, like myself, and that makes me *homo*sexual."

Yaakov was getting into his little bulldog stance. "My parents don't sex," he said, offended by my vile aspersion. His family's honor was at stake and he was getting ready to take on anybody who said they did: he put his hands on his hips and spread his feet apart, braced for an attack.

Moshe thought Yaakov was silly. "How do you think you got here, then?" he asked.

"You're stupid!"

Moshe turned to me confidentially. "He doesn't know about it yet."

"I'll fight you!" Yaakov threatened Moshe.

"I dare you!" Moshe shot back.

"I dare *you*!"

"Yaakov, he didn't insult you—it's just a word, it's not necessarily bad—"

"My parents don't sex!" he insisted.

Yaakov is one of the most aggressive little kids I've ever seen, and to see him defending his untenable position was painful to me, especially since everyone there knew he was wrong—or did they?

I looked around at the other little kids, Sruli's two little brothers and Moshe's sister Rachel, who hadn't said a word, and I wondered: What on earth must this conversation sound like to them? What could it mean? How did they explain to themselves what Yaakov and Moshe were fighting about?

"But *I* have sex," I explained, trying to get the conversation back to myself and ease the tension. I turned to Sruli. "And that's why the guy in the beit midrash shot me."

"How do you know it was one of the bochurs?" Sruli asked.

I suddenly caught sight of Yitzchak, sitting quietly on the little brick wall. He didn't say anything and I wondered if he thought I might tell on him.

"It's just a feeling I have," I said.

Later in the week some of the smaller children went on a field trip. A bus came to pick them up from school and parked across the street. I watched the kids get on the bus, and among them I noticed little Yitzchak. He sat by a window on the side of the bus facing the street. He saw Dovid and Yossi in their yard playing ball and waved to them. And then he saw me.

I was taking a break from the phone (calling in for work), and sitting on one of the stoops outside, watching the activity on the street. When Yitzchak recognized me he waved and I waved back. He had a big smile on his face and I was really happy and excited for him: he was going somewhere and we were staying here. Once I picked up my binoculars and looked through them to see him better and he laughed.

For some reason the bus didn't leave and then the engine was turned off. Apparently they were waiting for someone. I went in the house and put my hat on, and came back outside.

Several minutes later they turned the engine on again, and I got up and walked across the street to the window where Yitzchak was sitting. Looking up at him, I asked him where he was going.

"Camp," he said.

"Where?"

He shrugged his shoulders.

"Well, have a really good time," I told him and then I started back across the street. I had just gone a few steps when I turned around to see him again and wave. One of the bochurs was leaning over Yitzchak and pushing him back in his seat: "Don't be a troublemaker."

Yitzchak started to say something, but again he was pushed back in his seat and once more the injunction was repeated: "*Don't* be a troublemaker."

I was about to say something, but then thought better of it—I didn't want to get Yitzchak into any more trouble than he already was. I returned to my stoop and watched the proceedings.

Troublemaker.

Yitzchak was a "troublemaker" because he was talking to me. How insidious that was.

A moment later the bus finally started, and as it moved on up the street Yitzchak looked at me, no smile on his face, and I waved to him: I'm sorry.

Surreptitiously, he managed a small wave back.

31 / moshe

"I can tell if someone is Jewish just by looking at them."

Moshe made this self-confident assertion to distract me from my reading as we sat outside in front of my apartment one day.

"How?" I asked.

"There's something about the eyes, something about the way they look."

I looked around to see if there was anyone we could test this theory out on, but the street was pretty empty. A few minutes later, however, a good-looking man in his twenties with long black hair came by. He climbed the steps and said hello as he passed between us and started up the walkway. He was wearing a leather jacket, and I assumed he was a musician friend of the beautiful girl who lived in the back.

After he was gone, I turned to Moshe. "Is *he* Jewish?"

Moshe nodded his head. "Definitely."

"I bet he's not," I said. "We'll ask him when he comes back."

I'd been rereading some of my stories and went back to

them, but Moshe wouldn't let me concentrate, and so we made small talk while we waited.

About ten minutes later the guy came back, strolling along with a cool and self-assured manner.

"Excuse me," I said. "We were just wondering: Are you Jewish?"

The guy stopped beside us and looked from me to Moshe and back again before answering. "No."

Moshe and I looked at each other and I stuck my tongue out at him. The guy was watching us, and so I gave him the explanation: "We had a bet going. He thought you were Jewish and I said you weren't. I won."

The guy nodded his head as if he understood what we were talking about, and went on his way. If I'd heard right, he seemed to have been slightly offended at being asked such a question. But what did he expect from a man sunning himself in shorts and a black dress hat, and a little boy with fringes on his clothes and a skullcap on his head?

I picked up one of my stories and started glancing through it again.

"What are you doing?"

"I'm checking my stories for mistakes," I told him. "This one is about you—do you want to read it?"

"Read it to me."

"Why don't you read it for yourself?"

"I don't want to."

"Why not?" I asked.

"I like pictures."

And suddenly I felt as if a world had just opened up in front of me . . .

Moshe didn't like to read!

To live in that environment, where such a premium was placed on scholarship, and not to like reading . . .

Moshe suddenly stood up and came over beside me. "Tell me about sex."

I looked up at him. "What do you want to know?"

"Tell me about it," he insisted, and he put his hands on the arm of my chair and leaned over me.

"You tell me," I said.

"What?"

"What do *you* think sex is?"

Moshe contemplated the question for a moment and then said, "Sex is when you act out your embarrassment."

I was amazed at his definition and repeated the words to myself so as not to forget them: *Sex is when you act out your embarrassment.*

"How do you do it?" he asked.

"What?"

"When you touch yourself."

Moshe was still standing over me and now he was rubbing his crotch up against the arm of my chair. I felt a little nervous, looking up at this eleven-year-old boy—his determination only slightly softened by a seductive earnestness.

"Moshe," I said, "you should ask your father."

"My parents are divorced," he said.

"I know. But don't you ever see him?"

"He's in Israel."

God—I felt so sorry for him. He didn't like to read and his parents were divorced: he was certainly going to have a rough time of it for the next several years.

"Tell me," he said again, and he rubbed his crotch up against my elbow.

I was a little embarrassed. "I don't want to."

"Please! I'll give you a dollar."

I shrugged my shoulders.

"I'll give you five hundred dollars."

"Moshe!" I exclaimed, and then answered him brusquely, "You just touch yourself."

"That's all?" he asked.

I shrugged again.

I felt like such a coward, and I hated the fact that my embarrassment and my lack of forthrightness were based on the fear he'd tell his elders what I'd said. It is so important to be honest, and here I was afraid to be just that.

Looking morose, he moved away from me and sat on one of the walkway's little brick partitions.

God, how I hated these false constrictions!

If I wasn't such a coward I would have just told him to come inside and I would show him.

32 / the proposition

In August the TV season started up again and I got a job standing in for a cute fourteen-year-old boy on a situation comedy. After more than four months of sitting outside my apartment reading, I was now getting up at five-twenty in the morning, cycling to the gym for a workout, and then catching a bus down to Culver City for work.

What with my going to movies in the evening and seeing friends, my encounters with the boys were abruptly curtailed. After having been out later than usual one evening, I was cycling lazily home. I had on my black hat, loose black pants, white T-shirt, and sneakers: I looked like a casual Chassid. As I was riding down Waring I came to Poinsettia and saw one of the bochurs walking by himself. As I got nearer I noticed it was Levi, and I greeted him. He acknowledged me and so I circled back around in the street to talk to him.

"I just got a book on Rabbi Schneerson," I told him, "because you were reading one."

"What?" he asked.

I told him I would show him and struggled with my back-

254 / rick sandford

pack to get the book out, but before I could he said, "*Despite All Odds?*"

"Yes! What did you think about it, do you think it's any good?"

"Some of it's good."

"So, what do you think about New York?" I asked.

"What?"

"About the riots, about the Chassidic community—"

"What should I think?" he asked rhetorically.

I shrugged my shoulders. "I don't know. I'm really asking. All I know is what I read in the papers, and you're on the inside . . ."

In Brooklyn, a few days before, a car in Rebbe Schneerson's motorcade had gone through a red light and the driver, in an effort to avoid the oncoming traffic, had swerved his vehicle, jumped a curb, and killed a little black boy. Within hours the black community of Crown Heights was up in arms and a Lubavitcher from Australia had been stabbed to death. There'd been rioting ever since.

"Are you liberal?" Levi asked, as he continued on down the street—answering my question with another question.

I equivocated a bit as I walked my bike beside him. "Well, I'm way to the left of the Democrats, if that's what you mean."

"Do you like blacks?"

"I don't know," I began, a little uncertainly.

He redefined his question for me. "Do you like them as people?"

"Well, I don't know any blacks, really. None of my friends are black," and I ran through the black associations in my mind. "I've had sex with three black men. I'm not really attracted to them, though."

"Do you know who Al Sharpton is?"

"No."

"Alton Maddox?"

"No," I said. "Who is Alton Maddox?"

"He's a big fat nigger." Levi put it bluntly.

I was listening: Yes?

"He wants to kill—people," Levi said.

I nodded. Jewish people, no doubt.

"They're animals," he said.

We reached the corner and stood there for a moment in silence. I made to turn away, but Levi asked me if I was in a hurry. It was almost midnight and I had to be up at five-twenty in the morning, but—no, if Levi wanted to talk, I was willing to listen.

We crossed the street and headed up my side of Alta Vista toward my apartment, where we paused.

"You rent an apartment here?" Levi asked.

"Yes."

Levi knew that: this was a stall of some kind.

"One bedroom?" he asked.

"One *room*," I clarified.

He was just standing there, and suddenly it occurred to me that he might want to come in, and so I asked him, "Would you like to see my apartment? Would you like to see where I live?"

He indicated he would.

This *was* a surprise. I lifted my bicycle and carried it up the three steps of the walkway and led the way to number 1. I leaned the bike on its kickstand, got my key out, opened the door, and turned on the light.

It wasn't as bad as it could have been although, after the night air, it was very stuffy. The bed wasn't made and there were books and clothes strewn all over it. The floor was relatively clear of stuff, and the books on it were arranged in piles. The desk was littered with notebooks and paper but, for the most part, they were stacked neatly. Otherwise, the room was pretty much: books and more books, piled up, two deep, and lying everywhere you looked.

I parked my bike and stepped toward my desk as Levi came in the room. "It's kind of a mess, but this is it. That's my bed—I sleep with my head at the end, because that's what one of the characters in *Ulysses* did. This is my desk—and my computer—"

"So you *do* live in the modern world," he said.

"Yes, my computer and my answering machine," I said. "But that's it. No TV, no car."

I pointed to the books on the bed to impress him, a whole selection of books about Jews: Tanakh: The Holy Scriptures, the Mishnah, *The Indestructible Jews* by Max I. Dimont, *Judaism* by Isidore Epstein, *The Living Talmud/The Wisdom of the Fathers* selected by Judah Goldin, and *Legends of the Hasidim* by Jerome R. Mintz.

"I thought you'd have posters," he said.

"Well"—and I pointed to the poster above my desk—"that's *Follies*, that's the best musical I've ever seen, and a friend of mine gave me that one, *Without You I'm Nothing*, because I really liked it. *Sweeney Todd* is over there, and that's Dublin," I explained, pointing to a large map on the wall, "because I read Joyce, and I wanted to see where *Ulysses* took place."

(It wasn't until later, when I started writing all this down, that I realized he probably thought there were going to be posters of naked men all over the room.)

I looked around and noticed the photograph in the plastic frame propped against the wall. "Oh, and this is Aaron. He was my favorite Jewish boy," and I handed the picture to Levi to look at.

Aaron really was classic: the curly brown hair, the big nose, the full lips and sensitive eyes. Those Semitic ingredients which so often end in aesthetic disaster somehow combined in Aaron beautifully: he was the best Jew I had ever seen.

"He's dead," I explained.

"How did he die?"

"AIDS." What else?

Levi handed the picture back to me. He was very noncommittal. I didn't really know what to do, so I continued pointing things out: "Those are my notebooks by the desk, my Jewish books are over there on the second shelf. Oh, and"—taking from the bed the three-ring notebook in which I had arranged all my stories—"this is my book about you guys." I turned to the title page: *The Boys Across the Street.*

Levi feigned (or not?) indifference.

We hovered in the middle of the room. There was no place for him to sit and I didn't have anything to offer him. As he started moving back outside I realized that we might never be alone again. I'd thought about this before and I'd resolved that if I ever got the opportunity . . .

"Would you like me to give you a blow job?" I asked.

He stared at me with that noncommitting look of his and I suddenly got the feeling that this proposition of mine was the inevitable consequence of *his* conception of who I was.

"No."

The question, in and of itself, was *our* consummation.

"Well, you can't say you weren't asked," I told him.

He looked at me as we walked out toward the street. "Would you be interested in that?" he asked.

"Well, sure. I mean, you're nice-looking and you're a virgin, so—yeah, I'd be interested in giving you your first blow job. And, you know, my experience has been that the men who are the most repressed have the strongest erections."

"I'm not a homosexual," he said.

I felt like leveling with him. "Levi—all my straight friends? They all like getting blow jobs."

"So, did you think I was going to say yes?" he asked me.

"No. I mean, I was ninety-nine percent sure you were going to say no, but I wanted to give you the experience, I wanted you to at least be able to say, 'This guy wanted to suck my cock. I knew this guy once who made porno films. He was a world-famous cocksucker and he asked me if he could suck *my* cock.' That's all."

"I think you're crazy," he said, and we started walking together toward the corner on Waring.

I shrugged my shoulders and sighed. "Okay. 'Crazy'—meaning what?"

"I think you're absolutely out of your mind."

I shrugged my shoulders again. "That sounds like a negative value judgment. I know it doesn't have to be—"

"You're not normal."

"*Normal*"—I was contemptuous.

"You're not like most people."

"Who wants to be like most people?" and I turned on him: "*You're* not like most people."

"But you're not living the way you're supposed to."

"*Supposed?* According to who? I know, the Torah. The Torah says I should be killed."

"That's just about Jewish homosexuals. That isn't about you."

"Oh, only *Jewish* homosexuals should be killed. It doesn't matter who *I* have sex with." I was indignant. "In this book I read, *Tzitzith* by Aryeh Kaplan, it said that the world was created for the Jews—"

Levi acknowledged this: "God made the world for the Jews."

"But I want the world to be created for me, too."

"You're a part of creation—isn't that enough?"

I shook my head no. "*I* want to be a Jew. I want God to care about who *I* have sex with."

"Then you'll have to convert," he said.

I humbled myself before Levi with downcast eyes. "But I could never believe in God."

"So you'll never be a Jew."

I threw my hands up: What are you going to do?

"It's a waste of time your reading all those books about Jews," Levi said.

"What do you mean, it's a waste of time? I learn something all the time. I read Rabbi Schneerson's biography and then I open the paper and there's a story about him, and I already know about him. How can it be a waste of time?"

"You're sick," he said.

I held up my hands: Yeah, so?

"You read books and you can talk, you're not stupid, but you're sick. So why don't you kill yourself?"

I shrugged my shoulders again: What could I say? "I'm happy—why would I want to kill myself?"

"Because you're sick."

"Well, obviously, I'm not 'sick.' But, if I was sick, I think I *would* kill myself—I'm not into pain and suffering at all. So, if I ever do get sick—"

"How would you do it?" he asked me.

That was interesting, and I *had* thought about it. "Do you remember hearing about that guy who set himself on fire to protest the war in the Persian Gulf? I thought that sounded pretty good. There's getting drunk and taking the long swim to China, there's jumping off the Grand Canyon—I'm not one for guns—"

"What about poison?"

"No. I really want to experience my death if I'm going to do it."

"Being a homosexual is like being a murderer—"

"Levi!" and I started to reprimanded him. "Homosexuality is nothing like—"

"Can I finish talking, please?"

I acquiesced: Of course, *please*.

"A murderer has all these feelings building up inside him, but if he wants to badly enough he can stop his desire to kill."

"Levi, I was queer since I was a little kid—I didn't *choose* to be homosexual. It's a fundamental part of who I am. Your analogy is false."

"But you're not living the way you're supposed to."

"When I was a kid," I told him, "and I realized I wasn't like everyone else, you know what that made me do? It made me question everything, *everything*—and you know what I found out? I found out that everyone was lying to me: my parents, my school, my church, my country. When something comes from so deep inside you that it is beyond your understanding, then—you must judge everything by that standard."

"But it's not natural."

"Yes it is—and you know why? Because it comes from *inside* me. Levi, you wouldn't know anything about 'God' or Judaism unless you read a book or someone told you about it—everything you know about being a Jew comes from *outside* you. *That's* not natural. I wasn't *taught* to be homosexual: I *am* homosexual, and that's a million times more natural than your being a Jew."

"You're talking about being an animal—"

"I'm talking about being a human being! And my wanting to have sex with another man is *not* the same thing as wanting to kill someone!"

"I didn't say that."

"Yes you did."

"You can control your feelings," he said.

"I don't know where my feelings come from," I told him. "A murderer does. A murderer is involved in very specific situations to which he responds."

Levi regarded me for a moment, and then he suddenly changed the subject. "Do you like talking to me?"

"Sure, of course. You're interesting and what's really nice, compared to most people, is that you have a very definite point of view. That's exciting."

And then Levi spoke matter-of-factly what almost sounded like the supreme compliment: "I learn things from you," he said.

"What?"

"I learn what homosexuals are like, why they are like they are."

"That's great. I think I'm a good representative for homosexuality. I've never been in a relationship, though. I mean, that is one way in which I am not like other queers. Most of the people I know may not be in a relationship, and maybe the ones they do have don't last long, but at least they've had them. I've never been in a relationship at all."

We were silent for a moment.

"So what's the upshot?" I asked. "What are you finding out about 'homosexuals'?"

"I don't think you saw your father enough when you were a boy."

He was giving back just what I'd told him the last time we'd spoken, no arguing with that.

A cab stopped at the corner, and as it pulled away the man who got out saw Levi and they greeted each other effusively. Suddenly Levi wasn't the dour, defensive, and gloomy young man he always is with me. His eyes lit up and I could tell he felt let off a hook of some kind and was relieved that he had access to someone who could back him up. Levi introduced us and we shook hands. The guy's name was Danny; he was a Jew in his early twenties with reddish-brown hair, a frizzy beard, wire glasses, and—as opposed to Levi—a more practical, less ethereal sensibility.

"He's gay," Levi said, explaining me to Danny.

Danny looked at me and I shrugged my shoulders.

Levi then defined my situation in more detail. "He's sick."

I spoke to Danny in a mock whisper, "Our argument basically comes down to this: I think my homosexuality is below my consciousness, that it is prerational, and Levi thinks I have a choice."

Danny seemed to agree with me. "People don't know why they're gay. You probably don't know why you're gay."

"But you don't have to be gay if you don't want to," Levi interjected.

"But why would I want to have sex with a woman when I could have sex with a man? I think the erect penis is the most extraordinary thing in the world and I think a man's ejaculation is the most spectacular exhibition of life there is—so why would I want to deny myself that?"

The defining of explicitly sexual terms must have signaled a terminus for the conversation because Levi and Danny started back across the street, leaving me rather abruptly, without even saying goodbye.

"Goodbye," I called after them, in an effort to fill up the sudden silence. They looked back at me without answering.

And then I came home.

By paring down the civilities between us—by not saying goodbye—the understanding was affirmed between them that they weren't homosexual themselves. I felt sure that if Danny had known I was queer before we were introduced he wouldn't have shaken hands with me. A handshake validated me in a way that was not quite acceptable (all three of us were wearing black hats—might Danny have initially thought I was Jewish?).

It was late and I had to be up early, but I had a responsibility not to let Levi slip through my fingers, so I turned on my computer and started writing.

Tomorrow would just have to take care of itself.

33 / pennies

I came back from work about eight. I'd just bought some ice cream (chocolate–peanut butter swirl), and was about to sit down and enjoy it while I read the day's paper, when I heard the sound of kids playing.

I got up and went outside and there was Yitzchak, in the middle of the walkway, and Moshe, sitting on one of the low brick walls bordering it. They both had skates on.

"Yitzchak. Moshe. How's it going?" and I sat on the little wall opposite Moshe.

" 'How's it going?' " Moshe mocked me.

"I've been working," I said.

"So?"

"So—that's why I haven't been around."

" 'That's why I haven't been around,' " Moshe mocked me again. Obviously, there were no right answers.

"School began yesterday," I said, "but I can't tell—is it high school, or just the beit midrash?"

"So what?"

"I'm interested," I said.

"I *know* you are," Moshe almost spit at me, as if that was the reason why he was being so nasty.

While we were talking, Yitzchak got up and went into my apartment to look for money.

"You know what I did today?" I asked Moshe rhetorically, trying to lighten his mood, change the subject, divert his attention, something, anything: "I stood in on a TV show for a fourteen-year-old Jewish boy."

Moshe moved his head from side to side, parroting my words in a little singsong voice.

Oh, well. I tried. I sat still and contemplated him: the blue yarmulke on the back of his head, the peyos framing his face, and the little gap between his two front teeth. He wouldn't look at me.

"We're moving to New York in two days," he suddenly said, still turned away from me.

"Really?" I asked, concerned. "In two days? Where? To Crown Heights? Where the riots were? Both of you or just you? Is your mother going? Are you going to live with your father? Are you coming back?"

Moshe made fun of my questions, as if they were all incredibly irrelevant, insults unworthy of being answered. "What's Yitzchak doing?" he asked.

"He's looking for money," I told him. "Moshe, why are you mad at me?"

"You're so stupid," he said. "Give me your money."

"I don't have any money," I said, suddenly thinking of the money I *did* have: "I have this," and I showed him the check I had just received in the mail.

"Give it to me."

"No. It wouldn't do you any good anyway, because you'd have to get it signed to get it cashed."

"How much is it?"

"For one day's work," I began rather grandly, "they paid me one hundred and sixty-four dollars, but after taxes I only get one hundred and fourteen dollars."

"Give it to me and I'll cash it."

"No."

Yitzchak came back outside and sat beside Moshe, opposite me.

"What were you doing?" Moshe asked him.

"He was looking for money," I explained again.

"How much did you get?" Moshe asked. We could see Yitzchak had his hand balled in a fist.

"Fifty cents," Yitzchak said, and then, extending something in his other hand, he asked, "What's this?"

Moshe took the object from him.

"That's a light for when you go bicycle-riding at night," I told him. "You put it on your leg and it shines so people can see you. Since it's on your leg, it goes up and down."

I could see Moshe weighing the object in his hand. I reached over, not to take it but to try the switch, to see if there was still a bulb inside. There was, but the battery didn't work.

"Are you really moving to New York?" I asked Yitzchak, feeling he might be more responsive than Moshe.

He is shy anyway, but I wondered if his silence now was in deference to his older brother. It was strange to see them: Moshe in his belligerent, emotional mood, and little dreamy-eyed Yitzchak, watching, quiet.

"Are you coming back? Are you just going to visit? Are you both going?"

"Yes."

Apparently this information hadn't seemed too costly for Yitzchak to answer.

"If you're going away I won't get to see you anymore. I have to work tomorrow night—*am* I going to see you again?"

I suddenly felt panicked. If they really were going, and this was the last time I was going to see them, then—how could I see them enough? If they are so important to my stories, and I need to describe them, then—what? Who are they? How do they look? How do they sound?

Yitzchak went back into the apartment.

I looked at Moshe sitting opposite me, turned away, the bicycle light weighing in his hand.

"I'm going to miss you," I told him.

He wanted to smash the light, to break it, but his upbringing conspired against his instinct, and when he threw the light across the yard it was with an ease that precluded its breaking.

The phone suddenly rang in my apartment and I got up and ran in to get it. As I dashed across the room to pick it up before the machine did, I saw that Yitzchak was on my bed and pulling back the covers and mattress to see if he could find any money under the head of the futon.

It was a friend of mine who just wanted to talk. While I stood there listening to him, I noticed my ice cream melting and then watched Moshe as he came into the room. I told my friend I was busy now, that I would call him back, and hung up the phone.

"Get off the bed," Moshe ordered Yitzchak. "It's full of dick germs."

Yitzchak laughed at this concept and looked from Moshe to me, to see what I thought of what his brother had said.

Moshe glared at us and looked around the room almost desperately. He took a small battery-operated reading light from one of my bookshelves.

"That's for reading when it's dark," I said, taking it back from him and examining it as if I'd never seen it before.

Moshe suddenly grabbed my hat, my beautiful black hat, and asked, "How much did this cost?"

"Fifty-five dollars."

"Can I have it?" he asked.

"No. It's my favorite piece of clothing. I've never paid so much for something to wear in my life."

Moshe then started squeezing and mangling it, crumpling it up into a ball, which he then threw across the room. I felt reasonably certain it wouldn't be too difficult to return it to its original shape, but I wasn't nearly as disturbed by the attempted destruction of my property as I was by the violence of Moshe's feelings and the sense that I had somehow betrayed him.

Was my absence so important, so crucial to him? Had my sitting outside all summer long, reading, day after day, been such a solace to him? Was there something he needed to tell me? Was there something more he wanted me to explain? Had my company meant so much then?

Did he really like me?

Could all of this have something to do with love?

I wondered if Yitzchak shared in these feelings. He was kneeling on the edge of my bed now, watching his brother. Moshe looked around and saw the big glass jar of pennies on one of my file cabinets. He reached up and took it. Yitzchak made some objection: he remembered when I'd told him and Yaakov that they could have any money they found on the floor but that the jar of pennies was my "desperation money."

Moshe held the jar to his chest. "I'm going to take your money," he said.

"I don't care," I told him.

He then skated out of the apartment.

When I didn't make any objection to Moshe's action, Yitzchak got up off the bed and followed his brother. "You have to split it with me!"

I sat still for a moment, completely disinclined to run after Moshe because of the money and then feeling the necessity of running after him for himself.

He and his brother were skating away down the sidewalk.

"I'm going to miss you," I called after them.

They continued on their way.

"I really like you."

And then they were gone.

34 / avraham

Moshe and Yitzchak didn't actually move to Crown Heights, Brooklyn, for another couple of weeks, but because I was working I only saw them a few times. When I *was* at home, Moshe acted resentful and never spoke to me again without being sarcastic.

The last time I saw Yitzchak, I asked him about it. "Why is Moshe mad at me?"

"I don't know."

"Would you ask him why?"

"I don't want to."

"Why not?"

"Because then he would get mad at me."

Yitzchak was looking at my binoculars again, this time trying to figure out how the focus worked and actually unscrewing some of the pieces and putting them together again. I told him that some of the pieces that turned didn't come off, but that didn't stop him.

After he'd gone, I tried looking through them, but one of the lenses was broken and the two separate images wouldn't match up. Well, if anyone was going to break my binoculars, I was glad it was Yitzchak.

I continued to study the Jews.

I started buying *The Jewish Journal* each week, as well as the *B'nai B'rith Messenger*, which had a column by the Lubavitcher Rebbe on the Torah. In one of the issues I found out that the circled "U" on food products was administered by the Union of Orthodox Jewish Congregations. Over a period of a couple of months as a little project of my own, I went through every single product at my neighborhood market and listed each item that had a circled "U" on it: there were over four hundred!

Obviously, it was a much more widespread practice than I had imagined. And then I began to wonder if it might be part of some worldwide Jewish conspiracy ("And I will set a sign among them . . . and they shall declare my glory among the Gentiles": Isaiah 66:19): after all, not only had they invented "God," but they'd managed to get the whole Western world to actually worship one of their own! To say nothing of the fact that almost every boy born in the United States, including me, had part of his penis cut off before he even left the hospital!

And now they wanted to put their mark on all of our food!

Very scary.

I started reading *Likutei Amarim (Tanya)* by Rabbi Schneur Zalman of Liadi, the first Lubavitcher Rebbe. It was the most important book for Chabad, outside of the Torah, and they read a different section of it every day. It was the first book I'd ever read that went backwards, with the English on the right-hand pages and the Hebrew on the left.

It was tough going, but I read it carefully, using the glossary for almost every page. The general upshot of the book seemed to be an intellectual game in which Zalman was trying to reconcile the endless dichotomy of God Is One with the multiplicity of the world. Over and over, he states that God cannot be known and then goes on to offer what he knows.

On page 31, in the seventh chapter of the first part, I came across this:

> . . . Therefore the sin of wasteful emission of semen is not mentioned in the Torah among the list of forbidden coitions, although it is even more heinous than they; and this sin is greater because of the enormity and abundance of the uncleanness and of the *kelipot* which he begets and multiplies to an exceedingly great extent through wasteful emission of semen, even more than through forbidden coitions . . .

Kelipot means "bark" or "shell" and is a term used to denote evil. Another term for evil is *sitra achra*, "the other side." One day as I was passing in front of the school with my *Tanya*, some of the boys—who were amazed to see me reading one of their holy books—started talking to me. When one of the bochurs passed by and saw us speaking together, he told me to stay away from the school.

"What are you talking about?" I asked him, incredulous. "I live here."

"I'm just warning you," he said.

He turned away from me, but I advanced on his retreating back. "Why? Am I the *kelipot*? Am *I* the *sitra achra*?"

He didn't answer me, but a shudder constricted his back.

I wondered when it happened: just when does the eager learning of these kids turn into the brutish defensiveness of their elders? Is it when they realize it's all a lie but say yes to it anyway?

These poor despised people: in retaliation against a history of subservience, they make up a world of their own with which to defy creation—a world in which hope for a Messianic future denigrates the here and now, where the nationalist and racist assertion of the "chosen people" commands survival whatever the cost, where any effort is never good enough and self-pity blooms into righteousness, a world where beauty is evil and life, no longer reason enough for living, prevails only as an excuse for atonement.

And it was all predicated on the one "absolute": the Torah was the word of God.

Therefore . . .

A smell of semen was in the air.

In the autumn there is a carob tree up the street that emits a heady pungent aroma and for several months each year I feel as if I were awash in sex. One afternoon, when I didn't have to go to work, I set my things up outside to read. I was still trying to finish the *Tanya*. I was only wearing shorts and had on none of my Jewish accoutrements.

Shaul, our plumber, was installing new toilets that used less water, and occasionally he would pass me on the way from his truck to one of the apartments and back again. While I was sitting there, trying to concentrate on my reading, Avraham came back from school. When I saw him I set my book down. He was all dressed up in a black suit and had his black dress hat on. He was taking special classes in preparation for his bar mitzvah. As he walked toward me I noticed he had a package with him, a long clear container with two dark blue bags and a book inside. When he was adjacent to me he noticed the *Tanya*.

"You shouldn't put it upside down," he said, taking it in his hands and turning it over, then bringing his fingers up to his lips to kiss them. "It's like God."

"I'm just not used to reading a book backwards," I explained to him.

We looked at each other in silence for a moment.

"You know what this is?" he asked, indicating the package he had with him.

I shook my head.

"This is my tefillin," he said.

"Really? Did you just get it?"

"No, I've had it for a month."

"When is your birthday, September?"

"September twenty-third."

"According to the Jewish calendar, when is your birthday?"

"On the fifteenth day of Tishrei."

"Is it always on September 23?"

Avraham shook his head. "No, next year it's in October."

"Really? Did you get your tefillin, or did you have to buy it, or what?"

"It's very expensive. Mine was made in Israel. It cost eight hundred dollars. It was made by hand."

"If I wanted to buy one—"

"You want to buy tefillin?"

"Well, I already have a yarmulke and tzitzis and a hat. And I've got the Mishnah. I think the tefillin's next."

Avraham smiled, and a dimple high on his left cheek creased.

"How much," I asked him, "would a tefillin cost at Atara's, say, the cheapest tefillin I could get?"

Avraham thought about this for a moment. "A hundred and seventy-five dollars."

Suddenly Dimitri started playing his violin and the strains of his music began drifting out over the street, an aural counterpoint for the afternoon, saturated as it already was with the reek of virility.

"Well, I have to go," Avraham said and took off down the driveway, only to return a moment later. "My parents are gone," he said, and I felt he was glad to have an excuse to be with me, but he modified that possibility with an explanation: "I don't have a key."

He sat down on one of the little brick partitions across from me and turned to look up the street toward the carob tree. "That tree stinks," he said.

"Oh, I don't think so," I said. "I like it—I think it smells good. It reminds me of sperm—the primal seed."

Avraham smiled indulgently at me, and as we sat there looking at each other we listened to the music. It was beautiful. I'd spoken to Dimitri once and asked him what the music was that he played, and he listed a number of composers—Mozart, Bach, and Paganini—but the only piece he mentioned by name was one called "Gypsy Airs" by someone named Pablo de Sarasate.

Avraham suddenly interrupted my reverie. "Do you want to see my tefillin?"

"Sure."

He unzipped the clear container and took out one of the dark blue bags. I asked him about the lettering on the cloth. He said it just spelled out the word tefillin in Hebrew.

From the bag he removed a square object with a case. Part of the case was a red metal box, about an inch and a half square, and inside was a small black box that looked like it was made of wood, attached to a leather apparatus with straps.

"You put that on your forehead?" I asked.

"Yes," he replied, "and the other one is for your arm. We have two sets of tefillin," he explained, and then with pride, "Only *we* have two sets."

"Do you put these on when you're alone, or do you ever pray all together with your tefillin on?"

"You do it by yourself, but you also pray together."

That image seemed very funny to me: all these black-suited Jews praying together with one little black box on their forehead and another one on their arm.

I got my *Artscroll Weekday Siddur*, and Avraham showed me the prayers he had to recite when he wore his tefillin, as well as the four passages that are written down and sealed inside the little boxes.

"When you wear the tefillin," Avraham said, enticing me with its power, "it's like God is hugging you—tight."

Shaul passed us on the way to his truck, and on his way back he spoke to Avraham in Hebrew. He seemed to be angry, but Avraham just laughed at him. When he was gone, I asked Avraham what he'd said.

"He said for me not to talk to you. He said you're crazy."

Every time Shaul passed us he would say something and each time he seemed a little angrier, but Avraham wouldn't take him seriously, and finally, in exasperation, Shaul spoke to me himself. "He sh-should go home; he n-needs to study."

"But his parents aren't home," I explained.

I thought how strange it was that I should know two Jews with speech impediments—Shaul and Avi—and I wondered if there was a connection. Maybe it had something to do with the fear of God.

"Will your parents get mad if you talk to me?" I asked Avraham. "I talked to your mother."

"What did she say?" he asked.

"Nothing."

"She told me I shouldn't talk to you," he said. "Not because of you but because it causes trouble with the beit midrash."

I was touched. I'm sure that is not the case with Dovid and Yossi's mother. I bet she tells them outright that I am stupid or crazy or sick and not to talk to me just because she says so.

Shaul passed by us again and again said something to Avraham, more vehement this time, but Avraham still just laughed.

"What did he say?" I asked.

"He said you're stupid."

I shrugged my shoulders.

It was a beautiful day, and in the silence between us we could hear the sound of the violin scaling the heights of some ultimate pain and beauty, and I wondered if Dimitri could possibly comprehend the emotion his music seemed to be expressing.

"You know what I think of when I hear him playing?" I asked Avraham rhetorically. "Little Jewish kisses being blown to me from across the street."

Avraham laughed and I was suddenly very happy: we two together—there in the shade of the eucalyptus tree, seminal effusion in the air about us. It seemed like some kind of perfection, as if the world were coalescing around us.

And then, in contemplation of this juncture in time, I asked Avraham, "Do you really think the Messiah is going to come this year?"

"We hope so," he said. "We think it might be Rabbi Schneerson."

"You think Rabbi Schneerson is going to be the Messiah? But he's an old man."

"If he is the Messiah he will become like twenty again. When Moshiach comes everybody will be twenty forever."

"Oh, Avraham, that's horrible," I said. "You'll suddenly be twenty years old and you'll never get to know what it's like to be a teenager."

Avraham laughed. "No, I'll keep on growing *until* I'm twenty and *then* I'll stop."

I nodded my understanding.

He looked away across the street, subsiding into reflection— the sound of the violin tracing some line of thought in his mind—and a stillness overcame him until he was motionless, staring. It was lovely to look on him in that tranquillity, with his peyos curving back around his ears and his black hat emblematic of emulation: all dressed up and adorned for devotion.

When a few minutes had passed, he suddenly turned back to me. "You know what's going to happen when the Messiah comes?"

I shrugged my shoulders.

"When the Messiah comes, all the bad goyim—you know what that is?"

"Goyim? Gentiles, non-Jews—right?"

Avraham nodded and then continued, "When the Messiah comes, all the bad goyim are going to be killed, but all the good goyim are going to become our slaves."

"Oh, well," I mused, "I'll probably go up in a lightning bolt right here," and then I had an idea. "But if I don't—could I be *your* slave?" The idea appealed to me. "You would feed me, right? And maybe you could hitch me to a cart and I could take you for rides, and afterward you could rub me down. Like a pony. I'd love to be your slave! And if I was bad you could hit me!"

Avraham smiled at me, the dimple high on his cheek appearing for little moments and disappearing again. He knew I was kidding him, but he could also see that I *really* would enjoy being his slave and doing whatever he wanted me to do. "You know," he said, "if you're my slave, you'll have to give me all your money."

"But you would feed me, right?" I asked, just to make sure.

Avraham straightened himself, his dignity offended. "Of course I'll feed you!"

"Then I would *love* to be your slave and you can *have* my money. The next time you put your tefillin on—when you *daven*—ask God if it would be okay. Even though I'm a bad goyim I promise I'll be a good slave. I'll do whatever you want and *even* if I'm good you can hit me! It'll be fun!"

Avraham considered me for a moment and then said rather hesitantly, "I don't think slaves are supposed to have fun."

I sighed and shrugged my shoulders: What are you going to do?

35 / epilogue

At night, when I'm here in my apartment, I'll suddenly hear the sound of the gate clanging across the street and then I'll get up and go outside and invariably I'll be able to see one or more of the Jewish boys, either going into the compound or walking down the street.

Sometimes I recognize them as characters in my book, and then the idea of these people I have created—moving about as though they have their own three-dimensional autonomy—overwhelms me with proprietary warmth.

I think what I feel is love.